FULL CIRCLE

The new E.J. Pugh murder mystery

Someone is stalking romance novelist E.J. Pugh's fourteen-year-old adopted daughter, Bessie. The whole Pugh clan rallies round her to keep her safe – but Bessie has more problems than an average teenager. When she was a child, her entire family were murdered ... so who is this person claiming to be her dead brother Aldon? And who seems to be willing to take out her entire new family to get to her? The Pugh family is taken back, full circle, to where the horror all began...

*Recent Titles by Susan Rogers Cooper
available from Severn House Large Print*

The E J Pugh Mysteries
ROMANCED TO DEATH

The Milt Kovak Series
SHOTGUN WEDDING
RUDE AWAKENING

FULL CIRCLE

Susan Rogers Cooper

Severn House Large Print
London & New York

This first large print edition published 2012
in Great Britain and the USA by
SEVERN HOUSE PUBLISHERS LTD of
9-15 High Street, Sutton, Surrey, SM1 1DF.
First world regular print edition published 2010 by
Severn House Publishers Ltd., London and New York.

British Library Cataloguing in Publication Data

Cooper, Susan Rogers.
  Full circle. -- (An E. J. Pugh mystery)
  1. Pugh, E. J. (Fictitious character)--Fiction. 2. Women
  novelists--Fiction. 3. Women private investigators--
  United States--Fiction. 4. Stalkers--Fiction.
  5. Detective and mystery stories. 6. Large type books.
  I. Title II. Series
  813.6-dc23

  ISBN-13: 978-0-7278-7999-8

Severn House Publishers support The Forest Stewardship Council
[FSC], the leading international forest certification organisation. All
our titles that are printed on Greenpeace-approved FSC-certified paper
carry the FSC logo.

MIX
Paper from
responsible sources
FSC® C018575

Printed and bound in Great Britain by the
MPG Books Group, Bodmin, Cornwall.

to my favourite elizabeth,
who once was a bussie,
(russian for bessie)
but now is just
cousin liz.

ONE

BLACK CAT RIDGE, TEXAS, THE PRESENT

They're all asleep in there. Thinking they're safe. They stole her from me again. They won't win next time. Bessie's mine. She belongs with me. If I have to kill the whole family to get her, I will.

E.J., THE PRESENT

I woke up with a start. The clock said three a.m., but my body said something was wrong. Pulse rapid, breath coming in quick gulps. I counted heads. My husband, Willis, lay beside me, snoring as only he can. The kids had gone upstairs only a few hours ago, really – midnight, one a.m. God, I had no idea when we finally stopped going over it and over it and all of us went off to our respective beds. That's what woke me. It wasn't over. Not by a long shot.

I had been in Austin for four days for a convention. I'm a romance writer and this had been a biggie for me; I'd been nominated for a Lady, the most prestigious award in the romance biz. I'd lost, but still ... And then all that glory had come crashing down with the death of my roommate. Willis had rushed to my side, leaving our kids in the care of his mother, Vera.

But they'd had plans of their own, my children. Plans that nearly got them killed.

I climbed out of bed, careful not to awaken Willis, and moved to the window seat. The window was open to the cool night air of April, and I could hear the cicadas trilling their messages, the first sign of summer.

Summer comes early in central Texas. In a month the song of the cicadas would be muted by a closed window and the hum of central air-conditioning. After ten hours of hot Texas sun, even at midnight the roof tiles would still be hot to the touch.

But at that moment, the back yard was bathed in moonlight, washing the color out of everything: the redwood picnic table, the faded red and blue plastic swing set that had been sitting in that same spot for ten years. If Willis had his way, it would still be sitting there when we had grandchildren to play on it. And maybe that wasn't a bad idea.

Grandchildren. That all depended upon our ability to keep our current children alive.

I'm not a person who worries over what almost happened. I've been through enough in my life to glory in the almost-happened, to relish it, to cherish it. The problem now, this night, was that it wasn't over.

The kids thought it was. And thinking that, they could find the macabre humor lying beneath it all. I'd been in these situations enough to know that a threat like my girls had endured didn't just stop when the stalker ran away. No. Stalkers don't stop. They come back, and back, and back. Until they're satisfied in their sick-puppy minds. And I'm afraid the only thing that would satisfy this sicko was the rape or death of my daughter Bessie. And that was not going to happen. Willis and I would find this sicko, and he would go to jail.

Or die.

Where to start? It goes back ten years, really, to the day I walked next door to my neighbors to get the kids for carpool. The most horrible day of my life.

BLACK CAT RIDGE, TEXAS, 1999

It was my week to drive the carpool. After a long, wet weekend I was more than happy to bundle up my kids and get them to their respective schools. Rainy days and small children don't go well together. I got my two, Graham, six years old, and Megan, four years old, into the station wagon, got them buckled, and honked the horn for my next-door neighbor, Terry Lester. Her two younger children, Aldon, ten, and Bessie, four, were to ride with me. Her oldest, Monique, sixteen, was driven to school by her father. It was bad enough that I had to take my troops to two different schools – the expensive private pre-K for the two four-year-olds, and the public elementary for my Graham and Terry's Aldon.

There was no response from the house next

9

door. Cursing under my breath, I told my kids to stay put and ran to the Lesters' back door, dodging puddles from the weekend's rain. The door was unlocked as we usually didn't lock up much out here in suburbia. Stepping inside Terry's kitchen, I got my first hint: the coffee pot was sitting on the counter, cold and empty. Second hint: no boxes of cereal on the kitchen table, no spill of milk, no lights, no camera, no action. Diagnosis: the Lesters had overslept again. I called out Terry's name, then headed for the staircase leading to the bedrooms. This wouldn't be the first time I'd had to wake up the Lester family.

Terry's house was neater than mine and more formal than mine. Hell, the boys' locker room at the high school was more formally decorated than my house. I had to pass through the dining room with its Chippendale-style table, chairs, and sideboard into the foyer to get to the stairs. From there I could see into the living room, with its impossibly cream-colored couch and love-seat, the pale carpet without a spot on it, and the knick-knacks my children couldn't keep their hands off.

I headed up the stairs. I had only taken one step when I saw the stains on the walls. Then I smelled it. Two distinct smells, actually. One I recognized but didn't want to admit. One that matched the stains on the wall. The other was something new, something bad.

I stepped back, my mind gone suddenly blank. Something was wrong. Terribly, terribly wrong, but I didn't know what. And I didn't want to know what. Without much thought I ran out of the house, got my kids out of the station wagon and into our own home.

'Take your sister upstairs!' I yelled at Graham.

'Why?' he yelled back.

'Because I said so!' I said, grabbing the phone in the entry hall. I dialed 911 and told the operator to get someone out to the Lesters' address. While I was still on the phone with 911, I felt a presence on the stairs. I turned and saw my daughter Megan standing at the top of the stairs, tears in her eyes, her pretty face scrunched up.

'Megan, go back to your—'

'I'm not playing with Bessie no more—'

'Anymore,' I automatically corrected. 'Honey, I'm on the phone—'

'She won't even wave at me!' Megan wailed.

'Megan, I don't know what you're talking about—'

'She's just standing there at the window being mean!' Megan said.

The implications of what my daughter was saying finally dawned on me. I dropped the phone and ran up the stairs. The window in Megan's room overlooked the connecting driveways of our house and the Lesters' next door. Straight across from Megan's window on the second floor was Bessie's. And Megan was right: Bessie was standing at her own window, her face and clothes matted with rusty red.

I grabbed Megan and took her into her brother's room. 'Graham, watch Megan.'

'Is she gonna do tricks?' replied my smart-alec son.

11

'Do it!' I said. There must have been some-thing in my voice. For once, my six-year-old son actually obeyed.

I ran out of the house to the Lesters' back door. It was still open, just the way I left it. And some-where upstairs, beyond the blood I'd seen on the stairway, Bessie stood, obviously hurt but alive. I knew I couldn't wait for the police, or an ambulance, or anyone else. I was there. And so was Bessie.

I've never thought to ask myself if I'm brave. That's not one of those characteristics women think a lot about. That's a man's bailiwick. In retrospect, I don't think going after Bessie was all that brave, not if bravery is a conscious decision. I was running on instinct; there was nothing conscious about going into that house at all.

Once inside, I headed for the stairway, and turned on the light. The marks on the walls were reddish brown, and the smell was distinctive. I hurried up the stairs to the landing and, turning, started to head up the second half of the flight but tripped, falling face first. And landing on ten-year-old Aldon, lying on his back, his eyes opened, the formerly feisty blue eyes now almost opaque in death. The top of his pajamas was covered in blood. I scrambled off him, throwing myself backwards against the wall. I felt the bile rise in my throat, and jumping to my feet, ran back down the stairs for the clear air outside.

I gulped in lungfuls of warm spring air. My body was shaking all over and I knew I had to get home, back to my own babies and away from whatever had happened at the Lester house. After two steps in the direction of my own home, I remembered Bessie. Standing at the window, staring into space – covered with blood and gore. But alive. I couldn't leave four-year-old Bessie in that house. I couldn't.

I hugged the wall as I gingerly stepped around little Aldon, trying not to touch or disturb him in any way. At the head of the stairs I turned right again, starting toward the end of the hall where Bessie's room was. Terry and Roy's room was the first on the left. My eyes seemed to have a mind of their own and swiveled to the open doorway of the parents' room.

Sitting on the floor, his back against the open door, was Roy, or what was left of him. I only recognized him from the pajamas I'd helped Terry pick out last Christmas. Royal-blue Chinese silk. They'd cost $150. The top half was soaked in blood, the door behind him a Rorschach pattern of gore. Between the legs of royal-blue silk rested a shotgun, Roy's finger still on the trigger guard, although the muzzle had dropped across his left arm. His face was gone.

I gripped the doorjamb to steady myself. When I moved my hand to continue on down the hallway, I saw the bloody handprint – my own. I looked down at my hands and the front of my shirt, all covered with blood. Aldon's blood, no doubt. At some point I heard a high keening sound. It took just a moment before I realized it was coming from me.

I forced myself to go on. The last room on the left was Monique's, my babysitter, the girl who trusted me with her heart's secrets. The door was open. Monique was in a sitting position against the back wall, her eyes squinched shut, her mouth in a grimace. Blood from her body had spattered the wall behind her, leaving a bloody pattern on the colorful posters hanging on the wall. Terry lay across Monique's bed, the back of her nightgown covered in blood.

I moved to Terry's body and gingerly picked up her hand, feeling for a pulse I knew wasn't there. I sobbed out loud. One eye was hidden by the blanket, the other stared dully at me. I touched the lid softly, pulling it down to close over the big, cocker spaniel brown eye. I wanted to stay there forever, just hold her in my arms and cry. But I didn't. Turning, I quickly moved across the hall to Bessie's room.

She still stood where I had seen her from Megan's window. Staring ahead of her into space, her little arms by her sides, her back to me. She looked so angelic standing there, her pretty little pink nightgown, her long dark brown hair falling in tresses down her back.

I gulped in air, steadied myself against the doorjamb and said, 'Bessie, honey, it's me, Auntie E.J.'

There was no movement from the window. 'Bessie, honey, we're going to go to my house and play with Megan, OK? You want to do that?'

I moved cautiously toward her and gently turned her to face me. Her eyes, carbon copies of her mother's, didn't track. They moved where her body moved, but they weren't seeing anything. From the back she had seemed angelically aloof from all the mess around her, but turning her I saw the front: the blood-matted nightgown, clumps of something foul on her face and in her hair. I picked her up in my arms. 'We're going to go play with Megan now,' I cooed. 'Just you and me. How does that sound?'

I pressed her face against my breast as I made my way out of that house of death.

E.J, THE PRESENT

That had been more than ten years ago. Bessie was now ours, legally adopted years ago, emotionally ours from the very beginning. The loss of Terry Lester, my best friend, was something I'll never get over. I've made friendships since then, but none like that I had with Terry. I think that true friendship is like true love: you only get one chance at such a gift, and Terry was mine: My true friend. I will miss her until the day I die.

But I think I've done good by her. I love her daughter as my own; all of Terry's special things are still in storage until Bessie has her own home. And I've tried to keep Terry and Roy and Monique and Aldon alive in Bessie's mind and heart, as well as in my own. But this – how do I protect Bessie from the unknown? From a monster sick enough to pretend to be Bessie's dead brother to get to her?

All these things were still in my mind as I

prepared breakfast this fine Monday morning. I had the windows open to the beautiful April morning. My azaleas were beginning to bloom in the back yard, and the willow tree was budding out. Butterflies flitted by the open window. And all I could think was: Screw the lot of you. I'm not in the mood.

I poured juice as I heard the heavy clomp of size eleven shoes hitting the stair treads. Shortly thereafter, Graham burst into the kitchen. At sixteen, Graham was already three inches above my five-eleven status.

'Hey,' he said, flopping down on to a stool at the breakfast bar.

'Hey yourself,' I said, setting the juice in front of him. 'Captain Crunch or Frankenberries?' I asked.

My son saluted me. Assuming that meant Captain Crunch, I pulled the box from the shelf and handed it to him, just as his father wandered into the room.

'Have you seen my briefcase?' Willis asked, looking absently around the great room.

'Did you leave it in the car?' I asked.

'Maybe,' he said, taking a seat on the barstool next to Graham and grabbing the Captain Crunch.

I'd tried the first seven or eight years of having children to never have sugar cereals in the house. Then Graham, who was a great climber, found his father's stash of Frosted Flakes on the top shelf of the kitchen cabinets and all bets were off. I had to give it up.

'Graham,' I said.

16

'Huh?' he said, not looking up as he shoveled cereal into his mouth.

'Look at me, please!' I said, my voice sharper than I'd meant it to be.

'Whaaaat?' he whined, while looking at me, at least.

'I want you to keep an eye on Bessie today,' I said.

'Elizabeth,' he corrected. Last year Bessie had decided to go by her full name. I'm not exactly a fan of the idea. 'And how am I supposed to do that?' Graham asked. 'We don't exactly go to the same school, Mom.'

'I know that!' I said. His grandmother had given him her old car when she bought a new one, and today was his first day to drive to school. He'd already promised the girls a ride. 'When you drop them off this morning, just watch to make sure they get inside...'

Graham sighed loudly. 'Jeez, Mom, of course.'

'And when you pick them up don't be a minute late! I don't want them waiting outside the scho—'

'You pick 'em up,' Graham said, standing and taking his bowl to the sink. 'I've got soccer this afternoon.'

'OK,' I said, relieved. It would be disruptive for me to drive them to school this morning after Graham had promised them a ride in his 'new' car. 'But you needed to tell me that first thing.'

'I just did,' he said, heading for the back stairs.

'No, I mean...' But I was talking to air; my son was gone.

Then I heard them coming down the stairs.

17

'That is too my top!' Megan said, or screeched.

'I bought this with my own babysitting money!' Bessie declared. 'It's mine!'

'I bought that when we went to the mall that time with Meredith!'

'Excuse me,' Bessie said, 'but I don't think you *bought* anything when you were with Meredith!'

'What are you implying?' Megan said, now at the bottom of the stairs, hands on hips as she stared daggers at her sister.

'I'm not implying jack-squat!' Bessie shot back. 'I know and you know that Meredith Rhiengold is one of the biggest shoplifters in the whole school!'

'I *did not* shoplift! Ever! In my whole life!'

'Oh, well, did *Meredith* get this for you?' Bessie said, fingering the top she was wearing.

'Ah ha! You admit it!' Megan said, pointing a finger in her sister's face. 'That *is* my top!'

Bessie looked into the kitchen where two sets of eyes were staring at her. Willis said, 'She got you, hon.'

'Go upstairs and change,' I said.

Bessie's face turned red then she turned to Megan and ripped the top off, leaving her in just her bra. 'Here's your damn top! It's ugly anyway!'

'Then why did you want to wear it?' Megan said in that nasty way girls have of scrunching up their faces while taking sarcasm to its evil extreme. She was talking to her sister's back as Bessie headed for the laundry room.

'Mother, are there any clean clothes?' Bessie

demanded.

'I don't know!' I yelled so she could hear me. 'Did anybody do laundry while I was gone?'

'Then what am I supposed to wear?' Bessie yelled back, tears evident in her voice.

I heard Megan walking down the hall to the laundry room. 'Here, wear this. Just ask next time, OK?'

'I don't want to wear your stupid top!'

'Then go naked!' Megan said and slammed out of the room.

Megan was sitting at the breakfast bar eating Frankenberries when Bessie came in, wearing Megan's top. Megan handed her the box of cereal but Bessie shook her head. To me, she asked, 'Do we have any Fruit Loops?'

'No. It appears no one went shopping while I was gone.'

A big, trembly sigh, then, 'I'll just have a banana.'

'No fresh fruit either,' I said.

She grabbed for the Frankenberries. 'Just give me the stupid cereal,' Bessie said, and Megan laughed, which got her a noogie on her arm, which in turn caused Bessie to receive a wet willie, at which point I intervened.

'Eat! Next one to touch the other gets to ride to school with me in the Volvo.'

It was amazing how quickly they straightened up.

'Eat fast,' Graham said, coming in from the garage. 'I'm leaving in five.'

The girls finished up, put their bowls in the sink, and both ran upstairs for their backpacks.

And in five, they were gone. Out the door and away. Out of my sight but not out of my mind. This was just the first day. The first day to wonder when he was coming back and what he would do when he got here. The first day to try to know where Bessie was at every moment. Every second. My belly clinched up. And if he never came back? I asked myself. Then I guess, I answered myself, I'll worry about him for the rest of my life.

BLACK CAT RIDGE, TEXAS, 1999

One of Codderville's finest found me puking in the oleander bushes that separated Terry's yard from mine. Bessie was standing silently beside me, staring off into space.

I pointed back towards Terry's house and said, 'They're all d-e-a-d.'

'Ma'am?' the officer said.

I rolled over from my all-fours position into a sitting position.

'Ma'am, are you hurt?' he asked, obviously seeing the blood on my shirt and hands, and possibly my face.

'No, but I think she is,' I said, looking at Bessie standing just feet from me.

The officer squatted next to me and pulled Bessie gently to him. She came docilely. Together we checked her for cuts or shotgun wounds. We found none.

'What's wrong with her?' I asked, my voice dangerously close to a whine.

The officer stood up and headed for his car. 'I

don't know, ma'am. I'm not a doctor; maybe shock.' He shrugged. 'I'm calling an ambulance and some backup now.'

He made his call and came back, his hand on the butt of his gun riding low on his hip.

'Aren't you going to go in there?' I screeched. I really did. It was beginning to hit me. I wanted someone to *do* something, and he was the only someone within yelling range.

He started asking me questions: my name, address, relationship to the child, but not what happened. I tried to tell him several times, until he finally said, 'Save that for the detectives. They'll be here shortly.'

I stood up. My face dangerously close to his. 'They're all d-e-a-d in there. Can you spell? Do you understand the concept? D-E-A-D?'

He put his hands on my arms and gently push-ed me out of his space. 'Ma'am, just sit down there on the lawn with the little girl. We'll take a look at the house as soon as my backup arrives.'

'Backup!' I snorted. 'They're dead; they're not going to hurt you!'

I sat with Bessie and waited until the ambu-lance and the backup arrived. I saw three offi-cers go into the house, but then I was distracted helping get Bessie into the ambulance. An officer was dispatched to watch my children and I gave her Willis's number at work, asking her to call him to come home and tell him briefly what happened.

As I crawled into the back of the ambulance with Bessie, a plainclothes cop crawled in with me. Holding out his hand, he said, 'Detective

Stewart, Mrs Pugh. Mind if I ride with you and get your statement?'

I held up my bloody palms and he put his hand down. Shaking hands was not an option. I looked at Bessie then at one of the EMTs working on her. 'Can she understand me?' I asked.

He shook his head. 'I don't know, ma'am, but I don't think so. She's got all the symptoms of shock.'

I moved to the back of the ambulance with Detective Stewart and there told him everything, from the moment I first walked into the house, until the moment I came out and puked in the oleanders.

By the time I'd finished telling my story, we'd arrived at Codderville Memorial Hospital. They took Bessie quickly inside and, after several hours, I was told she was diagnosed as being in severe shock, borderline catatonic. I told my story to several more police officers, plain-clothes and uniform, and a couple of medical types and one social worker. Finally, the doctor came out and told me that Bessie had been given some medication that would make her sleep for several hours.

'The best thing you can do for her and your-self, is to go home and get some rest,' he said gently, an arm on my shoulder.

I thanked him and turned, finding Detective Stewart standing there. 'I'll drive you home,' he said, grabbing keys from a uniformed officer.

It was four o'clock in the afternoon before he dropped me off. All the vehicles that had been clogging the street earlier – the police cars, ambulances – were gone, and the house next door was cordoned off with yellow tape. I tried not to look at it as I rang the bell for my own home.

TWO

BLACK CAT RIDGE, TEXAS, THE PRESENT

The boy who calls himself her brother, I'll kill him first. I owe him big time. I'm gonna gut him like a fish. Fillet him. I can feel the smile on my face. Just the thought of him gone makes me happy. Maybe I'll let Bessie watch. She deserves that much for her part in trying to escape me! She's been bad, but I'll teach her how to be good. I've learned from the best!

OK, here's what happened:

APRIL, 2009 (LAST WEEK)

Elizabeth Lester Pugh was of two minds when it came to what she wanted to be when she grew up: a Nobel Prize-winning quantum physicist or the Poet Laureate of the United States. Maybe both. She had no concerns whatsoever about make-up, clothes, shaving her legs, all those things girls her age seemed to fixate on. She believed highly in personal hygiene, would never go outside without washing her face and combing her hair, and was always careful not to have a booger hanging out of her nose. But that was about it. Except – and this was a big exception – when it came to her sister Megan.

Megan was a total girly-girl. Her existence was tied up in her make-up, her clothes, and what boy said what about what girl. Megan's goal in life was to be a wife, mother, and fashion consultant, not necessarily in that order. So Elizabeth, who was smaller than Megan, was very careful to buy the clothes that Megan wanted but couldn't wear, borrow things from Megan's closet when Megan could never borrow anything from hers, and generally make Megan's life as miserable as possible. It was her duty: they were sisters.

On the other hand, nobody, and I mean nobody, said a bad word about Megan in front of Elizabeth, and visa versa. And that went double for their brother Graham. On the Graham front, the two girls were totally bonded.

On this beautiful Thursday in April, the two girls got out of the minivan that was their carpool vehicle of the week, and raced to the front door, Megan of the longer legs winning as usual. They knew that today they were latchkey kids, as Dad was still at work and Mom was off to her romance convention in Austin, so they dug the extra key out of the flowerbed and used it to get in the house.

Megan, heading for the kitchen, said, 'I'm hungry.'

Elizabeth answered with, 'You'll never lose weight that way. I'm going upstairs.'

Megan wasn't really overweight but Elizabeth never missed an opportunity to point out that she *could* be. She bounded up the stairs and into her room, throwing her backpack on the bed and heading straight to the computer. She turned it on and checked her email. And there it was: an email from Tommy.

Elizabeth wasn't really into boys, but Tommy was different. He was smart and funny and he understood her. She had to admit, to herself at least, that she was beginning to have a bit of a crush on him. The email was simple:

TO: Skywatcher75
FROM: T_Tom37
Home yet? IM me when you get there. T

So she did. They'd met in a chat room several weeks ago, one dedicated to astronomy nuts, which they both were. They were the only non-college-aged kids in there and had gravitated to each other. Now neither visited the astronomy site much, but talked to each other by email and IM as often as possible. Elizabeth sent out an IM:

Skywatcher75: 'T, u there?'
T_Tom37: 'Hey, E, been waiting for u.'
Skywatcher75: 'Just got home'
T_Tom37: 'Missed u.'
Skywatcher75: 'How was school?'
T_Tom37: 'Usual – u?'

Skywatcher75: 'Same'
T_Tom37: 'Gotta talk bout something'
Skywatcher75: 'What?'
T_Tom37: 'This is serious, E'

Elizabeth felt a stab of panic laced with joy. Was he going to profess his undying love for her? Was he going to say he couldn't talk to her anymore? What?

Skywatcher75: 'What?'
T_Tom37: 'I haven't been telling u the whole truth'
Skywatcher75: 'About what?'
T_Tom37: 'Me'

Oh, God, Elizabeth thought, *he's not a boy in the ninth grade like he said – he's some thirty-year-old freak...*

Skywatcher75: 'Go ahead'
T_Tom37: 'U have to be brave and hear me out'
Skywatcher75: 'T, stop. Just tell me'
T_Tom37: 'My name's not Tommy'

This was it, Elizabeth thought. His name is Herman and he's in his fifties. Oh, gross.

Skywatcher75: 'What is it?'

There was a long silence from the other end, so long that Elizabeth thought for a moment that Tommy, or whatever his name was, had gone away. Then her computer pinged and words she'd never expected to see popped up.

T_Tom37: 'My name is Aldon.'

Elizabeth stared at the letters, not sure she was reading them right. Finally, she wrote:

Skywatcher75: 'I don't understand.'
T_Tom37: 'I'm your brother, Bessie.'

E.J., THE PRESENT

When Elizabeth told me about the emails, and the stalker's 'confession', I was sick to my stomach. There was no question that this could be Aldon. I saw his dead body – tripped over it. Buried it. Cried over it. Bessie was so young when it happened that any memory she had of that terrible time would be shaky. The trauma of what she had experienced that night left her mute for several weeks. I'm not sure how much of that time she remembered. We used to make a pilgrimage every year to the Lesters' graves, but in the last five years or so, we've let Bessie set the tone. Some years we all go, some years just Bessie. And once, no one went. It's her call.

But I never suspected that she could be almost convinced that Willis and I had lied to her. That Aldon never died, that we were somehow in a conspiracy to cover up 'what really happened'. I cried when she told me that. I didn't even know tears were streaming down my face until she looked at me and her face began to crumble.

27

Then I felt the tears and wiped them away. 'I'm sorry, honey,' I said. 'So sorry you had to go through this.'

'I'm sorry!' she said. 'That I could believe that creep! I don't know what got into me!' she said, sobbing.

At fourteen, my youngest daughter is still tiny, still small enough that I can pick her up. I did, and pulled her into my lap, holding her tight. Megan was crying too, saying, 'I told her you and Dad could never ever do that! I told her!' Then I had ended up with both girls in my lap, holding them tight, all of us crying. Willis and Graham sat at the table, Willis with his face in his hands, Graham looking anywhere but at the crying females.

It had been the longest night I'd spent since childbirth. And it wasn't over. Not until he was found, and I managed to have a few words with him.

GRAHAM, THE PRESENT

Here's the strange thing: I didn't get grounded. Not one day. Actually, I came out of this whole thing looking pretty damn good, if I do say so myself. Semi-superhero status. The girls, my sisters, might disagree, but they sure as hell didn't when I was saving their asses! It's just when they got time to think about it and figure out how much they now owed me that they decided I didn't do much. But they are Wrong with a capital 'W'.

So I called Lotta that first Sunday, after I

finally got up, late in the afternoon, and asked if I could drive her home from school on Monday. I'd met Lotta the night before, riding around in the low-rider. Long story. Anyway, the guys in the low-rider were her cousins (one was an uncle, I think), and they picked her up from work. So she was with us when the whole thing with Elizabeth came down. And she was hot – Lotta, not Elizabeth, jeez – and she'd given me her number.

'Hey, I work, idiot,' she said.

'Who you calling an idiot?' I said, smiling when I said it.

'You! Who do you think?' she asked.

'I dunno. Thought maybe you had somebody else on the line who really was an idiot,' I said.

'Naw, I only talk to one idiot at a time,' she said.

'So I'll drive you to work,' I said.

'Um, you'll have to talk to my cousin,' she said.

'Which one?'

'You saying I got too many cousins?' she asked.

'Hey, if you can count 'em all, that's fine.'

'Are you saying I can't count?' she said, no longer playing around.

'No, I'm saying you got a lot of cousins!' I said.

''Cause if you're saying you think I can't count 'cause I'm Mexican, you can just take your white ass...'

'Whoa, there! Jeez, Lotta, where'd this shit come from?' I asked, totally confused.

There was a sigh on the other end of the line. 'Never mind,' she finally said. 'The school counselor says I got issues.'

'Hey, we all got issues,' I said.

'You saying your issues are better than my issues?' she demanded.

'OK, look,' I finally said, 'I guess this isn't gonna work, so, Lotta, enjoyed meeting you...'

'Sorry,' she said. 'I tend to get defensive. I think that comes from being the only girl with five brothers and fourteen male cousins. Not another girl in the bunch.'

'I can understand that – on a smaller scale,' I said, 'being the only boy with two sisters.'

'Yeah, but I met your sisters, and I think they're nice,' she said.

'That's 'cause you're not a boy sharing a bathroom with them. Underwear drying on the bathtub, hairy razors everywhere, face cream or some such shit all over the counter – and don't get me started on trying to get in there in the morning! I almost pissed myself last week.'

'Oh, thanks for that image!' she said, laughing.

'So,' I said, taking a deep breath. 'Can I drive you to work after school tomorrow?'

'Hum,' she said, like it was the first time she'd heard me ask. 'I guess so.'

'Great!' I said. 'I'll meet you at the door to the parking lot, OK?'

'See you then after last bell,' she said.

Then we both said goodbye and hung up. Then I thought, all I had to do was figure out how to get Mom's car. But that afternoon, that, and so many more of my problems got solved when my grandma came over.

She had her friend Miss Gladys with her and they were driving what I thought were both their cars. One was a fairly late model Ford Taurus and the other was Grandma's Valiant.

Once everybody got in the living room, she made Mom call me downstairs and then came the bombshell of all bombshells.

'I was looking at the Valiant,' Grandma said, 'and thinking about the horror Bessie went through in *my* car. And I thought she'll never want to ride with me anywhere again. And then I thought, I need to get her to ride in it a lot so she'll get used to it being my car again, and not that horrible place where she was held captive, but then I thought how she hardly ever rides with me, so then I came up with the perfect solution.'

Grandma looked from one to the other of us with a beaming smile on her face. Finally, her friend Miss Gladys said, 'Oh, for heaven's sake, Vera, just spit it out!'

Grandma glared at her but then turned to me with a smile. 'If it's OK with your parents,' she said, 'I want you to have the Valiant. I already bought me a new car,' she said, pointing toward the window, 'that Taurus out there. Fine little automobile. Now that Valiant has a lot of years left in it, Graham, if you treat it right!'

I whirled around to my parents. Mom was looking shocked but Dad was smiling, which meant he and Grandma had already discussed it, without talking to Mom about it. Oh, boy. 'Can I?' I asked. Or panted. Or whatever.

'I don't see a problem with it,' Dad said.

'Willis!' my mother said, staring daggers at my dad.

'What's your objection, E.J.?' Dad said, really putting her on the spot.

She opened her mouth and closed it, and then tried it again, with still no words coming out. Finally she shook her head, sighed, and said, 'No objection.'

I jumped up and hugged my grandmother and thanked her a bunch. Then grabbed the keys and headed out the door.

E.J., THE PRESENT

So I picked them up after school that day, and the next, and the day after that. He didn't show. I knew he wouldn't right away. He'd wait for us to let our guard down, to stop watching every move that Elizabeth made. Then he'd once again go after her. That's what stalkers did.

One afternoon, as Megan climbed into the backseat, Elizabeth stuck her head in the open window of the passenger side of the car. 'Mom, my friend Alicia wants me to go home with her. I told her it would be OK, right?'

'Who's Alicia?' I asked, never having heard of this particular friend.

'She's new in school...' Elizabeth started.

Megan cut in. 'And she's a total geek and a snob on top of that! Why in the world a geek would think they have anything to be snobby about, I don't know.'

'Shut up!' Elizabeth said.

32

'Bessie! We don't say shut up!' I corrected.

'Yeah, and we don't call me Bessie, remember, Mother?' she said, drawing the dastardly word 'mother' out as only a teenage girl can. To her sister, she added, 'And you're just pissed because she didn't invite you!'

'Elizabeth! We don't say pissed!' I corrected.

'Maybe you don't, Mom,' Megan said, 'but I think Bessie just did!' There was stress on the old nickname, which caused Elizabeth to stand up straighter and glare at her sister.

'Is anyone really talking to you?' Elizabeth said. 'Other than that skuzzy skater who tries to look down your shirt every day?'

I couldn't help looking back at Megan. She was turning blood red. This was something I'd have to delve into – later.

'Elizabeth. I don't want you going home with someone I don't know. Have her mother call me and we'll discuss having your friend come over to our house,' I said.

'Oh, gawd! You've got to be kidding! Alicia's waiting for me! What am I supposed to tell her? That my mother thinks I'm too young to have play dates, for God's sake!'

I was losing my patience. 'Get in the back seat now,' I said.

'No! I have to go tell Alicia I can't go!' she almost screamed at me.

I took off my seatbelt and opened the driver's door. Before I got myself out of the car, Bessie was in the backseat, buckling her own seatbelt.

Still standing outside the car, I said, 'Where is this Alicia? I'll tell her myself.'

33

'No! Don't! Please, Mom! Gawd, I'd die of embarrassment!' Bessie said.

I got back in the car. 'Tomorrow, tell her to have her mom call me and we'll set something up. That's the only way, Elizabeth. Do you understand?'

'Yes, ma'am,' she said. In the rearview mirror, I could see her folding her arms over her chest and glaring out the side window.

BLACK CAT RIDGE, TEXAS, 1999

I finally got to sleep sometime around three a.m. When I awoke the next morning, it was after ten and my mind registered the smell of bacon coming from the kitchen downstairs. And then the terrible events of the day before washed over me like a red tide.

I found a robe and put it on over my gown and headed downstairs. Willis and I had decided to keep the kids home from school another day. We had to tell them what happened; we didn't want schoolyard gossip to be their first hint of the tragedy that had befallen their friends.

Willis was leaning against the bar that separated the kitchen from the breakfast room, his back to me, bacon frying in a skillet on the stove.

'Where are the kids?' I asked, aware of the silence of the house.

Willis whirled around at my voice, the Codderville *News-Messenger* he'd been reading shoved behind his back. 'Ah, hey, babe. Mom came by early this morning and picked them up. She's taking them to a movie in Codderville.'

I nodded my head. The only good reason, I thought to myself, to have a mother-in-law in the first place. 'That's good,' I said. Then, 'What are you hiding behind your back?'

'Hum? Oh, nothing,' he said. 'Have some breakfast! I bet you didn't eat anything yesterday. You must be starving. What can I get—?'

I grabbed the paper from where he'd tried to hide it. The headline: 'Black Cat Ridge Family Victims of Murder-Suicide.' The story read:

'Codderville Police yesterday discovered the bodies of four members of the Lester family of Black Cat Ridge. In an apparent homicide-suicide, the father of the family, Roy Lester, manager of the Codder County Utility District, allegedly shot his wife, Terry Lester, and two of their three children, Monique Lester, age sixteen, junior at Black Cat Ridge High, and Aldon Lester, age ten, fifth grader at Black Cat Ridge Elementary, then allegedly turned the gun on himself. The Lesters' youngest child, Elizabeth, age four, is in undisclosed condition at Codderville Memorial Hospital.

At this time, the police can find no reason for the apparent murders and suicide.'

'You bet your ass they can find no reason!' I said, flinging the paper in the trash. 'Roy didn't do it!'

Then I looked at Willis, his head bent, one hand covering his face. 'Honey,' he finally said, 'the police said he was sitting there with the shotgun in his lap, his face...'

I walked up to my husband and gently pulled his hand away from his face. 'I know what they saw, Willis, because I saw it first. But that has nothing to do with anything. Roy didn't do it. You know it and I know it.'

Willis shook his head, tears streaming down his face. 'Ah, shit, baby...'

I put my arms around him and we both cried, long and hard. It was the first time I'd ever seen my husband cry.

Later, after we'd exhausted our tears and cleaned our faces, we sat at the kitchen table, coffee cups before us. 'Why would Roy do it?' I asked.

Willis shook his head. 'I don't know. He wouldn't – not unless he went nuts.'

'Why would he suddenly, out of the blue, go nuts? Have you seen any signs of impending nuttiness?'

Again, he shook his head. I placed my hand over his. 'Let's assume for a minute that he didn't do it.' Willis looked up at me. 'Let's assume,' I went on, 'that our funny, lovable friend we've known for four years did *not* kill his wife and two of his children.'

'If we assume that,' Willis the engineer said, 'then we must also assume that someone else did.'

'Yes,' I said.

'And if someone else did it, then that someone else manufactured things to make it look as if Roy had done it.'

'Yes,' I said.

Again, the shake of the head. 'But why? Why

36

in the hell would anybody – *anybody* – do this?'

'It's easier for me to believe somebody else did it than to believe Roy did. So there's a Charles Manson clone out there – I don't know! I just know Roy didn't do it.'

This time Willis put his hand on mine. 'Honey, statistically speaking more murders are committed by family members than by strangers.'

'Not in this case.' Then it hit me – the anomaly. 'OK, answer me this: Where in the hell did that shotgun come from?'

'The attic,' Willis said.

'What?'

He sighed. 'The shotgun had been his dad's – the only thing he had of his father's.'

'OK, so Roy, the most laidback person I've ever known, suddenly goes nuts, and instead of using a kitchen knife to kill his family, goes upstairs, pulls down the ladder to the attic, crawls around up there until he finds this shotgun – oh, and did he have bullets for it? – and then comes back down and proceeds to shoot his family. Is that what you're saying?'

Willis stood up abruptly, knocking over his chair. 'I'm not saying shit! We don't know what's in other people's souls, in their hearts! We don't know what went on in their bedroom! What deep dark secrets they had!'

I stood up and glared at my husband. 'Well, I do! I know they lost a baby between Aldon and Bessie and Roy cried for days! Did you know that? I know that Roy had an affair the first year they were married and Terry kicked him in the balls so hard he had to go to the ER! Did you

37

know that? I know that Monique went on the pill last year – just in case! Did you know that? I know that Roy's mother died in an alcoholic ward in Dallas. Did you know that?'

Willis shook his head as he sat back down. 'No, I didn't know that. Except for the ER visit – Roy told me about that.'

I sat back down across from him. 'I also know something else. If Roy Lester was capable of doing what was done at that house yesterday, then so are you – so is everybody! And I don't believe that! I could not go on living in this world if I thought for an instant that everyone – me, you, Roy – was capable of what I saw!'

'You don't think I'm capable of killing somebody?' my husband demanded.

'Yes, I do. I think you would shoot, stab, bludgeon or beat to death anyone hurting me or the kids or even a stranger, but I *do not* think you are capable of picking up a shotgun and chasing your children down the stairs and shooting them in the back!'

The tears were again running freely down my face. Sobbing, I got up and left the room, heading up the stairs, feeling the muzzle of an imaginary gun at my back.

ELIZABETH, THE PRESENT

It wasn't bad enough that I got kidnapped by that horrible cretin a while back, now my mother acts like I'm made of glass. I can't go anywhere by myself! Ever! I had to make up going to Alicia's house because there was no way my mother was going to let me take the bus to the new mall in Codderville. And she wouldn't even let me do that! Just go to Alicia's house! With her mother there! Alicia's cool and it would have been a blast at the mall. Half our class was going to be there. With the great big exception of Megan!

I can't do anything without Megan! You know, sometimes, I'd just like to be myself – not an extension of Megan. If that horrible incident taught me anything, it's that I'm entirely too wrapped up in this family! I have a family! They're dead, but they're mine! Sometimes my mother acts like I've always been hers! And that's not true! And sometimes I wish that guy really had been Aldon. Even if it meant Mom and Dad had been lying to me and were involved in some way in what happened to my family – the up side of that is I would have someone really mine. My blood.

In biology class we talk about bloodlines and genetics and I know nothing about mine! I know my grandma died of cancer. What about my real mom? Would she have succumbed to it too? Would I? There are so many things I don't know. Sometimes I feel like just taking off! Surely there's someone out there related to me. Somewhere!

E.J., THE PRESENT

So for six weeks Graham took the girls to school every morning and I picked them up from school every day. I had two more weeks until school was out, and needed to get the kids involved in something. There had been a flyer in the church program the Sunday before about the Methodist Youths doing a summer camp for the smaller kids. I figured that would be a perfect way to keep the kids occupied and watched the entire time. I knew Graham wasn't going to like the idea, but he was my ace in the hole.

It's funny how kids change. I always figured Graham would be my problem child. A smart-mouthed, in-your-face child, he turned into a relatively mellow teenager. And, as far as I can tell, the mellow isn't from anything he smokes. He's a straight 'B' student, does sports, has a lot of friends – albeit some of them not so bright – and does *some* of his chores without bitching. And the way he stepped in and took care of his sisters during that horror, well, I can't praise him enough for that. Actually, I can't praise him at all. All three of them get mad at that. The girls are all 'we didn't need to be rescued,' and Graham's all 'shucks, ma'am, I didn't do nothin'.' It would be comical if it wasn't so maddening.

I've always heard that the teenage years are the hardest, but who would have thought Bessie – excuse me, Elizabeth – would be the problem? She was an angelic child. Always the voice of reason when she and Megan were playing. Megan would say, 'Let's play fairies and jump off the roof!' and Bessie would say, 'But, Megan, we'd get hurt. Let's don't.' Megan would say, 'Let's put the cat in the dryer!' and Bessie would say, 'I think that would make her sick. Let's don't.' And Megan would say, 'Let's stick our Barbies in the oven and see if they come out with a tan!' and Bessie would say, 'I think they'd just burn up. Let's don't.' Megan would always argue, but Bessie would almost always curb Megan's enthusiasms.

But now it's different. I'm afraid Megan got thrust into the role of the reasonable one when she began reading Elizabeth's emails from her 'brother Aldon.' And Bessie, poor Bessie, still so desperate for her own family, wanted to believe. No matter what, she wanted to believe.

It breaks my heart a little more that this person did this to her. Someone attacking her for no other reason than the fact that she was a girl and available would have been bad enough, but for this person to seek her out, stalk her, play games with her head, bring up the past that we've tried so hard to help her understand and put behind her, is unconscionable. He needs to be put down like a rabid dog. Yes, I know, Texas's leading un-known liberal is talking. Sometimes politics are just words. I want this monster dead. Hey, I'm a mom.

I found the church program where I'd dropped it by the back door, and found the number for the youth summer program director, Myra Morris. She'd been with the church for three summers, directing the youth summer programs, and the kids loved her. I figured with Myra involved, at least I had a fighting chance of getting all three to go. Especially Graham, who, as I mentioned, was going to be my ace in the hole. Myra was twenty years old, had blond hair that she usually wore in a perky ponytail, blue eyes as big as an anima character, and legs at least twice the length of her torso. She was a serious beauty – a former UT sorority girl who'd seen the light and transferred to SMU to finish up before going on to seminary.

'This is Myra,' she said when she picked up the phone.

'Hi, Myra, it's E.J. Pugh, Graham—' I started.

'And Megan and Elizabeth's mom! Hi, Ms Pugh! I hope you're calling to enroll all three as counselors!'

When I was a teenager and young adult, full of angst and anger and rebellion, I would have hated Myra Morris. But as a mom, these things change. I wanted the Myra Morrises around my kids. The perky, head cheerleaders with the Type A personalities and an overload of spunk. I would gladly kick a clone of myself as far away from my kids as I could get her.

'Actually, that's exactly why I'm calling. And, Myra, I need to tell you confidentially that Elizabeth was being stalked this spring. We never found the guy who did it, but he did try to kidnap her—'

'Oh, dear Lord!' Myra breathed. 'Is she OK?'

'She's fine, Myra, but actually it's me. I'm scared shi— to death,' I said, remembering I was talking to someone at the church and trying desperately to clean up my language. 'I was hoping I could enlist you to keep a clandestine eye on her.'

'Of course! We've got a lot of safe guards in place for the little ones, and I'll just make sure we follow them for the older kids too. Is there anything else I can do?'

'Would it be possible for Elizabeth and

Graham to work together? He'll be coming to keep an eye on her.'

'I'll make sure of it. What a good big brother he is!' Myra said, of course finding the bright side. OK, I didn't say these perky types weren't still annoying as hell, just that they'd be better around children than I would have been at that age. Personally, more than two minutes around her gave me hives.

'That's great, Myra,' I said. 'Thanks so much. When does it start and when do they need to be there?'

She gave me all the pertinent information, including location, which, unfortunately, was not on the church grounds. They would be bussed every day to the church sleepaway camp that had a day-camp area, and was about fifteen miles from Black Cat Ridge.

I hung up and sat back in my chair, thinking about my idea. Maybe not such a good one, I thought. I didn't like the idea of the kids being fifteen miles away from help (and on the road the camp was on that translated into thirty to forty-five minutes), if they needed it. OK, in my mind *when* they needed it. Myra had told me who would be driving the bus, Gus Mayhew, a forty-five-year-old former Marine with arms like ham hocks and legs like sides of beef, who she'd talk to about staying the day. If Gus, one of the deacons of the church, agreed to do it, and I thought he would, then it was on.

Willis and I had been raised in different faiths – Willis as a Southern Baptist, me as an Episcopalian – and, at the urging of Terry and Roy, found ourselves firmly in the arms of the Methodists within weeks of moving to Black Cat Ridge. Willis's mother, Vera, wasn't happy, but then, I really didn't care about making the woman happy. OK, we had issues. Everything was fine the first year, but the minister we had moved on and our church was punished for some reason with the entrance of The Right Reverend Berry Rush. The only thing worse than Berry Rush was his wife, Rosemary Rush. Separately they were both pompous, arrogant, self-righteous, and holier-than-thou. Together they were royal pains in the ass.

He called at noon on Wednesday.

'E.J.,' he said when I picked up the phone. 'This is Reverend Rush.'

'Oh, hello,' I said, finding the nearest chair to sit down. Along with everything else, Berry Rush was long-winded.

'I was so terribly sorry to hear about what happened at the Lesters.'

'Thank you,' I said.

'Do you have the names of the next of kin so I may call and offer my condolences and any services they might possibly need?'

I found my address book and read off the name of the only viable next of kin.

'I understand that you found them, E.J.,' Reverend Rush said.

'Yes.'

'How are you doing?' he asked.

'I'm OK, Reverend Rush,' I answered, gritting my teeth. 'Thank you for asking.'

'If there's anything Rosemary or I can do...'

The thought made me shudder. 'No really, I'm all right. But I do appreciate your concern.'

'Well, we'll be praying for you and your family, and of course, little Bessie.'

'Thank you,' I said, but was talking to dead air.

Thinking about Mrs Karnes, Terry's mother, the number I'd given Berry Rush, I decided the first voice she needed to hear from her daughter's neighborhood should be mine and not Berry's. So I dialed the number, hoping to beat Berry to the punch.

'Hello?' a female voice answered.

'Mrs Karnes?' I asked.

'I'm afraid Mrs Karnes can't come to the phone,' the woman said. 'She's not taking any calls right now.'

'Oh, of course,' I said. 'I'm sorry. This is E.J. Pugh. I was Terry's next-door neighbor—'

'Oh, my goodness!' the woman exclaimed. 'You're the poor thing that found ... Oh my goodness!'

There was a commotion on the line. I could hear the woman say, 'Now, Irene, you shouldn't be up ... E.J., Mrs Karnes wants to speak to you.'

'E.J., is that you?'

'Yes, Mrs Karnes, it's me.'

I heard her sob. 'I don't believe any of this,' she said.

'I know, I know.' I hadn't realized how hard

45

this was going to be. My own tears were welling up and spilling over. This woman had been through so much, so damn much.

'How's Bessie?' she asked. 'Are you taking care of Bessie?'

'She's still in the hospital, ma'am, but I saw her yesterday. It's too soon for the doctors to know much.' Know what, I hope she didn't ask. She couldn't take the possibilities – the horrible possibilities that went through my head a thousand times a day.

I heard her take in a breath. 'Do you have a copy of their will?' she asked.

'No, ma'am, I don't know that they made one.'

She sighed, and I could tell she was in pain – her words coming out in short, staccato sentences. 'They did. Last Christmas. Up here. I made them. The cancer was back. I couldn't be ... responsible ... for the ... children. I thought I'd be dead ... long before...'

'Yes, ma'am.'

Again, the long intake of breath. 'Terry didn't tell you?'

'No, ma'am.'

'You – and Willis – are executors. Lynda was ... but...'

Lynda, Terry's sister, had died in a car wreck the year before. 'Yes, ma'am,' I said.

There was a sob on the other end of the line. 'A woman shouldn't outlive both of her children, E.J.! It's not right!'

I was gasping for my own air. Terry hadn't said a word, but then, when was there time? Why would that be on her mind? Her sister dead, her

46

mom dying, why would she even think to mention it?

'I hate to break it to you like this, E.J.,' Mrs Karnes said. 'You're listed as guardian of the children in case ... Oh, Lord.'

'Mrs Karnes...'

'I can't be responsible, don't you see?'

'Ma'am...'

'E.J., I'm dying. The chemo, it's not working. They're talking about calling in Hospice.'

'Mrs Karnes, I'm so sorry...'

'Thank you, but that's not the point! The point is Bessie! I'm going to have my lawyer send you a copy of the will. You need to get your own lawyer. Somebody's going to have to pay for Bessie's hospital bills, and the funerals...'

'Mrs Karnes, we'll take care of it,' I heard myself saying. 'Please don't worry about it.'

'Oh, I'll worry about it, I'll worry myself sick about it, but there's not a blasted thing I can do!' I heard another deep intake of breath, as if she were fighting for each one. 'E.J. Roy ... Roy was like a son to me...'

'He didn't do this, Mrs Karnes,' I said.

I heard her sob again, then the phone went dead.

THREE

BLACK CAT RIDGE, TEXAS, THE PRESENT

I have so many plans! Bessie and I will be so happy. My sister, my lover, my sweet, sweet Bessie. She's like a Hershey's kiss, a tiny morsel you can eat in just one bite! Ha! That's my Bessie! And she'll be happy, once I get her away from her captors, she'll be so happy.

E.J., THE PRESENT

I took the kids to their orientation meeting for being day counselors and sat in the back, trying to be a large, redheaded fly on the wall. Graham had been the hold out. Even the thought of seeing perky blond Myra Morris every day wouldn't budge Graham.

'I have plans for this summer!' he said.

'What?' I inquired.

'I dunno. Plans.'

'What plans?' I demanded.

'You know, plans!'

I stood up from where I'd been sitting across from him in the family room, the TV thankfully muted for a moment. Without looking at him, I headed into the kitchen, saying, 'You're going.'

'Mom! Listen!'

'What?' I said, opening the freezer to find something to put out for dinner. Chicken, again? There was that roast – doctor said no red meat for Willis. Oh, those pork chops! Pork's the other white meat, right? My hand reached for the pork chops just as Graham said:

'Mom. I've got a girlfriend.'

The pork chops fell to the floor with a loud thunk.

'You what?' I demanded.

Graham looked at me funny. 'I have a girlfriend. That's not a bad thing is it?'

'You get a car and immediately get a girlfriend! I knew that car was going to get you in trouble...'

'Jeez, Mom! Chill! She's not pregnant!'

My right hand flew to my breast where my heart was reacting at jackhammer speed. 'Oh, God, you're having sex!'

Graham blushed scarlet. 'Jeez, Mom! No! Gawd! I'm just saying, I don't want to go baby-sit a bunch of kids because my girlfriend ... my friend who's a girl ... whatever ... works nights, and if I work days, I'll never see her!'

I was overreacting. I knew I was overreacting. Graham knew I was overreacting. But I didn't seem to be able to stop myself. 'Who is she?' I demanded.

'A girl from school,' Graham said.

'What's her name?' I demanded.

'Lotta,' he said quietly.

'Is this a joke?' I demanded.

'What?' he said, getting angry.

49

'Lotta What? Lotta Fun? Lotta Woman? Lotta Babe? Lotta What?'

Graham turned away from me, throwing his arms up in the air. 'Jeez, Mom, you are most definitely getting weirder!'

I took some deep breaths. Picked the pork chops up off the floor and put them on the counter. Walked back into the family room where Graham was pointing the remote at the TV.

'Don't un-mute it,' I said. I sat down next to him on the sofa. 'I'm sorry,' I said. 'I over-reacted.' I sighed. 'Please. Tell me about this girl.'

He put the remote down and turned to me, actually looking me in the eye. 'Her name is Lotta Hernandez. Lotta is a nickname for Carlotta.' He grinned at me. 'But I think I will tell her you said it stood for Lotta Woman.'

I smacked my son on the arm. 'Don't you dare! Not until I see her and decide if she is or not!'

'Oh, great! That's not gonna happen. No meeting.'

'Why? Who are you ashamed of? Her or us?'

'Y'all, of course,' my son said. Sobering, he said, 'She's already met the girls. That car full of boys I was with – they were her cousins, and I think one was her brother. Anyway, they picked her up from work so she was with us when we found Megan and went after Elizabeth.'

I nodded my head. 'Then I have to meet her,' I said. 'If only to thank her for helping.'

'So you see why I can't babysit at the youth

camp, right?' he said.

I shook my head. 'I understand why you don't want to, but you have to, Graham. I don't want Bessie – Elizabeth – alone at the camp.'

'Then don't send her or Megan! Why ruin my summer just for her?'

I looked at my son and bristled. 'Aren't you being a little selfish?'

'Jeez, Mom, everything's always been about Bessie! Don't you think Megan and I have suffered enough for Bessie? Our lives turned upside down, your attention and Dad's attention totally on her—'

'That's not true, Graham...'

'Oh, yes it is!' my son said, standing up and glaring at me. 'She's always come first! It's always, always about Bessie—'

'Then maybe it's time I left,' came a small voice from the doorway. Graham and I both whirled around to see Elizabeth standing there.

Graham turned his glare to her. 'Yeah, kid, maybe it is,' he said, then left the room.

ELIZABETH, THE PRESENT

I didn't realize Graham hated me. And I guess Megan, too. I'm so out of here. I just don't know where to go. I have no one. I'm totally alone now. Maybe I'll hitch-hike to Austin or Houston, try living on the streets. I won't sell my body, though! And I won't do drugs! I promise myself that right this minute!

Jeez, could I be more of a geek? I can't believe the kid heard me say that, and I can't even believe I said it. I was just pissed, you know? I mean, yeah, they've always paid a little more attention to Elizabeth than to me and Meg. But so did we. I mean the kid saw her whole family murdered, you know? She needed special attention. Things were finally getting to normal, I guess you'd call it, when that asshole up and tried to kidnap her. So now Mom's paying special attention to her again. And why not? *She's* the one who got kidnapped, not me or Megan. Jeez, I can be such a jerk sometimes.

I talked to Lotta about it. She agreed. I'm a jerk. Except she wasn't that nice about it.

'What were you thinking? And she heard you?' Lotta said.

'Yeah, unfortunately she was right there—'

'Unfortunately my ass!' Lotta said. 'It was God's will! You say something like that, even think it, it's gonna bite you in the butt! You're such an idiot! What were you thinking?'

'I guess I wasn't—'

'No, I guess you weren't! Now what are you gonna do about it, idiot?' she demanded.

'Uh...' I started.

'You're gonna apologize to her is what you're gonna do, you stupid gringo!'

'Hey! What would you do if I called you a stupid Mexican?' I demanded.

'Well, first you'd be wrong! I'm not stupid and I'm not a Mexican. I'm an American. So you'd be wrong on both counts!'

'Well, don't call me a gringo!' I said.

'OK,' she said, her voice softer. 'That was wrong. I won't do it again. I'll just call you an idiot! Which you are!'

'She won't even speak to me...' I started.

'She doesn't have to speak to you – you speak to her!'

'Whatever. It still won't fix the fact that I'm not going to be able to see you much,' I said.

'We'll work on that. Does this church thing pay money?'

'Nope. Strictly volunteer.'

'Well, that sucks. What are the hours?'

'It's day camp. Eight a.m. until one p.m.'

'I don't have to be at work until six at night. Hey, why don't I volunteer?' she said. 'Then we'll have the mornings together and the after-noons. If you can stand to see that much of me,' she said, her voice teasing.

'Oh, I can stand it,' I said. 'But it's like a Methodist Church thing. Aren't you Catholic?'

'What? You just assume because I'm of Mexican descent that I'm Catholic? Gawd!'

'I'm sorry, I just thought—'

'Yeah, I'm Catholic but so what? God won't mind if I take care of little heathen Methodist babies!'

I laughed. 'Well, at least you have the right attitude.'

She laughed back then said, 'Go take care of Elizabeth. You're a bad big brother. You want I should send Ernesto over to teach you how to be a good big brother?' she said, mentioning her

300-pound older brother who didn't like me dating his baby sister.

'No, that's OK,' I said quickly and she laughed. 'I'll make it up to her, I promise.'

'OK,' she said, 'but just remember, Ernesto's only a phone call away!' With that, she laughed and hung up on me. God, isn't she great?

I knocked on Elizabeth's bedroom door, which is something I don't usually do. I figure the girls shouldn't be doing anything in their rooms that their big brother doesn't have a right to see. Except changing clothes. I walked in on that twice, both times with Megan and, believe me, it was pretty gross. But this time, I knocked on Elizabeth's door. There was no answer but I knew she wasn't anywhere else in the house – I'd already looked. So I said, 'Liz, it's me. I'm coming in.' I opened the door and walked in.

She was lying on the bed, a book in her hand. Which wasn't unusual for her. 'I need to talk to you,' I said.

She turned her back to me. 'No,' she said.

I reached over her prone body and pulled the book out of her hands. She turned around and glared at me. 'You don't have to say anything,' I said. 'Just listen.' She grabbed for the book and I put it behind me, out of her reach. 'I'm sorry I said or even thought what you overheard,' I said. 'I'm an asshole. It was unfair and I didn't mean it, I was just pissed at Mom.'

'Give me my book,' she said, the most words I'd heard her speak at one time in two whole days.

'No,' I said. 'You listen.'

She slapped me in the face, then burst into tears. The slap didn't hurt, she's awful small. But I put my arms around her and held her. At first she tried to pull away, but I didn't let her. Finally she put her arms around my back and sobbed into my chest.

'Kid, I'm so sorry I said that. I'm so sorry you've been through everything that's happened to you. And I'm really sorry you have such an asshole for a big brother.' I pulled her away and held her face in my hands and looked her square in the eye. 'But let me tell you, kid. I knew your brother Aldon better than you did. He was my friend. And I swear to you, he woulda been an even bigger asshole than me,' I said, and smiled at her. 'He was mean!'

'I'm just all messed up,' Elizabeth said, looking down at the bed, rather than into my eyes. 'I don't know who to trust anymore. I feel so alone.'

I pulled her face up so I could look into her eyes, so she'd know I was talking the truth. 'You're not alone. You have your family. We're your family. We always have been. We always will be. And I won't speak for Megan 'cause she can be a real douche, but you can trust me. I swear to God, you can trust me. And,' I got off the bed and moved toward the door, 'cause I didn't want to be looking at her when I said this, because, well, you know, 'I love you, kid.'

BLACK CAT RIDGE, TEXAS, 1999

Willis and I left our home and went into Codder-

55

ville to pick the kids up at his mother's house. We had to tell the kids what had happened, explain why they were not in school today, why they'd spent the day at their grandmother's house.

We sat the kids down on the couch together, risking the pinches, kicks and bites that happened whenever the two of them were within arm's reach of each other.

'We have some very sad news,' I started.

Willis nodded. 'You know yesterday something happened at the Lesters' house, right?'

Both little heads nodded.

'Well...' I said. 'Um, something bad happened—'

'I knew it!' Megan jumped in. 'I knew Bessie was doing something bad! She was all dirty and I bet her mama's gonna beat her butt! She can't play no more, right?'

'Anymore.' I took Megan's tiny hands in mine. 'Honey, Bessie's not in trouble. She was hurt. She's in the hospital.'

Megan's lower lip began to tremble. 'She gonna be OK?'

I stroked her hair. 'Yes, darlin', she's gonna be fine. But her mommy and daddy aren't. They've gone to Heaven. And they had to take Monique and Aldon with them.'

Graham stood up, hands fisted at his side. 'Where's Aldon?' he demanded.

I let go of Megan and tried to grasp Graham's hands, but he pulled away from me, darting out into the middle of the living room.

'Where's Aldon?' he yelled.

56

Willis stood and went to Graham, grabbing him and holding him close. Kneeling in front of him, Willis said, 'Son, I'm sorry. I'm so sorry. But Aldon's dead. He's gone. Do you understand?'

Graham squirmed from his father's embrace and backed away to glare at Willis. 'Shut up, you shit!' he yelled.

Megan, still sitting in front of me on the couch, began to cry. 'Mommy?' she said, looking up at me. 'Mommy, what's a matter?'

How do you tell a six-year-old and a four-year-old that other children, their friends, are dead? Children aren't supposed to die. Grandmas and grandpas die. Not their peers.

Graham pulled away from his father and ran toward the kitchen. Willis started after him, but I said, 'Leave him alone, honey. Just let him be.'

But then Graham was back, that morning's Codderville *News-Messenger* in his hands. He looked his father square in the eye. Unfortunately for this moment, my son read at a fourth-grade level. 'Why, Daddy?' he asked. 'Why did Uncle Roy do this?'

With Megan still in my arms, I stood up and all of us waited for Willis's answer.

'Uncle Roy didn't do this, honey,' my husband said. 'The police are wrong.'

ELIZABETH, APRIL, 2009

Dad wasn't much of a cook, but he gave it his best effort. Wieners chopped up in macaroni and cheese and salad out of a bag. Elizabeth played

57

with her food, not seeing her brother and sister scarfing down Dad's efforts like they were good. Normally she'd take a shot at Megan's eating habits and style, but tonight she didn't even think about it. She had too much on her mind.

Aldon, he'd said. Her brother. Her dead brother. The brother who'd died when she lost the rest of her birth family, nearly a decade earlier. Elizabeth didn't understand what game Tommy was playing, or why he would do this. Aldon was dead; she knew that; she went to his grave at least once a year.

After Tommy had written those words, Elizabeth had blackened the monitor, too numb with fright and bewilderment to even think about responding. It had taken her so long to lay her family to rest in her mind, and here was this guy bringing it all back up again. What was he doing? Aldon was dead. Just like her sister Monique and her real mom and dad. She knew who had killed them and why. Mom – E.J. – had told her the whole story when she was eleven. She didn't have all the details – she didn't want them – but she knew enough to know that her brother Aldon was definitely dead.

Elizabeth nibbled on a slice of wiener. What was Tommy up to? she wondered. Why in the world would he say such a thing? And how did he find out about her brother Aldon?

The taste of the wiener made her sick to her stomach. She sat at the table hoping she would not puke into her plate – one of those personal hygiene things she was so fond of.

'What's wrong with you?' Megan asked from

across the table. 'You're acting weirder than usual.'

'Nothing,' Elizabeth answered.

Graham and Megan looked at each other. No come back. No shot at Megan having cleaned her plate. Something was definitely wrong. Megan looked at her father who sat oblivious at the end of the table, going for his second helping of wieners and mac and cheese. Best not bring anything up now, Megan thought. Not in front of Dad.

So they left her alone. Elizabeth didn't notice; she was too wrapped up in the 'what ifs' and 'maybes' Tommy's IMs had aroused in her. What if Aldon wasn't really dead? What if he had somehow survived that awful night? Then why wouldn't Mom – E.J. – know that? And if Aldon had survived, who was buried in his grave? Elizabeth shook herself internally and told herself to stop it. No way had Aldon survived that massacre. No way had he been wandering the world from the age of ten until now. Tommy was playing some horrible joke on her, but she would refuse to be anybody's punch line. She just wouldn't talk to him again. That's all there was to it.

E.J., THE PRESENT

It was at the orientation meeting that I finally met 'the girl', Graham's friend Lotta. Both my girls were hanging all over her after the meeting when I walked up to the group.

'So, what did y'all think?' I asked.

'Lotta's gonna be one of the counselors!' Megan said, practically jumping up and down.

'Ah, Mom,' Graham said, 'this is my ... friend, Lotta. Lotta, this is my mom.'

Lotta stuck out her hand and we shook. 'Nice to meet you, Mrs Pugh,' she said.

'Nice to meet you, Lotta. I wanted to thank you for your part in rescuing my girls,' I said.

'It was my pleasure,' she said. She put her arms around Megan and Elizabeth. 'It was a strange way to meet my new buddies, but at least I got to meet them!'

'Yeah!' Megan said, and Elizabeth, thank God, just grinned. Somehow she and Graham had worked out their differences and gotten around his harsh words.

'So what do y'all think about the camp?' I asked again.

Graham shrugged, Megan said, 'It's OK,' and Elizabeth said, 'Whatever.'

Then Lotta spoke up. 'I think it's gonna be great!' she said, a big smile on her face. 'What an opportunity to shape young minds! And get them interested in sports and physicality. I can't wait to see the camp!'

Oh, gawd, I thought, *she's perky*. Then she won my heart. She said, 'But that Myra, she's a little hyper, don't you think?' I decided then and there, Lotta and I were going to get along just fine.

ELIZABETH, THE PRESENT

I don't like kids. I'm not going to have any.

60

They're small pests. Bigger than a bug, but smaller than a grown-up, but still pests. It's going to be a long summer. It's hot as hell out there in the woods, and speaking of pests!!! There are a lot of the bug variety out there! I've got bites all over me and, ugh! I found a tick in this little girl's hair and Myra said I had to get it out and deal with it!!!! How does one *deal* with a tick???? Then she told me – I had to burn it! Burn a living thing! That's so gross I don't even want to think about it! I refused to do it, so she made Graham do it! I noticed she didn't do it herself! Myra's getting on my nerves. Graham is so fawny over Lotta that I'm about to puke! I like Lotta a lot – ha! – but Graham is so lovey-dovey with her it's embarrassing! I think even Lotta is a little embarrassed by the way he acts! Well, I know I would be if a boy acted like that around me! I can't believe there's another week of this session then three more sessions to go! What did I do in a past life to deserve this hell??????

GRAHAM, THE PRESENT

This camp counselor thing's pretty cool. I'm the oldest counselor – well, me and Lotta – and all the little kids think we're like junior gods, and the other counselors, the oldest a freshman in high school, tend to agree with the little kids. So, it's OK. My sisters are the hold-outs, of course. Liz is acting like she's too good to be there, and she's pretty mean to the little kids. They don't like her much. And Myra is starting to catch on

61

to Elizabeth's game. She's not giving her any slack, which I think is cool. If Lotta wasn't in my life, I'd definitely make a move on old Myra! God, she's hot! But I can't act like I'm aware of that fact, because even if Lotta didn't catch me drooling, Liz or Megan would, and they'd rat me out in a New York minute.

Anyway, things went pretty smooth the first week. They've got this set up in two-week sessions, so we'll have the same kids next week. Then the week after there will be a new bunch for two weeks, and so on, for a total of eight weeks. It's not so bad, a lot of fresh air, time to sneak into the woods for some grubbin' time with my baby, and being idolized by little snot-noses. The problem time for me is arts and crafts. I'm not so good at that. Actually, I suck big time. I can teach them sports all day long, take them canoeing in the lake, no problem, supervise swim time, I'm there, but arts and crafts? Give me a break. That's for girls. I don't even think they should be teaching the boys that, but Myra ignored my suggestion that the boys do something manly during that time. Unfortunately, the little snots seem to enjoy it, so what do I know?

Mom clued me in that Mr Mayhew, who drives the bus and is a deacon at the church, is going to stay to help keep an eye out for the faux Aldon. That's French for phony. Sometimes I worry about my mother. Mr Mayhew's like fifty or something, and already retired from his job at the post office because he had to have something replaced – like a hip, I think. Anyway, what's a fifty-year-old guy with only one real hip gonna do if something goes down? I'm worried the old guy's just gonna get in my way!

So anyway, that's the set-up. Me and Liz work with one group of five kids, Lotta and Megan work with another, and then there are two more groups with two counselors each. And then Myra oversees all of us and Mr Mayhew sits in the bus and reads the newspaper. Real helpful, this guy. The day camp part is about half a mile from the headquarters of the sleepaway camp, but we do see the older kids running through the woods sometimes – or at least hear them.

So, the five kids me and Liz are accountable for are three boys and two girls, ages five and six. All the kids do stuff together in a big group, mostly, but we're responsible for our five, helping them with their, excuse the expression, arts and crafts, and the sports stuff. And breaking into smaller groups for swimming and canoeing.

Like I said, things went great the first week, but on Sunday at church we found out that Myra had a car accident over the weekend and broke her leg. She was in the hospital and we were getting a replacement. And then we met her: her name was Christine and she was butt-ugly. That solved my drooling problem.

On Monday, when I drove the girls (Lotta included – I pick her up on our way) to the church parking lot, Christine was standing by the bus, clipboard in hand. She was wearing khaki shorts and the camp T-shirt, and I gotta say, butt-ugly as she was, the girl had some legs. Lotta caught me looking at them and elbowed me in the gut. I'll try not to do that again – my girl's got a powerful elbow. Not to mention a wicked tongue and a hell of left hook. Don't ask me how I know about the last one. It's embarrassing.

The new supervisor, Christine, didn't smile much, and seemed to be of the Marine Corps boot camp school of counseling. She wore a whistle! Truth! At least she seemed to agree with me on arts and crafts. She decided an hour was too much time to spend on that crap, and cut it by half. Which was fine by me. Megan – of course it had to be Megan – wasn't thrilled.

'I don't think that's a good idea, Miss Christine,' she said. 'Especially today. I think it would be a good idea for the kids to spend their time today making Miss Myra something. Cards, or something. After all, she *is* in the hospital.'

'Yeah, I think she's right,' Lotta said, then glared at me until I agreed. Some of the other counselors also agreed.

Christine stared at Megan for a moment, then said, 'OK. You're right.' Then she blew her whistle and, as she walked out of the arts and crafts pavilion, said over her shoulder, 'Make cards!' And blew her whistle again. It's only Monday and I've already got some serious issues with that freaking whistle.

ELIZABETH, APRIL, 2009

By her digital clock on the bedside table it was three a.m. when Elizabeth woke up. Her computer was pinging. It took her a moment to figure out what it was, then she remembered Tommy and the horrible things he'd said. She stared at her computer like it was a cobra about to strike her heart.

The pinging continued and she finally got up and moved to her desk, lest the noise wake up the rest of the family. She turned on her monitor and saw the IMs.

T_Tom37: 'E, u there?'
Skywatcher75: 'What do u want?'
T_Tom37: 'Sorry if I scared u'
Skywatcher75: 'U didn't scare me – just pissed me off!'
T_Tom37: 'Didn't want 2 do that either'
Skywatcher75: 'I don't want 2 talk 2 u n-e more, Tommy, or whatever ur name is'
T_Tom37: 'Bessie, ur n danger'

The only danger Elizabeth felt she was in at the moment was from flying glass when she punched in her computer monitor. God, what was he up to?

T_Tom37: 'Do u want me to prove I'm Aldon?'
Skywatcher75: 'Yeah, u do that'
T_Tom37: 'Our parents were Roy and Terry Lester and our older sister's name was Monique'

Elizabeth felt her stomach turn over.

Skywatcher75: 'U could find that out n-e

65

place. Big deal'
T_Tom37: 'U have a mole on ur R hip, shaped like a star'

Elizabeth felt the bile rise. Not many people knew that. Her mom, Megan ... Oh, yeah, and anybody in any gym class she'd ever taken! Again, big deal.

Skywatcher75: 'So u no some-1 I took gym w/, huh?'
T_Tom37: 'What do I have 2 do 2 prove I'm Aldon?'
Skywatcher75: 'B dead'

Elizabeth wrote those words, then turned off the monitor and the computer at the box. No more pinging in the middle of the night, thank you very much.

BLACK CAT RIDGE, TEXAS, 1999

The hospital administrator handed me a slip of paper with the estimated amount of the twenty per cent we would owe the hospital after the insurance paid out. It equaled to two house payments, a summer utility bill, a car note, and groceries for a month.
'Looks like we're releasing her tomorrow,' the jovial, very young man said. 'That's good news, huh?'
I returned his beaming smile. 'That's wonderful news.' I stood up and said, 'I'll go see Bessie now and talk to her doctors. You'll have all this

ready tomorrow when I check her out, right?'

'No problem, Mrs Pugh,' he said as he ushered me out of his office.

I made my way to the elevators and up to pediatrics and Bessie's room. She was sitting up in bed and a girl in a candy striper uniform was feeding her Jell-O.

'You are such a brave little thing,' the girl said. 'You're my brave Bessie. Look at how you eat this stuff! Why, you're the best little girl on this whole floor, you know that?'

I smiled and said, 'Hi.'

The girl looked around and blushed. 'Hi,' she said.

I came into the room and kissed Bessie on the forehead. 'Hey, Bessie, honey, how are you doing?'

She didn't answer, she didn't smile. What she did do was look at me. Right into my eyes. I thought my heart would break wide open. 'You're going home tomorrow, honey! Back to my house! Megan's so excited. We'll fix up the extra bed in there just for you! Like when you spend the night. How does that sound?'

She leaned forward, taking the Jell-O from the spoon in the candy striper's hand into her mouth. She squashed it around a minute, then looked at me and nodded.

'Can I have a hug?' I asked. She put her little arms around my neck and squeezed. Real live communication. As she let go, I kissed her cheek. 'I'm going to go see your doctor, then I'll be back, OK, honey?'

She didn't respond but went back to her Jell-O.

I found her doctor, a new one I hadn't met. This was a beautiful young woman named Ashma Rajahri and we introduced ourselves.

'Such a tragedy,' she said, shaking my hand. 'I am so sorry for your loss.'

'Thank you. I just wanted to say what a great job you've done with her. She looks wonderful.'

Dr Rajahri smiled. 'Do not thank me. Thank the incredible recuperative powers of children. She is a very brave little girl.'

'Yes she is,' I agreed.

'One thing you should be aware of, Mrs Pugh,' the doctor said, leading me to a couch in an alcove where we both sat down. 'Elizabeth is not speaking. I don't know how long she will be thus, but as of now, she is not talking. There is nothing wrong with her physically. I had an ENT specialist check her, and there is nothing wrong. Yet, she does not speak.'

'You can't say how long—'

Dr Rajahri shook her beautiful head. 'I only wish that we could. I would suggest that at your earliest convenience you seek psychiatric counseling for the child. She has been through a very traumatic experience and I can only assume this is what has made her speechless.'

I nodded my head, wondering how Megan was going to handle this – how any of us was going to handle this.

FOUR

BLACK CAT RIDGE, TEXAS, THE PRESENT

I'll infiltrate their little 'family', as they like to call it. Charles Manson had a 'family'; Jim Jones had a 'family'. I'll teach them what family is really all about! A lesson they'll take to their graves.

E.J., THE PRESENT

This is the best summer I've had in I don't know how long. Pre-kids, at least! I have the entire morning and part of the afternoon to work, or talk on the phone, or catch up on inappropriate TV that I've DVR'd, or just sit and watch my hair grow. Oh, and of course worry about Elizabeth. But I think I have everything under control in that area. Graham is right beside her the entire time she's at camp and Gus Mayhew is there for backup.

Then the second week of camp, on a Tuesday, Elizabeth came home and said, 'I'm going over to my friend Alicia's this afternoon.'

'Alicia? I don't know her, do I?' I was folding clothes and catching a missed episode of 'Project Runway'. I don't know why I watch the show religiously – I couldn't get my big toe in one of the outfits they're making – but I still love it.

'She was new at school this year,' Elizabeth said.

I looked at my daughter and muted the TV. 'Oh! She's the one you wanted to go spend the afternoon with without me talking to her mother.'

Elizabeth rolled her eyes. 'Gawd, Mom.'

I shook my head. 'Her mother still hasn't called,' I said, un-muting the TV.

My daughter took the remote out of my hand and muted it. 'Alicia's mother is a drug addict. Alicia was taken away from her when she was ten. Alicia lives in a foster home. We won't be going to her house, needless to say, we'll be taking the bus to the mall in Codderville.'

I smiled at Elizabeth. 'There!' I said. 'Doesn't the truth feel better?'

She smiled. 'Yes, it does, Mom. So I'll be back around five—'

I shook my head and took the remote back. 'No. You may invite Alicia to come over here. I'll even go with you to pick her up. But ... You. Are. Not. Taking. The. Bus. Anywhere. Do you understand?'

'Gawd, Mom, you are such a...'

I waited. Finally, 'Such a what?'

'A pain in the ass!' my daughter finally said.

'Why don't you talk to Alicia about coming over *next* week?' I said. 'Because you're grounded for the rest of this week.'

'Gawd! Mother!' At that point she whirled

around and stomped up the stairs, while I un-muted the TV to find out what Tim Gunn had to say.

At about that same time, Megan came flying down the stairs, heading for the front door. I sighed and muted the TV. 'Where are you going?' I asked her.

'Out,' she said, door opening.

'Stop!' I yelled.

Her entire body heaved a giant sigh as she turned and stared at me. Not a word passed her overly lipsticked lips.

'Where are you going?' I repeated, a phony smile on my face.

'Out,' she repeated.

'Shut the door. You're letting the air-conditioning out and the heat in!'

She shut the door, standing with one hip stuck out and her hand on the doorknob. Her shorts were too short, both top and bottom, her top showing too much cleavage and too much tummy.

In the time-honored tradition of mothers everywhere, I said, 'You're not going anywhere in that outfit.' She rolled her eyes, still keeping her hand on the doorknob. Oh, Lordy, this was going to be a fun year. 'Upstairs. Change. Then we'll talk about where you're going. And *if* you're going.'

'Gawd, Mother,' she said, letting go of the doorknob and stomping back up the stairs.

It was heavenly quiet for almost fifteen minutes before the doorbell rang. I muted the TV, sighed my own sigh and headed for the

71

door, almost getting knocked over as Megan jumped down the stairs to beat me. We grabbed the door at the same time. I wrestled the knob out of her hand and opened the door.

The boy standing there was a vision. Shorter than me, he wore a knit cap pulled low over his head, touching his eyebrows, with grungy-looking long brown hair falling out of it. His eyes were covered with shades, and he wore a baggy T-shirt over even baggier cut-off jeans. He wore high-top red sneakers that had seen better days and was carrying a skateboard under one arm. I caught all this in the thirty seconds the door was open before Megan slid out on the porch to join him, trying to pull the door closed behind her.

'Megan—' I started.

'I won't leave the porch without telling you,' she said and the door closed.

She had at least changed her top to a T-shirt that covered her from neck to shorts. Unfortunately it was tight, showing off how well-endowed my fourteen-year-old daughter was. Which is, needless to say, way too well-endowed to my way of thinking.

At that point Elizabeth came down the stairs. 'Alicia's on her way over,' she informed me.

'I told you next week,' I said, heading back into the family room. 'What part of being grounded did you not understand?'

She made a sound of great indignation. 'I didn't think you were serious!' she said, as if totally shocked.

'When have I not been serious about grounding?' I said. The one parenting tip I took from my own mother: stick to your guns on punishment.

'That's just ludicrous!' she said.

'Do you want to go for next week, too?' I said, looking at her with what I hoped was a stern eye.

'But she's on her way over here!' Elizabeth said.

'Call her and tell her she can't come.'

'Mom, she's a foster kid! She doesn't have a cell phone, for God's sake!'

I moved closer to her and glared down at her. 'Watch your tone, young lady, or you'll be grounded for the rest of the summer!'

Tears popped into her eyes. With Megan I couldn't trust tears – she was way too dramatic and could conjure tears at the drop of a hat. Bessie, on the other hand, rarely cried. 'Mom, she's riding a bike she borrowed from someone to come over here. It's like two miles away or more,' she said, her voice softer now, as she tried to keep the tears from spilling.

Ah, hell, what could I do? I sighed. 'You are in real trouble, young lady. But after Alicia leaves. Do you understand?'

Elizabeth's shoulders slumped in relief. 'Thank you!' she said, and ran back upstairs.

When I was in the sixth grade, a new girl transferred to our school. Her name was Teeny, like some very large men are called Tiny. She was an Amazon by our grammar school standards. In sixth grade I had grown to the gargantuan height of five foot four inches. Before Teeny, I had been the tallest girl in my class, even taller than a good many of the boys. Teeny towered over

73

me – and *all* the boys – and I loved her for it. For the first time that year I could stand up straight, shoulders back, as my mother dictated umpteen times a day.

I will always remember Teeny for that, and for one other rather important detail. She and my best friend Mary Beth and I were walking to the store after school one day and Teeny let slip that her older sister was going to have a baby. Mary Beth and I were very excited, talking about showers and new houses, and all the other things we knew our aunts and our mothers' friends did when they were expecting. So I asked the question I always heard my mother ask: 'Is it her first?'

Teeny looked at me as if I was crazy. 'Well, yeah,' she said. 'She's like fifteen, ya know.'

Well, no, we didn't know. 'And she's married?' Mary Beth asked.

Teeny sighed. 'No, she's not married!'

And then I asked the most important question I'd asked anyone up to that point in my life: 'Then how'd she get pregnant?'

And Teeny told us. In detail. OK, so maybe Mary Beth and I were incredibly naïve for eleven-year-olds in the 1970s, but that's neither here nor there. The point is, when Elizabeth's new friend Alicia walked in the front door, I could have sworn Teeny hadn't aged – she looked that much like the girl who stole my innocence all those years before.

But where Teeny had been full of bravado, Alicia was shy, barely raising her head when she spoke to me, and then only saying, quickly and

74

quietly, 'Nicetomeetya.' She had long, straight, dusty-looking brown hair hanging in wings that covered most of her face, and what hair didn't cover, large, black-rimmed glasses did. She was dressed in a mixture of Goth and Pentecostal – no make-up that I could see, but a long-sleeved black turtleneck under a gunmetal gray jumper that hung way below her knees, black tights, and large, clunky black shoes. And she was wearing this while biking in the afternoon of a central Texas summer day. She had to be part reptile.

She and Elizabeth ran up the stairs to Elizabeth's room, without even giving me the chance to ask her if Megan was still on the front porch with skater-boy. So I took that opportunity to open the front door and look. They were sitting on the two-seater swing on the front porch, bodies touching, hands entwined, staring into each other's eyes. I turned around and shut the door. There are some things I just don't want to know.

BLACK CAT RIDGE, TEXAS, 1999

'Lester, Roy, L-E-S-T-E-R. Lester. Yes, I'll hold.' I'd been on the phone for four days – OK, maybe just an hour – with the Codder County Utility Commission trying to find out about Roy's insurance. Finally the woman came back on the line. 'I'm sorry, ma'am, but I can't give out information on Mr Lester unless he gives his permission in writing.'

'Look,' I said, my already anorexic patience wearing exceedingly thin, 'as I've explained to just about anybody who will listen at your company, Mr Lester is dead.'

'Excuse me?' she said.

I sucked in a deep breath, counted to five – ten was totally out of the question – and said, 'Mr Lester is deceased, so therefore he will not be able to write to you to give you permission to give me the information I need. Are you with me so far?'

'Look, lady, don't go getting snippy with me, awright?'

I sighed. 'I'm sorry,' I said. 'I just need to explain what's going on...'

'Look, they don't pay me enough to take guff offa nobody!'

'I understand that. Is there a supervisor I can talk to?'

'One moment please.'

And I was on hold, again. Finally another woman came on the line. 'This is Mrs Harp. May I help you?'

'Mrs Harp, hello!' I said. 'My name is E.J. Pugh and I'm the executrix of the estate of Roy and Terry Lester. Mr Lester is the late manager of your utility.'

'I'm aware of that,' she said.

'Good. As you may have read in the papers, his youngest child, Elizabeth, is in serious condition in the hospital. As executrix of the estate, I need to assure the hospital that the bills will be paid. I assume Mr Lester had his health insurance through the utility?'

'We'll need confirmation from Mr Lester's attorney that you *are* the executrix of the estate before we can give out any information.'

'I understand that you won't be able to pay the bills until you get such information, Mrs Harp, but all I want to do now is to be able to assure the hospital that there *is* insurance so that they won't toss Elizabeth out in the street. The child is very ill, Mrs Harp, and she's only four years old.'

'Maybe Mr Lester should have thought about that before he took that shotgun to his family, Mrs Pugh. I'm sorry, there's nothing I can tell you at this time. Goodbye.'

I sat there with a dial tone buzzing in my ear, wishing I'd gone down to the utility in person so I could slap Mrs Harp's face. I was so angry that my hands were shaking as I put the phone down. And I knew instantly that I was going to have to become very thick-skinned to get through this – for Bessie's sake, if not my own. I was sitting there, my hand still on the phone, when it rang, startling me.

'Hello?' I said.

'E.J.?'

'Yes?'

'Reverend Rush here.'

'Hello, how are you?'

'Very well thank you. How are you?'

'Fine,' I said, and sighed. I would ask no more questions – with Berry Rush this could go on for days.

'I spoke with Mrs Karnes,' he said.

There was a silence. Finally, I said, 'Yes?'

'She said she had just spoken to you.'

I felt as guilty as necessary, then said, 'Yes.

77

She was quite upset.'

'Of course. I understand you and Willis are the executors of the estate.'

'Yes.'

'Then you and I must get together to make funeral arrangements.'

I sighed. 'Yes, I suppose so.'

In his most officious tone, he said, 'I think we should consider a private funeral with closed caskets, under the circumstances.'

'Closed caskets, certainly,' I said. 'But why a private funeral?'

'Under the circumstances, E.J., I'm afraid we will be inundated with curiosity seekers.'

'That is certainly a possibility,' I said, consciously speaking as pompously as the good reverend. 'But Roy and Terry had a lot of good friends in this town. I wouldn't want anyone to think they were being slighted. Everyone has a right to say goodbye,' I said, thinking except Mrs Harp. She can definitely stay home.

There was a long, chilly silence. Then he spoke: 'I really think a private funeral would be best.'

Having had run-ins with Berry Rush prior to this, I knew he was used to getting his way. After my run-around with the utility, I just wasn't in the mood to lose this one.

'Well if you really think so, Reverend Rush, I suppose we can get David Bailey at the Codderville Methodist to officiate and have the service there.'

'Now, E.J.—'

'I know it would be best at Black Cat Ridge

Methodist, but I understand your feelings.'

There was a silence. I smiled into it.

Finally the Reverend Mr Rush said, 'Of course I'll officiate, E.J. If you want an open service, then as executrix that is your prerogative. I would just like to go on the record as opposing the idea.'

'So noted,' I said.

GRAHAM, THE PRESENT

I come home from taking Lotta to work and found some longhaired skater-dude grubbin' my sister! I almost slammed his head into the wall, except I knew Mom would hear it and come out and then there'd be hell to pay. So I said, 'Hey!' real loud.

The dude jerked up from where he'd been lip-suckin' my sister and jumped to his feet. 'Whoa man!' he said. 'Nothin' happenin' here!'

'Megan! Go to your room!' I said.

'Yeah, and who made you King of the world, asshole?' she said.

Such language! I thought. 'You!' I said, pointing at skater-dude. 'Outta here!'

'See ya, Megs,' he said, and rode his board off into the sunset.

Megan whirled on me. 'Mom knew we were out here! If she didn't mind, then who are you to butt in?'

'Some day you'll thank me,' I said, opening the front door. 'That dude's a real loser.'

'Well it takes one to know one!' my witty (and I'm being sarcastic here) sister said.

Inside I found Mom in the kitchen starting dinner. 'You know what your daughter was doing?' I demanded.

'Which one?' Mom asked, not paying nearly enough attention to what I was about to tell her.

'Megan—'

'On the front porch with the skateboard boy. Touching. I don't want to know.'

'Yeah touching! He was all over her—'

'Graham, did you not hear what I said? I don't want to know!' she said.

I sighed and finally had to ask it. 'Mom, have you had the talk with the girls?'

That got her attention. She put down the knife and whatever vegetable she was abusing, and looked at me. 'What talk would that be, Graham?' she said.

Ah, man, that woman loves to put me on the spot. 'You know what talk, Mom.'

'Have you had a talk with them, Graham?' she said, emphasizing my name for some reason.

'It's not my place to have the talk with them,' I said, enunciating clearly, afraid that she was going through early onset Alzheimer's. They did a segment about that on TV once.

Mom sighed. 'Yes, I had the talk with them. Two years ago. Are you having sex?'

'Mother!'

She shrugged her shoulders. 'Just thought I'd throw that out while your mind was on something else. See if you'd actually answer.'

'I answered you the last time you asked! No, I'm not having sex!' Although, and I kept this part to myself, I think about it 24/7 and I'm

80

practicing like crazy.

Then it dawned on me. Megan hadn't come in behind me. I was so busy trying to teach my mother how to be a parent that I'd totally forgotten. I whipped around and headed for the front door, slamming it open.

They were back on the swing. The asshole's board was on the porch. I picked it up and flung it out to the street.

'Hey!' skater-dude yelled.

'Hey, yourself, asshole! I told you to get the hell outta here!'

He got up and headed for the street at a slow pace, trying to show me he wasn't afraid of me, although I think he shit his pants, just between you and me. 'Hey, Megs,' he said over his shoulder, 'get rid of the babysitter and maybe I'll see you again!'

At which point my sister jumped up from the swing and, with all her weight, shoved me, knocking me on my ass. It was embarrassing.

ELIZABETH, APRIL 2009

Elizabeth's cell phone rang as she was leaving fourth period English, heading for her geology class. She didn't recognize the number. Flipping it open she said, 'Hello?'

'Bessie, it's me, Aldon.'

Elizabeth stopped dead in the hall. The girl behind her bumped into her, said, 'Retard!' and kept going. Elizabeth barely noticed her.

'How did you get this number?' she asked.

'That's not important,' he said. 'What's important is that you're in danger. I need you to meet me—'

'This stopped being funny a long time ago, Tommy, or whoever you are. Don't call me, don't email me, don't IM me. If I hear from you again, I'm calling the po—'

'Bessie, whatever you do, don't call the police! They're in on it. At least that friend of E.J.'s is – that Elena Luna. She and E.J. were both in on this from the beginning—'

'In on what?' Elizabeth said, stopping traffic around her. She'd spoken louder than she intended. Seeing kids staring at her, she moved closer to the lockers that lined the hallways and spoke more softly into the phone. 'What are you talking about?'

'You didn't buy all that bullshit they told you, did you? This goes high, Bessie. Way high. You know Dad worked for the utility commission, right? At the beginning, when they were setting it up. Who do you think was the utility commissioner back then? J. Patrick Reynolds, that's who. You know who he is now? Railroad commissioner, Bessie! Do you know what that means? That makes this guy the most powerful man in Texas, next to the governor. Do you know what the railroad commissioner does, Bessie? He's in charge of transportation, sure, but he's also in charge of oil and gas. What's the biggest cash crop in Texas, Bessie? Oil and gas. And where do you think he'd be right now if Dad had been able to get the information he had to the right people? In prison, that's where. No railroad commission, no millions of dollars to control – and take. Like he took from the utility commission. And none of this came out back then, did it? No, it was all swept under the rug. By who? By your precious E.J., that's who. Along with her pal the police detective. I've been in hiding for nine years, but it's time I came out. I want to see you! I want what's left of my family back, Bessie! You're all I have! But once E.J. and Willis and that Luna woman find out I'm back, we're both in danger. Do you think they'd let you live now that you know what's really going on?'

'Go away!' Elizabeth hissed into the phone. 'You're insane!'

'No, Bessie, I've finally come to my senses. I've been hiding too long—'

'OK, if you're Aldon, then who did we bury ten years ago?' Elizabeth demanded.

'I hate to think who it might have been,' Aldon said in a hushed voice. 'Some poor kid, a runaway maybe. They killed him and put him in my place.'

'My God, you sound like a bad made-for-TV movie!' Elizabeth tried, attempting a laugh. It came out sounding slightly deranged even to her own ears.

'I need you to meet me, Bessie—'

'Stop calling me that! I haven't been "Bessie" in years! My name is Elizabeth!' she said.

'You'll always be Bessie to me,' the voice said. 'My baby sister.'

Elizabeth hung up, turning the phone off.

BLACK CAT RIDGE, TEXAS, 1999

I had to go to the funeral home and pick out caskets. This was all new to me. No one in my family had died as of yet, except for one grandfather, who died when I was twelve, and I had nothing to do with that funeral. Willis had taken care of the arrangements for both his father and his brother, but I hadn't been involved in anything other than fixing food and trying to be supportive. This time, it was all on my shoulders. I figured, hey, I'm five foot eleven, weigh 170 pounds, my shoulders should be big enough.

I selected the caskets: three adult-sized oak cases with tufted sateen lining, and a fifty-year guarantee. One child-size casket, painted white, with a pale blue sateen lining. We arrived at a figure that took my breath away, but I signed on the dotted line. I figured I was in this for the long haul.

I spent that evening with my family, not telling anyone about the cost of the day. The hospital bill of over $1,000, the bill that would be coming from the funeral home for more money than I made on three books. I don't know why I was shielding Willis from this. I guess, in some deep recess of my soul, I was afraid he'd leave me. I'd never worried about that before – about Willis leaving. But I guess I wasn't all that sure about his strength. Oh, I knew he could bench press 300 pounds on a good day, but intestinal fortitude? That I wasn't sure of. Dealing with the deaths of family members is one thing, but dealing with the deaths of friends is quite another.

For one thing, you can reject that. Would Willis? Would Willis reject Bessie? I didn't know, and I didn't want to push it to a conclusion. So I kept quiet.

The next morning I called Megan's school and told them she'd be in later, and took her to the hospital to see Bessie. On the ride over, I told her, 'Honey, Bessie's not talking right now. She's sick and she can't talk. Do you understand?'

'Why?'

'Why what, honey?'

She sighed. 'Why can't she talk?'

'Because she's sick,' I said.

'She got a sore throat?'

How does one explain psychological repression to a four-year-old? Answer: One doesn't. 'Yes, Megan, she has a sore throat.'

As we were driving along, I noticed Megan looking out the window and up at the sky.

'Honey,' I asked, 'what are you doing?'

'Where are they?' she asked.

'Who?'

'Aldon and them. Are they in the clouds? Do the airplanes run into them up there in Heaven? How come they don't fall down? Can you walk on clouds? Do they have bottoms?'

Megan has a tendency to run on and on, so I ignored her and kept driving. Finally from the back seat I hear, 'Mommy!'

I turned to look at her. 'What, honey?'

'How come the airplanes don't hit Heaven?'

'Because Heaven's higher than airplanes go,' I answered.

'Then what about spaceships, huh?'

Well, she had me there. 'Spaceships go right by Heaven and don't even know it's there.'

'Why?' she asked.

Where was the Right Reverend Rush when I actually needed him? 'Just because,' I finally answered. Megan's only four. She bought it.

When we finally got in to see Bessie, the private duty nurse we'd hired was sitting in a chair reading the *Ladies Home Journal* and Bessie was watching TV.

'Hi, Bessie,' I greeted. 'Look who came to see you!'

Seeing Megan, Bessie didn't smile, but she did lift her hand in a small wave. Megan ran over to her bed.

'You sick?' Megan asked.

Bessie nodded.

'You gonna get better?'

Bessie shrugged her shoulders.

'You're gonna come live with me!' Megan announced.

Bessie just looked at her.

Megan's pouty look came to her face. 'You wanna, dontcha?'

Bessie shrugged her shoulders.

Megan turned to me, a not so nice look on her face. 'Mommy!'

'Sit, Megan,' I said, indicating a chair. 'And don't talk so much. Bessie's not feeling well.' I took Bessie's hand in mine. 'Honey, we love you very much and we're going to be very happy to have you come stay with us.'

Bessie's hand lay limply in mine. How much

did she know? How much should I tell her, and when? And how did I keep Megan from blurting it all out? By leaving quickly, that's how. And talking at some point to a shrink.

We said quick goodbyes and headed home. Later that night, as I lay in bed trying to sleep, Willis sat up with contracts spread over his lap, reading glasses on, and his bedside lamp lit. I was at that point somewhere between sleep and wakefulness – that twilight state. I saw the hospital corridor. It was dark, with only light from the nurses' station spilling on the children's wing carpet, all ABCs and 123s. I saw Bessie's private duty nurse going down the hall – on her back. Someone was dragging her by the hair...

I sat up in bed gasping. Willis pushed his reading glasses down on his nose. 'What?' he asked.

'She's not safe there!' I said, jumping out of bed and pulling on sweats.

'What are you talking about?'

'She's a witness! If Roy didn't do this, and I know he didn't, then somebody else did and Bessie is a witness!' I took a deep breath. 'They may try to eliminate her.'

Willis burst out laughing. I swear to God.

'You asshole!' I said, grabbing my shoes and socks and heading for the door.

'Honey, do you realize how silly that sounds?' he said.

'About as silly as what happened next door,' I said, and left the room.

There was a guard at the door of the hospital when I got there. He opened the door a crack and I told him, 'The doctor just called. My child's taken a turn for the worse. I have to get up to pediatrics. Fourth floor.'

'Yes, ma'am,' he said, leading me to the elevators.

'Thank you,' I said as the elevator doors closed. I only felt a little guilty.

Once on pediatrics I looked down the long corridor. It was better lit than in my dream, but not much. The nurses' station was empty. My feet made the only sound as I walked down the empty corridor. I opened the door to Bessie's room slowly. The room was dark. A hand grabbed my arm and flung me to the floor.

FIVE

BLACK CAT RIDGE, TEXAS, THE PRESENT

Walking among them is such joy! They talk to me as if I'm one of them, and I have to hide my laughter at how stupid they are! Even my Bessie! She's probably the stupidest because she saw me more than the others, and yet she still doesn't see me! The real me! And it's so easy to find out the things I need to know. Little things. I've had all the big things from the beginning. So easy to find out everything you need to know by just looking them up on the Internet. The man's business is right there, telling me so much, and the woman's dirty books are all over the Internet, all the filthy-minded women wanting to read her trash. And once I had those sites, so easy to get into the home computer and find my Bessie talking to her friends. And so easy to become one of her friends. I miss those idyllic days, when we were lovers on the verge, so happy getting to know each other. Ah, memories. So sweet.

E.J., THE PRESENT

My lazy summer was turning into a nightmare. Graham and his Lotta probably on the verge of doing the deed; Megan with her skater-boy out on the front porch doing God knows what; and Bessie – excuse me, Elizabeth – upstairs with Wednesday from the Addams Family, probably on the Internet finding hexes to put on me. Willis was on a project at work that kept him there all hours, and took him out of town at a moment's notice. So I was basically on my own trying to corral my hormonally charged teenagers. At least Elizabeth wasn't ... Oh, Lord, she wasn't gay, was she? I pushed that to the back of my mind and concentrated on dinner.

Still no move on the part of the stalker. It was hard not to be lulled into a false sense of security. It's difficult to be on the defensive all day, every day. I felt somewhat safe at home because of my next-door neighbor, Elena Luna, who's a detective with the Codderville PD. She's also the closest thing I have to a friend, I'd guess you'd say. She's been next door now for almost ten years, with just one other owner between her and

89

the Lesters. She has two sons, one starting his senior year at the Air Force Academy in Colorado in the fall, and the other who will be going into his sophomore year at UT, my alma mater, come August, and a husband who will have served his twenty years at Leavenworth in eighteen more months and be on his way home. I'm anxious to meet him.

Luna had kept Willis and me abreast of the forensic findings from the cabin where the stalker had taken Elizabeth. There had been plenty of fingerprints – those of Elizabeth herself, as well as Graham and Manny, one of Lotta's cousins, and several unidentified ones. Several of those were discovered to belong to hunters who had used the cabin over the past year – one of them having been fingerprinted for his job at the post office, two with fingerprints on file for military service. Leaving three other unidentified prints. One of those turned out to belong to the son of the man from the post office, a fourteen-year-old African-American boy. All of those who'd seen the stalker, even from a distance, were certain he'd been Caucasian. That left two still unidentified, with no hits on any of the files kept by law enforcement. The owner of the cabin wasn't much help, Luna had told me, not keeping records of who rented it and taking only cash. There was also a good chance the stalker had used the cabin without permission – had never rented it in the first place.

'The cabin's a forensic nightmare,' Luna had told me. 'There's trash everywhere. If we tried to get DNA off the gum droppings or the toilet, it would take close to one hundred years to get all the results and cost the department near to $1 million. So, chances are, we won't be doing any DNA tests. Other than that, this asshole didn't leave a credit card or his driver's license that we've found yet. Which will probably be the only way to catch up with him.'

Dismal results, I know. I wasn't sure how or if this maniac was going to be caught; I only knew I would never feel safe for my children until he was. How could I feel safe when Elizabeth went off to college, moved out on her own, got married and started a family? I don't know that I ever could. But something told me this guy wasn't going to wait that long.

BLACK CAT RIDGE, TEXAS, 1999

I felt a heavy weight on my chest. Then the lights were turned on, blinding me momentarily. When I could see again, I saw Bessie standing on tiptoe by the light switch.

A voice said, 'Well, Eloise Janine, how nice of you to join us.'

I looked up into the face of Detective Luna, who sat astride me. 'Would you mind getting your fat ass off?' I asked.

'You don't have to get personal,' she said, sliding off and standing up, one arm extended to me.

'If I've ruptured a vertebra, who do I sue, you or the city?' I asked as I grabbed her hand to stand up.

Bessie scurried back into bed, sitting up and

watching us, her cocker spaniel brown eyes taking in everything.

'Have to be me personally. I'm not on duty.'

'Then what the hell are you doing here?' I asked.

She sat down in the chair next to Bessie, her face turning red. I couldn't help but break into a big grin. 'I'm just this crazy lady,' I said, 'with this crazy theory about...' Seeing Bessie out of the corner of my eye, I said, 'You know what. Whatever can an actual police detective be doing here?'

'On the off chance you might be right, I thought I'd just...' She waved a hand as if swatting away her embarrassment. 'Anyway.'

'Were you here last night, too?' I asked.

Elena Luna and Bessie exchanged glances. Bessie looked at me and nodded. I grinned again. 'Bessie goes home tomorrow. You gonna come stay with us for a while? I can fix up the sofa bed in the living room.'

'Go to hell – ma'am.' She shrugged. 'My mom's in town for a couple of weeks. She's staying with my boys. I didn't have anything better to do...'

'Luna, admit it!' I said. 'Admit you just *might* believe me!'

Again she shrugged. 'There's always the possibility you're not totally wacko.'

I bowed. 'Thank you.'

The next morning, before my ten o'clock appointment with Reverend Rush, I needed to do something. I needed to go into the house next door. Bessie would need clothes, toys, and other essentials. I took the key off the inside of the door to the Tupperware cabinet in my kitchen and, steeling myself, walked from my back door to Terry's back door.

The large, square kitchen was the same. The butcher-block countertops, the Mexican tile floor, the almond appliances. Terry's thatched roof canisters lined the back wall of one counter-top in precise stair-step fashion, the matching cookie jar a space over. A spider web had formed in the stainless-steel sink. Glass canisters of pasta lined another counter. A letter and a couple of bills were stuck between the spinach noodles and the rigatoni. I stuck the letter and the bills in my pocket to take back to my house. The kitchen was, as always, spotlessly clean.

Except it smelled bad. Really bad. I got busy emptying trash and the fridge of perishables, dragging the stinking bags out the back door to where the large garbage cans resided. I put the bags in one and dragged the can to the street. The next day was garbage pick-up, thank God. I went back in the house. The smell was still prevalent. I looked under the sink and found the Lysol. I sprayed it generously, knowing it would help the smell. What it wouldn't help was the fact that I still had to go up those stairs and down that long hall to Bessie's room. I knew, standing there in the kitchen, that the stairs would be the same as I'd left them, minus little Aldon's body. All the blood and gore would still be on the stairs and down the hall, and in the bedrooms.

At this point I could do one of two things: bite the bullet and go upstairs and get Bessie's things, or go to the mall and buy her all new. Mentally figuring the balance of my checkbook at the moment, I headed up the stairs. I hugged the inner wall – the clean one – of the stairwell and made my way upward. I averted my eyes from everything until I got to Bessie's room, where I ran inside and began grabbing the necessary items. But leave it to a four-year-old not to have matched luggage. There was nothing to pack it all in. Why didn't I grab a Hefty bag while I was messing with the garbage? Because I'm stupid, that's why. OK, at this point there were again options: I could go downstairs and get said Hefty bag, or I could go into Terry and Roy's bedroom and into the master closet where they kept their luggage and get a suitcase.

I went downstairs and got a Hefty bag.

Back at my house, I took the clothes and bedding to the laundry room. The stale smell of the house next door permeated the clothes. Or maybe just my nose – and a few other senses. Anyway, I wanted them washed. With the bundle under my arm, I headed for the washer. There on top sat a manila folder.

I dropped the clothes and looked at the folder. Friday, after school, while Terry was gone picking up the little kids, Monique, Terry's sixteen-year-old, had come over, asking me to hide the folder for her. I opened it. Inside was an imitation leather-bound book with 'Journal' stenciled in genuine faux gold on the front. I leaned against the wall, the tears beginning to spill yet again.

I loved Terry as much if not more than my own

sisters. But she, like everyone else in this world, had her flaws. One of them was not giving Monique her privacy – or even some space. Not yet being the mother of a teenager, I might be a bit off the mark, but I didn't agree with Terry's habit of rummaging through Monique's drawers and closets, looking for her secrets. That's why, the year before, I'd agreed to let Monique receive mail at my house from a boy I knew her parents didn't approve of. He dropped out of school the year before and joined the Marines. Monique and this boy corresponded regularly for three months, a letter every two days arriving at our house. Then one of them, Monique, I think, found a new love and the mail drop became a thing of the past. I truly believe that if Terry had had her way, banning Monique from writing or seeing this boy, the relationship would have lasted a lot longer, maybe all the way through boot camp and back home on leave, and God only knew what might have happened then. Or maybe I'm still rationalizing my own betrayal of my friend. Terry must have continued going through Monique's drawers, and the teenager hadn't felt it safe to leave her diary where her mother could get her hands on it.

I stroked the imitation leather and the faux gold lettering and thought of that beautiful young girl whose life had been snuffed out at so young an age. That beautiful girl who had so much to look forward to in life. I put the journal back into the manila folder, thinking I'd save it for Bessie. It would be a way for her to know her big sister. I stuck the manila folder on the top of the shelves in the laundry room, picked up Bessie's bundle and loaded the washer.

ELIZABETH, THE PRESENT

The camp is really a beautiful spot. There are oak trees hundreds of years old – great climbing trees, with limbs growing low to the ground, but thicker than my waist – heck, thicker than Megan's waist – and that's thick! Haha! It's shady there all the time, there are so many trees. Some of them pine trees, dropping their needles and cones everywhere. I've started a pinecone collection – only the biggest ones! I'm going to buy Mom a basket and buy some of that Christmas spray – you know the kind, smells like apples and cinnamon and other Christmassy things – and put the cones in it for her as an early Christmas present. I think it would look really good next to the fireplace. I saw that in one of Mom's magazines.

The skies are always blue at the camp, and sometimes I let my kids lie down in the one open spot by the lake where there aren't trees in the way, and we watch the clouds and I make them tell me what kinds of clouds they are (I'm very good at that) and then we just start saying what shape we're seeing! It's a lot of fun and the kids love it.

It's not as awful there as I thought it was going to be. It's hot, sure, but this is Texas! It's always hot here, even in the winter sometimes. But the shade helps the heat; sometimes you almost forget about it. Besides, we're in the water half the day anyway, and it's hard to stay hot when you're in the middle of a lake, ya know? I love canoeing – who knew? I'd never done it before, but Christine says I'm a natural. Graham doesn't like her because he says she's ugly. Like that's a reason not to like somebody! I keep telling Graham that it's not her fault that she's not good looking, and he says, 'Well, she coulda stayed home.' Which I guess is funny, 'cause everybody else laughed when he said it, but I think it's cruel too. I like her. Christine's kinda bossy, but she's helpful too. She showed me how to use a canoe in about ten minutes flat. In the week that Myra was here, she didn't teach me squat!

Mom makes us each pack a whole tube of sunscreen, but even so I'm getting a tan! I think it looks good and makes me look older. Megan just burns, no matter how much sunscreen she wears. Ha! She's always going on about her 'beautiful red hair' and how 'unfortunate' it is that I have just this 'plain brown hair'. Well, red hair goes with freckled fish-belly white skin that only burns!! Ha, ha! Guess who'll get the summers around here, sister-mine??? Yes, I know. I'm a bitch. And I'm reveling in it!

E.J., THE PRESENT

I took the kids to the hospital one afternoon after camp to see Myra Morris and take her all the cards the children at camp had made for her. It had been a compound fracture, and her leg was still elevated by a sling extended from the ceiling. She was pale and her blond hair was a mess.

Both my daughters bounded into the room and threw themselves on Myra, causing her casted and elevated leg to sway and Myra to let out a piteous moan. I grabbed the girls. 'Be careful!' I said and pointed to her leg in its sling.

'Oh, gosh, I'm sorry, Myra!' Elizabeth said.

'Me, too!' Megan said. 'We didn't mean to hurt you!'

Myra gave a pitiful smile. 'That's OK, you two. I know you didn't mean to.'

'I'd ask how you're feeling,' I said, 'but I think it's pretty obvious.'

'I have my good minutes and my bad minutes,' she said, with a lopsided grin. Looking toward the door, she said, 'Hi, Graham, hi Lotta.'

Thinking they'd been right behind me when the girls and I came in, I couldn't help but wonder what had held them up. Yeah, like I didn't know.

Lotta moved to Myra's bed and leaned over to gently kiss her on the forehead. 'I'm so sorry about your car wreck! What happened?' she asked as my gallant son pulled a chair up for her to sit next to the bed. I noticed he didn't pull one up for me. The fact that there was only one chair in the room was of little significance.

'I was leaving the camp, and you know that hill right after you turn on County Road Fourteen?'

We all nodded. It was a bitch of a hill. County Road 14 hadn't been paved since the 1950s, and the potholes along that stretch, and especially on the downhill slope, were legendary.

'Well, I was gaining speed, so I touched my

98

brakes to slow down and my foot went clear to the floor! And then I hit that really big pothole and the car flew into the air and next thing I knew I was wrapped around a tree with the engine on my leg and the On-Star lady saying sweet things to me. She's very nice, that On-Star lady.'

'Had you been having trouble with your brakes?' I asked her. As closet champion procrastinators, Willis and I both knew a thing or two about the steps to losing your brakes entirely. There are a lot of steps, and we believe (don't try this at home – we're semi-professionals) that you don't have to actually do anything about your brakes until the fourth step.

'No, actually, I'd just had new brake-shoes put on two weeks ago. And they checked out the entire system and said everything was fine! I had them tow the car to my dad's mechanic and not the brake place. Because if they missed something, I'm going to sue the socks off 'em!' she said, and the look on her face was, well, for a seminary student, very un-Christian.

Being a suspicious person who watches entirely too much TV, my mind immediately went to 'Somebody cut her brake lines!' I wondered how easy that would be. For me, fairly hard as I actually have no idea where the brake line is or what one would need to cut it. The aforementioned 'steps' are for me an intellectual conjecture. But when I see that brake-cutting stunt pulled on TV, I always wonder why someone would use it. It seems awfully chancy. How do you know that person is going to crash? What

99

if they run off into a field and are able to stop just from being in too tall grass, or get stuck in the mud or something? No guarantee that they'll get killed or maimed. I figured chances were much better that Myra's brake mechanic screwed up than someone tried to kill her or incapacitate her for a length of time. I mean, the girl is annoying, but not bad enough to kill.

Megan and Bessie gave Myra the cards the kids had made. Some were pretty cute, with stick figures on crutches, or one – a little creepy but unique – with only one leg and a stump and opulent use of a red crayon.

'When are they letting you out of the hospital?' I asked.

'Next week,' she said. 'My friend Christine, who took my place at the camp, is staying at my apartment, and she'll be helping me out.'

Everyone except Graham and me gave Myra a hug goodbye and headed for the two cars in the parking lot. Graham and Lotta got in the Valiant and the girls and I got in the Volvo and headed for home. I was just grateful that Graham and Lotta never had alone time in the dark of night.

ELIZABETH, THE PRESENT

I wish I was blond. Not strawberry blond like Megan is in the summer, but blond-blond like Myra. Sometimes blonds, like Myra, have skin that tans really well. Maybe I should bleach my hair! My skin is a lot like Myra's, and I bet I'd look great with blond hair and a tan. Of course, I'd have to bleach my eyebrows, too, 'cause they're like black. And my eyelashes are really black. Does one bleach one's eyelashes? No, then what would be the use of mascara? Jeez, Lizbutt, get a grip. I'd look good as a blond. But the first time I probably shouldn't do it myself. I should probably go to a professional. I wonder how much that costs? Probably more than five dollars, and that's all I get for allowance. I'll call some place tomorrow and see how much it costs and figure out how long I'd have to save up. I've still got my birthday money Grandma Vera gave me. That's twenty. It can't cost that much!

GRAHAM, THE PRESENT

Lotta only gets one night a week off, and of course, it's a week-night – Wednesday. But that doesn't really matter. No school, so who cares? I can do this counseling thing with my head up my butt. Some would say I *do* do this counseling thing with my head up my butt! Haha! Seriously, I love Wednesday. What's not to love? I get Lotta in the morning at camp, some in the afternoon, when she doesn't have to babysit for her younger brothers, and then most of the evening. It must really suck being a girl. She's the only one who ever has to babysit, because she's the only girl. And her parents have a curfew for her on her one night off – ten o'clock, can you believe it? They let her work till midnight or later, but going out with her boyfriend she has to be in by ten. That seriously sucks. Her brothers don't have any curfew and never have had one. I think some of that is cultural; I don't think the

101

parents of most girls do that, but still. Girls have it rough. That whole period thing, for instance. And having babies. That's gotta suck.

Anyway, I'm getting what my parents consider a hefty allowance these days (twenty bucks a week – gee, I'll go get me that Porsche I've had my eye on) and an extra five for doing the camp thing. I think it should be an extra fifty 'cause I could have gotten me a real job that pays money, but they don't see it my way. So anyway, I've got twenty-five bucks a week to take my lady out, buy gas, dinner and maybe a movie. Can't be done. Even if we get to a movie before six o'clock, which is the witching hour that magically changes the cost of a movie from six bucks to like seven-fifty or sometimes more, that's twelve bucks for the movie, leaving me thirteen. So we have to eat at McDonald's if I'm going to drive us there, 'cause that old Valiant guzzles the gas. So thirteen minus ... let's round McDonald's off at eight bucks. That leaves me five bucks. Dad went with me the first time I filled up the Valiant. It cost thirty-two dollars to fill up what is considered a small gas tank. Then we drove to the church and back, and multiplied that mileage by five and Dad added to my allowance exactly, and I mean *exactly*, what it would cost to drive to the church and back five days a week. So I've got the extra five dollars a week to pay for the gas for any running around. Let me tell you, some weeks, by Friday I'm bringing the girls home on fumes. I'm telling you, life is not easy for even a good, God-fearing American teenager like myself.

Lotta tried to give me some money, and at first I said, 'No way, Jose,' which pissed her off 'cause that's offensive to her Mexican heritage. But she's saving for college with the money she makes at the fried chicken place, and I don't want her dipping into that. But she said if I didn't take money for coming to pick her up every morning, then she'd stop riding with me and take the bus, then have to walk halfway 'cause no bus goes all the way to the camp. Well, she knew I wouldn't let her do that, so she pays me ten dollars a week for coming to pick her up. Which is cool. That way I can buy Cokes when we're tooling around town or, on those days when I hang out with my buds, I can make a dollar bet on a B-ball game, get me a Slim-Jim on occasion. So, what I'm saying is, that ten bucks a week is cool. And I'm man enough to let my woman help me out. Just don't tell my boys, ya know?

So anyway, me and Lotta are hanging out on a Wednesday. We been to McDonald's and snuck some French fries into the movie. We're sitting there watching a Bruce Willis movie (one of the greatest Americans to ever live, even if my parents don't like his politics!), when in walks my sister and her skater-dude. Now I've gotta wonder if my mom knows about this. Surely she wouldn't allow Megan to hang out with this dude? And was this like a real date? Megan's like fourteen, isn't that kind of young to be dating? Is Mom setting her up for all sorts of trauma and misguidance? Is that a word? So I excuse myself and go out to the lobby and use my cell phone to call home.

Mom answers on the second ring. 'Hey, Mom,' I said. 'It's me, Graham.'

'Oh, I thought it was one of my other sons,' she said. She thinks that kind of thing is cute. Someone, other than me, needs to tell her it's not.

'I'm here at the movies with Lotta—'

'Oh? What are you seeing?'

'That new Bruce Willis. That's not—'

'You know I don't like Bruce Willis. Well, his politics. I thought he was great in *Die Hard with a Vengeance*—'

'Mom, that's not the point! Megan's here! With that skater-dude!' I finally managed to get out.

'Is Margi Compton there with her?' Mom asked.

'I didn't see her,' I said.

'Go in and make sure Margi's not there,' she said.

'Hold on,' I said with a sigh. I'm not sure what Margi Compton had to do with it.

I went back in the theater and had a look. There was a family sitting on the other side of Megan, and it wasn't Margi Compton's family, and skater-dude was sitting on the aisle. I went back into the hall. 'No, Mom. I don't see Margi.'

'Well, then it was an out-and-out lie,' Mom said.

'Hell, Mom, even if Margi was there, what difference would it make?' I asked.

'She said she was going to the movies with Margi—'

'Mom, even if Margi was here, she still made plans to meet up with this asshole—'

'Graham, stop cussing. Just stop. I don't need it.'

'Yes, ma'am,' I said.

'Don't call me ma'am,' she said.

'So what do you want me to do? About Megan and skater-dude?' I asked.

'You? Nothing!'

'I can go get her and make her go home—'

'Graham, you're not the parent. I am. I'll deal with her when she gets home.'

'You mean you just want me to sit here and watch her lip-suckin' that a-hole?'

'Watch your movie. Unless you can find a Tommy Lee Jones movie to watch,' she added. Tommy Lee Jones used to be Al Gore's roommate, so that made him politically correct in my mother's eyes.

'Nothing. You want me to do nothing.'

'Graham. Do not warn her.'

'Oh,' I said, realizing my mother had plans to catch my sister.

I went back into the theater and sat next to Lotta. 'Let's get out of here,' I whispered in her ear. I had plans for a little one-on-one, and besides, I didn't want to take the chance that Megan would see me and blow my mother's torture to come.

ELIZABETH, APRIL, 2009

It was Friday afternoon and the girls were home alone again, Dad still at work, Mom still at her convention. Elizabeth had gone straight to her room. She'd been in there less than five minutes when there came a knock on the door.

'Who is it?' she called.

'Who do you think it is?' Megan said, coming in without permission.

'I want to be alone right now—'

'Uh uh,' Megan said, flopping down on Elizabeth's bed. 'You're going to tell me what's going on. Don't deny that something is, because you haven't been riding my ass in two days, and that's just not you. So I know something's up and you're going to tell me what it is.'

'Nothing's up—' Elizabeth started.

Megan rolled on to her stomach and stared up at her sister who sat cross-legged on the bed. 'Tell me.'

Elizabeth began to cry.

BLACK CAT RIDGE, TEXAS, 1999

I drove to the church for my meeting with Berry Rush. His office was plush: a teakwood desk, a six-foot silver and teakwood cross on the wall between rows of built-in bookshelves, an antique settee, and a winged rocker. All new since our last pastor.

He met me at the door with outstretched arms, grabbing me by the arms and squeezing. 'E.J., it's so good to see you! I'm so sorry it had to be under these circumstances! Come! Sit! Coffee? Tea? A soda, perhaps?'

I came, I sat, I declined refreshment. I pulled the paper the Lubbock attorney had sent me out of my purse and handed it to him. 'This proves power of attorney.'

'As if I would doubt it?' He chuckled.

'Now, about the service,' I said.

'Since you declined a private service, I suppose we'll need to have it in the sanctuary,' he said with a sigh. 'The chapel would be too small for the hordes of curiosity seekers bound to attend.'

I smiled stiffly. 'I doubt if we'll have that many. Now, about the service...'

'I've selected some hymns I feel appropriate for the occasion.' He then read off three of the drier selections in the Methodist hymnal.

I shook my head. 'I don't feel...'

'I've spoken with Choir Leader Johnson. He feels under the circumstances a soloist would be out of the question. A few flowers, possibly. Sedately scattered—'

'Reverend Rush!' My voice was loud so as to be heard above his.

'Why, yes, E.J.?' His look of hurt surprise would have withered a lesser person.

I shoved a piece of paper into his hand. On it were written the titles to three songs. 'These were Terry's favorite hymns. These are the songs I want sung at the funeral.'

He laughed nervously. 'But these songs are inappropriate for a funeral, E.J.'

'I really don't care, Reverend Rush. These were Terry's favorite hymns. These hymns will be sung in her honor. And I'm sure as a friend of Roy's, Tom Johnson would be happy to do the solo honor himself on "Amazing Grace". As for the flowers, there will be no flowers. People will be instructed to give any money they want to donate in the Lester family's memory to the Codderville Children's Foundation, a favorite charity of both Terry and Roy. The family will be buried at Memorial Hill Cemetery where Terry and Roy bought plots several years ago.' I hesitated. Then I said, 'I'll have to see about two more, I guess.' I stood up. 'Now if you'll kindly draw up a bill for the use of the church and your services, Reverend Rush, and mail it to me, I'll be happy to add it to the pile of other bills awaiting probate. Good day.'

I left the room to an amazing quiet. Not a sound. Not a peep. It took every ounce of will-power I had not to turn back for a look.

SIX

BLACK CAT RIDGE, TEXAS

I watch her every day, knowing in my heart that we'll be together soon. I know I messed up last time, not giving her a chance to get to know me. But now she does; she sees me as a friend. Friendship can easily move into love. It happens all the time. She'll love me soon, as much as I love her. And we'll be together forever. And there will be no one to stop us. The rest of them will all be gone.

I waited outside the theater in the ninety-degree heat, all the windows in the Volvo rolled down, fanning myself with a piece of paper I found on the floor. It was eight o'clock, but the sun hadn't completely set for the night, and the heat was still stifling. There was a crowd at the ticket booth, paying admittance for the many movies playing at the quadraplex. The doors opened and Graham and Lotta came out. I waved and they came over to the car.

'Why are y'all leaving?' I asked. 'The movie's not over yet, is it?'

'No, not yet, but I didn't want Megan and that dude seeing us, so I thought we should leave,' Graham said.

Feeling guilty, I rummaged in my purse until I found a twenty and handed it to my son. 'It's my fault you had to leave, so this is reimbursement,' I said.

'Ah, Mom, you didn't have to do that,' my son said as he hurriedly stashed the bill in his back pocket.

'Shoo now before they come out,' I said, smiling at Lotta. I didn't need to say it twice. They were off.

It was another twenty minutes before the exit doors opened to the throngs of movie-goers exiting the theater. Megan and her skater-dude were halfway back in the crowd. She wasn't wearing the jeans and oversized T-shirt she'd had on when she left the house; no, instead she was wearing a very short miniskirt I'd never seen before, and a very tight top that showed a belly ring I'd never seen before and way too much fourteen-going-on-forty boobage. Skaterdude, his oversized shorts about to fall off, the dirty watch cap still pulled down to his eyebrows, and still wearing the shades, had his arm around my daughter in a very possessive way, fingertips only a half-inch from aforementioned boobage.

I got out of the car and walked up to them. Because of the crowd and eyes only for each other, they didn't see me until skater-dude stepped on my foot.

'Xuse me...' he started, then looked up and froze.

Megan looked up too, and her pale skin turned a purplish shade that clashed with her red hair. She tried to pull away from skater-dude. The sudden movement started a reflexive move on skater-dude's part, and his hand grasped Megan's breast. She screamed and bolted and he jerked his hand away and started shaking it like it was on fire. I just stood there and watched while the dwindling throngs moved around us.

Finally I said, 'Megan, get in the car.' She did.

Turning to skater-boy I said, 'At this point I don't like you. But I know I'm just going on instinct. Come to dinner Friday night and I'll see if I like you or not.'

'Huh?' he said.

I left him standing there trying to figure out what I'd said, and got in the car to drive Megan home.

'I invited your friend over Friday night for

dinner,' I said casually as I started the car.

Megan turned all shades unbecoming and said, 'Huh?' Skater-dude was definitely influencing my daughter – at least her grasp of the English language.

'Do I really have to repeat myself?' I asked.

'Mom, you didn't!' Megan wailed.

'Daughter, I did,' I said calmly.

'Ground me!' she pleaded. 'Take away my electronics! All of it! Even my MP3 player! Beat me! Anything but that!'

I smiled. 'We'll all have a lovely time,' I said.

ELIZABETH, THE PRESENT

We're having a sort of anti-party Friday night. Sometimes I wonder about my mother. Megan lied to her, got her belly button pierced, and did all sorts of stupid things, and instead of grounding her for the rest of her life, Mom's inviting her – excuse the expression – boyfriend over for dinner Friday night. She said we could all bring someone and it will be like a party. I'm just not sure what she's up to, but I know it can't be good. I'm inviting my friend Alicia to come over. Lotta got permission from her boss to be a couple of hours late to work, and Graham's going to pick her up at her house and he'll pick up Alicia on the way back. I'll go with him, 'cause Alicia's way shy and she'd feel uncomfortable with just Graham and Lotta. Oh, and Dad's going to be home. So, everybody, including Mom, is going to have a 'friend' over. Ha! Ha!

Megan is totally flipping out! She knows Mom and Dad are going to do something to torture and humiliate her (one can only hope, haha!), but she's just not sure which. And (I can't help but laugh here – yes, I'm a bitch!) her belly button is infected! Ha! Green stuff is oozing out of the hole but she won't take it out because *he* bought it for her. The reason it's infected, I'm sure, is because it's made out of some nasty stuff from a third world country, or he bought it out of a bubble gum machine and Meg is allergic to plastic!!!

BLACK CAT RIDGE, TEXAS, 1999

I got Bessie down for a nap in her new house and her new bed, then went back outside to pick up the Codderville *News-Messenger* that was sitting by the front door. I hadn't looked at the paper since Monday, and wondered what page my friends warranted by Friday.

Page one. But at the bottom. Above the fold was an article about the death by car wreck of the beloved Mrs Olson, the counselor at the high school where Monique had attended. That article, along with one about misappropriation of funds at the Codder County Utility, had bumped the Lester family from above-the-fold status. A small article in the right-hand corner below the fold was all the news fit to print about the Lester family. 'Police sources say they are wrapping up their case on the Lester family murders, which will be listed as murder-suicide.'

I threw the paper in the recycle bin. Nobody

was going to do anything! Nobody! Four people murdered and everyone in Codderville and Black Cat Ridge was just going to look the other way. I picked up the phone and called the police station, asking for Detective Luna.

'Detective Luna,' she said on answering her line.

'I read the paper this morning,' I said.

'I'm glad you're able to read,' she said. 'It's astounding the number of adults in this community that can't. You should be congratulated. Possibly the Adult Literacy Program at the high school could use your—'

'Can it, Luna,' I said. 'I'm not in the mood.'

'Is there something I can do for you, Mrs Pugh?' she asked in a mockingly serious tone. OK, it could have been serious, but to me it sounded mocking.

'You can get off your butt, you and the rest of the jerks at that place, and find out who killed the Lester family!'

'Mrs Pugh, after an exhaustive investigation—'

'Of four days!'

'—we have discovered nothing to prove anyone else was involved in the murders of the Lester family. There was no break-in—'

'They rarely locked their doors!'

'—no indication of a disturbance of any kind, no neighbors heard anything—'

'No one asked me!'

'Did you hear anything the night before you found the Lester family's bodies, Mrs Pugh?' Luna asked.

'Well, no, but that's not the point...'

'Mrs Pugh, I haven't gotten to the most incriminating and disturbing piece of evidence to indicate this was a murder-suicide,' she said. 'Roy Lester was discovered with the murder weapon in his possession in a position of suicidal indication.

'Therefore, the verdict has been handed down that Theresa Lester, Monique Lester, and Aldon Lester were murdered by Roy Lester, who then shot and killed himself.'

There was a long silence. Finally, Detective Luna said, 'E.J., I'm sorry. I know this is not what you want to hear.'

'Look, Detective, I know that's what it looks like, because that is precisely what it is *supposed* to look like! But I'll tell you one damn thing for sure, and you can take this to the bank: Roy Lester did not kill his wife and children!'

'You come up with any proof of that, ma'am, and we'll be happy to reopen the case.'

'You know, I'm sitting here thinking what in the hell do you do when you can't get the police to investigate a murder? Well, I've just figured out what it is I'm supposed to do! I just remembered. I think the Codderville *News-Messenger* might be interested in a little muck-raking of the police department! They might be interested in the truth!' And with that, I hung up.

E.J., THE PRESENT

Willis and I lay in bed that night talking. It had been a while since we'd had this indulgence.

He'd been working late or out of town. Any other guy and I would have suspected something untoward, but not Willis. For one thing, he's too lazy for an affair; for another, we don't have enough cash on hand for an affair, and thirdly, he once said to me, while watching a Lifetime movie about cheating husbands, 'Why would you give up your whole life – your wife, your kids, your house, everything – just for a piece of ass?' I'll always love him for that less than tactful statement.

'Remember when we brought her home from the hospital?' I said.

'Yeah, when we thought all we had to do was get her to talk and everything would be OK,' he said.

'Well, we had to do a little more than that, but still. I thought it was all OK. I thought she was stable and ours.' I felt tears spilling down my face to my pillow below. Willis must have felt them.

'Hey, baby,' he said, his fingers wiping away the tears. 'It's going to be OK.'

'Is it?' I asked, looking into his big brown eyes that I so loved. 'How? Please, baby, tell me, how is it all going to be OK?'

He rolled over on his back, staring once again at the ceiling and not at me. 'It just is,' he said unconvincingly.

'I need you home more,' I said.

Again on his elbow looking down at me, he said, 'And which of our children do you suspect will get a full scholarship to college? And which should we send to mechanics school? 'Cause without this deal I'm working, there won't be enough money for college for three kids.'

'Well, Bessie might get a scholarship but she's the only one.'

'She's the only one who won't need it. She's got the Lesters' money for college.'

'What happened to that money we put aside for Megan and Graham? The money Terry's mother left us?'

'It hasn't accrued quite as fast as a college education has,' my husband informed me.

I sat up in bed, my stomach now upset for an entirely different reason. 'How bad is it?'

'A year each without them working. Maybe two if they pitch in.'

'Why didn't you tell me? We didn't have to use my book check last year to go to Disney World! We could have stuck it in the kids' college funds!'

'Things looked OK last year. Besides, I would not give up that trip for anything,' he said, pulling me down to lay my head on his shoulder.

'Yeah, that was a good trip,' I said, smiling to myself, remembering all three kids laughing so hard they almost fell down, running, teasing each other. Even Graham having his picture taken with Mickey Mouse.

We fell asleep that night in each other's arms, both, I hope, thinking of better times, better places.

That Friday night we had a cookout in the backyard. Skater-boy turned up ten minutes early, wearing regular blue jeans and a button-down collar shirt. All but the fringes of his scraggly hair were still covered by the dirty watch cap, and he still wore the shades, but I'd give him an 'E' for effort. We did discover that his name was Cyril and he was a sophomore at the high school. In actual years that was only two, but the maturity level between an eighth grader and a high school sophomore is counted in dog years, which made them sixteen years apart. This is only a theory, but I'm sticking by it.

My son Graham, bless him, stared daggers at Cyril all night, barely taking his eyes off him to drool over Lotta, who appeared to be taking it in stride. Megan, however, was not, and was staring her own daggers at her brother. Willis and I just sat back and enjoyed the scene. We knew enough to be cordial if not downright friendly to Cyril, maybe even insisting Megan go out with him. Because the minute we forbade her seeing him, Romeo and Juliet would begin. Seeming not to care might, hopefully, make Cyril seem less exciting.

It didn't work. After Graham and Elizabeth left to take Alicia and Lotta home, Megan went out to the front porch to wish Cyril a good night. And stayed out there for almost an hour, with me having to hold Willis back from going out there with his imaginary shotgun. We don't own any guns, but he has every intention of telling any boy coming after one of his girls that he does: a shotgun, a backhoe, and a big enough backyard to bury a body.

The weeks went by with nothing much happening. Cyril and Alicia both became fixtures at our house, and Graham wanted to quit working the day camp and get a real job, but I repeatedly said no. This was what the stalker wanted: for us to let down our guard. Gus Mayhew had already resigned his due diligence, saying he had better things to do than sit in the bus all day waiting for nothing. He was much nicer about it than that, but that's what it boiled down to.

Elizabeth became very close with Christine, Myra's replacement, and had her over for dinner one night. I can't say I liked her much. She definitely wasn't Myra – not a perky in sight – but a little too butch for my taste. She did not, however, bring the infamous whistle to dinner.

I suppose she was a nice enough young woman. When she came in she was wearing khaki shorts and a pink polo shirt with Birkenstock sandals showing off pink polished toenails. She had a lot of auburn hair in a shoulder-length pageboy with bangs, dark framed glasses, and entirely too much make-up. Even so, she wasn't a very attractive young woman, but she tried, I'll give her that.

We'd met briefly at church that first Sunday after Myra's accident, when she was announced as Myra's replacement at the day camp, so when she came in, I shook her hand and said, 'Nice to see you again.'

She smiled, showing off very white straight teeth. 'You too, Mrs Pugh.'

'Please, call me E.J.,' I said, then turned to my husband, 'and this is Willis, the kids' dad.'

She shook Willis's hand, said hello to various and sundry kids (which included the new add-ons: Lotta, Cyril, and Alicia) and we all sat down for dinner.

Willis had grilled fajitas and veggies outside and I served them with guacamole, tortillas, Spanish rice and black beans. Everyone dug in.

'So how do you and Myra know each other?' I asked Christine.

She swallowed and said, 'We met online. On a Christian chat room.'

'Oh,' I said. I didn't know there were Christian chat rooms. 'So how did you find out about her accident?'

'Well, she wasn't online for a couple of days, and I got worried and called her. We'd exchanged cell phone numbers a while back, so I had hers. And she told me about what happened. I couldn't believe it! I'm in seminary myself but hadn't secured a summer job yet, so I immediately volunteered to take her place. And then she volunteered her apartment for me to stay in. So it all worked out nicely.'

'Where do you live?' Willis asked. 'When you're not down here, of course.'

'Dallas,' she said.

'Oh! Do you go to seminary with Myra at SMU?' Megan asked.

Christine took a bite and held up a finger while she chewed and swallowed, then said, 'Yes, actually. But it's so big we hadn't met. We had to both come here to meet!'

'I'm so glad Myra has a friend like you. Not just to take over the day-camp job, but to be there for her when she comes home,' I said. 'She's going to need a lot of help.'

Christine smiled. 'She certainly is. And I'm glad to do it.'

'When is she coming home?' Lotta asked.

'It could be tomorrow. She'll find out in the morning. If so,' she said, looking at Graham, 'I might need you to cover for me while I get her out of the hospital and back to her apartment.'

'Sure,' Graham said. And under his breath I heard him mutter, 'Bet I'll get paid double for that.' As he wasn't getting paid at all, I suspected he was being sarcastic. I'm quick that way.

Cyril looked up for the first time since sitting down, a frown barely visible on his face. 'You're gonna be a preacher?' he asked.

'Yes, I am,' Christine answered, a smile on her face. 'It runs in my family.'

'Huh?' Cyril said, now totally confused.

Christine smiled at him. 'I'm sorry, I meant my father was also a minister.'

'Oh,' Cyril said. Then added, 'Why?'

It was Christine's turn to frown. 'Why was my father a minister?'

'No, why do you want to be one? You're a girl.'

Uh oh. The kid was now bordering on pissing me off.

'I mean,' he said, 'aren't y'all – girls, I mean – usually nuns?'

Christine coughed, almost choking on whatever bite of food had been in her mouth. I quickly took a drink, Willis found something he needed to look at on the floor, and Graham laughed out loud.

Megan turned to her – excuse the expression –

boyfriend. 'We're Methodist. As in Protestant. Catholics have nuns and priests, and as of yet, women aren't allowed to be priests. But Methodists have had women ministers, like, almost forever.'

'Oh,' Cyril said. He shook his head. 'I dunno. Seems like a lot of work for a girl.'

Megan looked at her Lothario for a long moment, shook her head and said, 'Whatever,' as she bent her head to her food. I kicked Willis under the table, thinking this boy is toast.

ELIZABETH, APRIL, 2009

'So who is this guy?' Megan demanded.

'I don't know! I thought he was just a nice guy I met, but then he started this whole Aldon business—'

'Aldon?' Megan said, taken aback. 'Like your brother Aldon?' Elizabeth simply nodded her head. Megan asked. 'What did he say about Aldon?'

Elizabeth took a deep breath and finally said, 'That he's him. That he's Aldon.'

'That who's Aldon? Tommy?'

'Yes,' Elizabeth answered.

'Aldon's dead, Liz,' Megan said quietly.

'Yes, I know,' Elizabeth said.

Megan tilted her head, looking at her sister. 'You're not sure?'

'What if—?' Elizabeth started, then stopped.

'What if Aldon is still alive? Is that what you mean?' Megan asked.

Elizabeth nodded.

121

'Then whose grave is it we go visit every year?' Megan demanded.

'He said it was somebody they killed and put in his place,' Elizabeth said.

'Somebody *who* killed?' Megan asked.

Elizabeth shrugged her shoulders.

'Who did he say, Liz?' Megan demanded.

'Mom and Mrs Luna,' Elizabeth said quietly. 'And Dad, I think.'

Megan let out a heavy breath, her cheeks puffing up with the effort. 'Wow, that's pretty heavy stuff,' she said.

Elizabeth nodded, her head bent, staring at the moon and stars on the comforter that covered her bed. Megan reached out and lifted her sister's head to stare into her eyes.

'And you believed him?' she asked.

Elizabeth looked back at Megan, and shook her head. 'No, not really. I know that Mom and Dad, I mean...'

'Let me ask you something, Liz,' Megan said, her hand still on her sister's face. 'Which makes more sense? That Mom and Dad, along with Mrs Luna, conspired to kill your entire family and, failing to get Aldon, killed some poor runaway and put him in Aldon's place, or that this asshole you met *online* is bullshitting you?'

Tears streamed down Elizabeth's face. 'Bullshit,' she said.

'Damn straight,' said Megan. 'Tell me exactly what he told you.'

So Elizabeth did, detailing the stuff about J. Patrick Reynolds and the Utility Commission and the Railroad Commission, and everything

122

else Tommy/Aldon had said.

Megan moved to the computer and turned it on.

'What are you doing?' Elizabeth demanded.

'Don't worry. If he IMs you, I'll ignore him. I just want to check out his story,' Megan said, finding a link to Texas government. Sure enough, J. Patrick Reynolds was the Texas Railroad Commissioner, former Codder County Utility Commissioner. He had been instrumental in trying to get the county utility hooked up to the only nuclear power plant in the area. He was a Republican (surprise, surprise, thought Megan), and was married with two children, one a son in high school, the other a daughter in college. His wife was a homemaker and he had formerly belonged to the Knights of Columbus, the Kiwanas, the Galveston Chamber of Commerce, and was past president of the Galveston JCs. Before moving to Codder County and becoming utility commissioner, he had owned an insurance agency in Galveston and had won the prestigious Canary Award from the American Independent Insurance Agency Association. According to Wytopia, J. Patrick was lily white and squeaky clean.

Megan checked all the other listings for Reynolds on Google and found only listings for newspaper articles mentioning him, speeches given by him, and speeches given about him by his buddies. As far as Google could tell her, J. Patrick Reynolds was fiscally, socially, morally, and personally conservative.

She read all this to Elizabeth.

'OK,' Elizabeth said, 'so what does any of that mean?'

'Absolutely nothing,' Megan answered. 'There wouldn't be any dirt here, and if the guy was involved in this big conspiracy ten years ago, I doubt it would be mentioned on Google.'

'So what do I do?' Elizabeth asked.

'You mean what do *we* do, right?' Megan said.

'I don't want you involved in this, Meg,' Elizabeth said.

'Forget that noise. I'm involved. Where you go, I go. Got that?'

Elizabeth started crying again. Megan left the desk chair and sat on the bed next to her sister. Putting her arm around the smaller girl's shoulders, she said, 'If you don't stop the blubbering, I'm going to smack you.'

BLACK CAT RIDGE, TEXAS, 1999

The next day I spent five minutes at the Codderville *News-Messenger* trying to get the editor to retract the story stating that the Lesters' death had been a murder-suicide. I explained that it wasn't murder-suicide – just murder, that Roy Lester did not kill his family. I told him flat out there was someone else out there who might kill again. His only response was, 'Do you have any proof?'

Royally pissed, I threw my arms up in the air in frustration and said, 'No I don't! But I'm going to get some if I have to hire a private detective!' And with that Bessie and I were out the door.

Imagine my chagrin the next morning when I picked up the Codderville *News-Messenger* and saw the following article on the front page:

Mrs E.J. Pugh, neighbor and executrix of the Lester family estate, claims that Roy Lester did not kill his family and then himself, as police sources have indicated. Mrs Pugh cites possible cover-up by the Codderville Police Department. 'At the very least,' Mrs Pugh said, 'they've dropped the ball on this one.'

Vowing to hire a private detective, Mrs Pugh claims there is evidence to prove the Lester family was killed by outsiders. Mrs Pugh lives at 1411 Sagebrush Trail in Black Cat Ridge and is the wife of Willis Pugh of Pugh Oilfield Engineering Consultants in Codderville.

I was incensed and scared shitless at the same time. It's an interesting feat to accomplish, but then I'm a talented woman. Willis, however, was not amused. I, single-handedly, had just blown the contract he was working on that meant we might be able to eat the rest of the year. He turned his back on me and didn't speak to me for the rest of the day.

That's why I decided to take the kids to the movies mid-afternoon.

Willis and I met in the early eighties at the University of Texas in Austin. It was our junior year and we fell madly in love fairly fast. One night toward the end of our first month together, we went to see a revival of *Bullitt* at the theater on the drag. Afterward we took Willis's 1968 VW to the parking lot of the football stadium and practiced 180-degree turns at high speed. Willis never did get it right, but I was great. I had that VW spinning like a dreidel every time I tried it.

There is a reason for this journey into the past of the Pugh parents. The kids and I had been to the movies in Codderville and were coming back in heavy rain. We were on Highway 12 heading towards Black Cat Ridge. The rain was coming down in sheets, my windshield wipers were on phase two, and the kids were arguing as usual. Well, Graham and Megan were. From what I could see in my quick glances in the rear-view mirror, Bessie was sitting quietly between the two, walking her Ernie doll across her knees.

We were nearing the bridge crossing the Colorado River that separated Codderville from Black Cat Ridge when a black van pulled up beside me on the four-lane road. At first I paid no attention. When he swerved, hitting my left front fender, my attention was gained.

I stepped on the brakes, slowing the wagon down, only to have the van slow down and swerve into me again, pushing me towards the bridge abutment. A second's glance into the window of the van showed me only my own reflection. All the windows appeared to be heavily tinted.

Flashing back to my *Bullitt* training, I hit the brakes as hard as I could, cut the wheel, and pulled a true 180, heading down the highway in the wrong direction. With two of the three kids screaming in my ears, I bumped over the divider in the highway, getting to the correct side, the van more slowly following my example.

I had a fairly new American wagon. It weighed a couple of tons and therefore does not go fast. But somehow, at this point, I got it up to ninety, hightailing it back to Codderville and civilization. I was hugging the inside lane when I saw the van moving up fast behind me. When we were almost level with the entrance to the last exit to Codderville, I cut the wheel ninety degrees and went sideways across the highway, bumping over dividers and grassy shoulder to get to the feeder road into town. The van kept going straight. The next exit wasn't for fifteen miles.

I pulled in front of the Codderville Police Department, slammed on the brakes and killed the engine, jerking open the doors and grabbing the kids in one smooth move. We were inside before even they knew what had happened.

I told my story to three different uniforms in three different sittings at three different desks on three different occasions. On Saturday evening in Codderville, Texas, nobody seemed to be in charge and none of the uniforms really seemed to care.

'Call Detective Luna,' I said to anyone who'd listen. Finally someone dialed her number and handed me the phone.

'Luna,' she said upon answering.

'Hi, it's E.J. Pugh.'

There was a sigh on her end. 'Yes, Mrs Pugh?'

'My kids and I just got run off the road by somebody who must read the Codderville *News-Messenger*.'

'Details.'

So I gave them to her.

'Where are you?' she asked.

'At the police station.'

'Stay. Don't move. I'll be right there.'

I hung up and called my husband.

'Hello?'

'Willis?'

Silence.

'I know you're not speaking to me but you really don't have to. Just listen. A big van tried to run us off the road by hitting my car.'

'Jesus! Honey, are you OK? The kids?'

'Well, I'm a little shook up and so are the kids, but we're really OK. Nobody was hurt.' I grinned. 'Willis, remember *Bullitt*?'

There was a silence while he slid back in time. 'Jeez, Eeg...'

'Pure one-eighty,' I said. 'It was beautiful!'

He laughed. 'Woman, what am I gonna do with you?'

I grinned again. 'I'll tell you when I get home.'

'I'm on my way now to pick you up.'

'That's OK, babe,' I said. 'The car's still drivable.'

'No,' he said, his Master of the Universe voice showing. 'We'll change cars. Throw them off.'

I grinned again and hung up.

SEVEN

BLACK CAT RIDGE, TEXAS, PRESENT

I feel sorry for them, really. They pretend that they're just one big happy family, when anyone can tell they're just acting! My Bessie isn't happy, that's easy to tell. She wants out and I'm going to give her an out. The pitiful thing is I know these people, both the mother and the father and the two kids, aren't going to just let her go. They'll try to follow us, sic the police on us, search for 'their' Bessie until I do something about it. So that's why I have to do something about it before we even go! I'll do only what I have to do. Kill them all. I won't enjoy it, but it has to be done.

E.J., THE PRESENT

All went according to plan the next day. Myra was released from the hospital and I offered to help Christine get her home. What with crutches, a suitcase, and a whole bunch of flowers, plants, balloons and cards, I figured Christine could use some help. Since my Volvo was bigger than Christine's car, I picked her up at the garage apartment behind the Canfields' house. The Canfields were a family at the church who lent out the small apartment every year to the day-camp director. Although they never rented it the rest of the year, I'm sure they took a healthy chunk off their income tax for those three months. Or maybe I'm just projecting.

Myra was looking her usual adorable self when we got there, with just the addition of her crutches. She'd ordered them special from the medical supply company and they'd just come in that day: brushed aluminum with pink patterned covers over the underarm cushion and the hand cushion. She had a matching ribbon tied around her perky blond ponytail. She had on tight, short blue jean shorts, and a white camp shirt tied at the waist. One pink thong adorned her one uncasted foot.

We helped her with all her stuff, which included two stuffed animals – a pink and blue teddy and a correctly colored giraffe. Myra didn't shut up from the time we walked into her room until I pulled up in the Canfields' drive-way.

'Oh, I'm so glad to be out of there!' Myra said. 'You just can't believe the food! I know they try, they really do, but it's just so hard to fix tasty food for so many. I know it's nutritious though, it says so right there on the thing you fill out for your food. You know, the thing that says what you can order for breakfast, lunch, or dinner? It tells you how healthy the food is. So I know they try. But you know, some people can't have salt, and some people can't have sugar, and some people can't have fat...'

And on, and on, and on. My ears were sagging by the time we got to her apartment. If I'd been wearing earrings, they would have fallen out. Unfortunately, the Canfields' garage apartment is, as most are, on top of the garage, which meant a flight of stairs. I held the crutches while Myra used the handrails and jumped up each step. Since she only weighed about ninety pounds, I'm sure it wasn't that much of an ordeal for her. Christine carried up the suitcase and the stuffed animals, and one of us would go back down for the flowers, plants, balloons and cards. My vote was on Christine.

This was the first time I'd been in the Canfields' garage apartment. I'm sure the bare bones of the place were just that: one large room with a partitioned-off bathroom and partitioned-off closet. Between those two partitioned areas was the kitchen: two cabinets on either side of the smallest stove-top and oven I've ever seen. Underneath one of the countertops was a dorm-sized refrigerator. A bar with a single sink cut off the kitchen from the rest of the area. Two bar stools were tucked under the bar. The living room held a futon couch that doubled as the bed, and one old, used armchair and an ottoman. Myra's touches were evident: a small bookcase crammed full of religious texts and romance novels, a tiny TV set balanced on an even tinier yellow plastic table, brightly colored throw pillows on the futon and the floor, a beaded curtain behind the futon that hung from the ceiling and, when the beads were all lined up, displayed the picture of an angel with wings spread wide.

Behind the beaded curtain was a desk and chair. Whether that came with the apartment or was brought from home I was undecided about.

Two walls had windows covered in mini-blinds (came with the place, I'm sure), but framed with draped gauzy material, one in purple, the other in bright orange. The wall space not used up with windows was covered with framed and unframed posters and pictures, the subjects of which I would expect: angels, kittens, babies, and a last supper poster where the apostles were played by dogs but Jesus was, thankfully, still Jesus.

Christine turned the futon into a bed and I helped Myra get settled. 'Where are you going to sleep?' I asked Christine.

She pointed to a sleeping bag almost hidden behind the easy chair. 'I've got my sleeping bag and Myra has a float I can blow up and use. I'll be fine. I love to camp out,' she said, showing that smile that made her almost pretty. 'Why don't you stay with Myra for a minute, while I go down and get the rest of the stuff?' she added.

'Oh, no!' Myra said, waving a dismissive hand. 'You're going to the day-camp, right?' she asked Christine, who nodded. 'So I'm going to be alone then! No reason for Mrs Pugh to stay with me!'

'Myra, E.J., remember?' I said.

'E.J. Right.' She banged herself on the head. 'Nothing up here, I swear!' she said and laughed. I wondered what they had her on.

I leaned down and kissed her on the forehead. 'OK, then, I'm going home. But if you need anything, you have my number, right?'

She grabbed my hand and squeezed it. 'Yes, I do! And thank you, E.J., you've been a peach. And to think I used to think you didn't like me!' Her smile was so bright and so white I felt like shielding my eyes.

'Now what would ever make you think that?' I said, wondering if I always gave that much away, or whether, despite her perkiness, Myra Morris was a little more astute than I gave her credit for. Waving and smiling I made it out the door before she could give me a blow by blow on how openly hostile I'd been to her over the years.

Christine was at the trunk of the Volvo, loading up her arms with the remaining items from Myra's hospital room. 'Can I give you a hand?' I asked her.

'If you'll just put that potted plant on the top here, I think I can get it all,' she said.

I did as she asked and as she headed up the steep flight of stairs, I called to her, 'Call me if you need anything.'

She breathed out an 'OK', as she made it up to the landing. I got in the Volvo and headed home.

GRAHAM, THE PRESENT

I think I'm seeing way too much of Lotta. In both ways – I'm with her every day from like eight in the morning until six in the evening. And then there's the other way: like she's in this skimpy bathing suit half the morning. How's a guy supposed to concentrate? We can't have sex

133

until she graduates high school. That's what she told me. So OK, I'm a nice guy. A respectful guy. I'm not pushing her, but how much am I supposed to take? At least she could wear shorts over her bathing suit, and a T-shirt maybe. That would help.

Meanwhile, I'm supposed to be keeping an eye on Liz, and I'm telling you, this is getting old. Nobody's roaming around the woods with binocs, spying on the shrimp. And I doubt that she's even thinking about it. She seems to be having a good time. The kids love her, and Christine gives her special little projects all the time, so Liz is basking in the glory. And I'm stuck babysitting when I could be out in the world making some bucks. I have to save every nickel I get to take Lotta out on her night off, which leaves me with nada when me and my boys go out, know what I mean? Can't even buy a Coke. I'm too old for this crap!

ELIZABETH, THE PRESENT

Alicia is a pain in the ass. I feel sorry for her and all, but she never wants to DO anything! She just wants to sit in my room in the air-conditioning, and play games on my computer. When I told her what happened to me last spring, she just shrugged! Can you believe it? I mean, I was kidnapped, for God's sake! I guess with her history, a little kidnapping is no big deal. I want to stop answering the phone when she calls because I don't want her coming over here, but she's a foster kid, ya know? What am I supposed to do?

Maybe I'll try to be more assertive and insist that she go do something with me. Something indoors. Mom could drive us to the roller rink in Codderville, or we could go to the movies, or just hang out at the mall! Anything but sit in my room every day staring at that damned computer! I've had more than enough of that to last me a lifetime.

E.J., THE PRESENT

As the week went on, I fixed a little more dinner than usual and took casseroles and sundry over to Myra's house. I figured Christine had enough to do; she didn't need to have to cook on top of it.

While grocery shopping on the Thursday of that week, the store had their own fully cooked briskets on sale, along with a free pint of mashed potatoes, a free bottle of gravy, a free can of green beans, and a free roll of store-brand crescent rolls. I picked up two of everything and had one bagged separately and headed over to Myra's garage apartment. Christine kept the door unlocked so Myra didn't have to get up every time someone came over, which, according to Christine, was often. So I carried up the separate bag of goodies and knocked on the door as I turned the knob, hollering out, 'Myra! It's E.J.!' and walked in.

I so wish I hadn't.

Myra was lying in the doorway to the bathroom, her broken leg twisted under her, one crutch on top of her, the other lying on the floor.

Blood covered everything. I dropped the groceries and backed out on to the stoop, grabbing my purse off my arm to search for my cell phone. Finding it, I dialed Elena Luna and the Codderville PD.

BLACK CAT RIDGE, TEXAS, 1999

Willis picked us up at the police station and we headed home, hoping the difference in cars would throw off whoever had tried to run us off the road. We got home and got the children to bed, then Willis and I fell down on the couch in the living room. 'You still mad at me?' I asked him.

'Nothing like a near-death experience to take the sting out of being pissed,' he said. He put his arm around me and pulled me close. 'I woulda missed you, babe,' he said grinning.

'Yeah?' I grinned back. 'How much?'

'At lot!' he said. 'I'd have to hire a maid to clean and cook, then worry about carpooling with the neighbors for the kids, and then, of course, all the extra expense of call girls on a weekly basis.'

'Weekly?' I showed surprise. 'How come they'd get it more than I do?'

He threw me down on the couch and straddled me. 'Oh, now I understand! Is that the whole problem, ma'am? You ain't been getting enough?'

I giggled and squirmed. 'Not in the living room!'

'They're asleep!' he said, his tongue going for

one of my shell-like ears.

'Bessie,' I said.

Willis sat up, rubbed his face, and looked at me. 'Bessie,' he said.

'Sobering thought,' I said as I too sat up and put my head on his shoulder.

'What are we going to do?' he asked.

I shrugged. He took one of his huge hands and placed it under my chin, lifting my face to his. 'Do you really think somebody could be after her?'

'It looks like it,' I said.

Willis, pragmatic, practical, yet always one to put off anything disagreeable, got up and locked all the doors and windows. He came back and threw himself on the couch next to me, laying his head in my lap, reached for the remote control and flicked on the TV. It was ten-thirty, time to watch *Saturday Night Live*. Last week we'd sat in the same room, watching the same program, a bottle of wine on the coffee table, the kids upstairs, and Terry and Roy laughing at the Prime Time Players right along with us. We turned the show off halfway through without even discussing it and headed for bed.

GRAHAM, THE PRESENT

Day camp has been cancelled. I'd say 'thank God', but under the circumstances, maybe not. I'll never say this to my mother, but she was right and I was ... well, not right. When Mrs Luna, or I guess I should say in this instance 'Detective Luna', showed up at the scene where

Myra had been murdered, they discovered some things. Like, in the bathroom, little tiny hairs – like stubble – covering the sink in the bathroom, rubber boobies in Christine's drawer, along with a couple of heavy-duty jockstraps. So Mom had been right – the stalker had been among us all along, still stalking Liz, but this time as her friend. Elizabeth has been stuck in her room for two days now, and I'm not sure for which: grieving Myra's death, or dealing with the betrayal. Even her friend Alicia can't get her out of her room. Hell, Alicia can't even get *in* her room.

Mom told me that Detective Luna had Myra's car brought in from the junkyard and had the techs check it out. The brake line had been cut. So the broken leg was on purpose – well, maybe not the broken leg exactly, but the injury. I'm sure stalker-boy didn't care if she broke her leg or her neck. Just so long as 'she' could get in to take Myra's place. I figure he must have been planning this for a time, what with becoming email buddies with Myra and all. What I can't figure out, at the moment, is how he knew we'd end up at the day-camp as counselors. Maybe he just figured getting a job with the church was close enough. I don't know. Either he's a very lucky bastard, or he had some inside information that even we didn't know. Nah.

ELIZABETH, THE PRESENT

I feel like screaming. But if I start I may never stop. The primal scream. I've read about it. That's where I'm headed. Why is this happening

138

to me? God, how selfish! I'm at least alive! That's more than I can say for poor Myra! Oh, God, and that's all my fault! If this freakazoid wasn't after me, Myra would be alive today! I can't stand this! I just can't stand it!!!!!

ELIZABETH, APRIL, 2009

Megan sat at the computer, Elizabeth standing behind her, staring at the screen. They'd already emailed 'Tommy/Aldon', and were waiting for an IM. The computer had just pinged, letting them know he'd finally answered. Elizabeth had been too nervous to respond, so Megan had taken over.

> T-Tom37: 'E, u there?'
> Skywatcher75: 'I'm here, A'
> T-Tom37: 'So u B-lieve me?'
> Skywatcher75: 'Not sure'
> T-Tom37: 'What can I do 2 help?'
> Skywatcher75: 'B patient w/ me – this is all so confusing'
> T-Tom37: 'I'm sorry. I no it is – if we met n person I could x-plain it better'
> Skywatcher75: 'I'm not sure about that'
> T-Tom37: 'I understand. This is scary 4 u. Just no I love u, little sister'

'God, this guy really lays it on thick, doesn't he?' Megan said to Elizabeth.

'But what if he is? Aldon, I mean?' Elizabeth said.

Megan turned to her. 'How can he possibly be

139

Aldon, Liz? Do you really think Mom and Mrs Luna are in on some big conspiracy?'

'No, of course not, it's just—' Elizabeth started, but the computer pinged again.

T-Tom37: 'Bessie, u there?'
Skywatcher75: 'Sorry – just thinking about what u said'
T_Tom37: 'I'm glad. We can meet where ever u want, whenever u want. It's up to u.'

'Ask him where he's been,' Elizabeth said.

Skywatcher75: 'Where hav u ben 4 all these yrs?'
T_Tom37:'I was hurt when it happened, but some people got me out of the house. They new what was going on and protected me. They've raised me as their own.'

'Coyotes, maybe?' Megan asked Elizabeth. 'I swear this is total Lifetime movie.'
'Does sound familiar, doesn't it?' Elizabeth said.
Megan wrote:

Skywatcher75: 'I want 2 see u. Do u hav a pic?'
T_Tom37: 'Downlding now'

A picture began to fill the screen. Elizabeth sat down hard on the bed behind her. 'Oh, my God,' she said. 'It's Aldon.'

The picture was of a man in his late teens,

early twenties, with dark hair, fair skin and freckles. He was smiling and had a chipped front tooth.

'I remember when he chipped the tooth,' Elizabeth said softly. 'It was my fault. I was on the top bunk of his bed, and I wasn't supposed to be. And I was playing with his baseball bat and he told me to drop it. And I did. Hit him right in the mouth and chipped his first permanent tooth.'

'I wonder how hard it is to get age-progression software?' Megan mused.

'What?' Elizabeth asked her, as if coming out of a trance.

'You know, like they use on those shows about missing kids. They show a picture of what they looked like when they went missing, then show a picture of what they'd look like now – even if it's like years later. They call it age progression.'

Irritated, Elizabeth said, 'I know what age progression means.'

'Then why did you ask?' Megan demanded, as irritated as her sister.

'But how can we tell? I mean, if this is real or age progression?' Elizabeth asked.

Megan shrugged. 'I have no idea, but I think it's safe to assume that it's age progression. Isn't that a more likely scenario than the Lifetime version he's spouting?'

Elizabeth sighed. 'Yeah. It is. But why would Tommy or whatever his real name is go to all this trouble?'

Again Megan shrugged. 'No idea. I don't think your average pervert has to try this hard, do you?'

Elizabeth said nothing, just stared at the picture on the screen. Again, the computer pinged and Megan went back to the IM screen.

T_Tom37: 'Bessie, u there?'
Skywatcher75: 'Yes'
T_Tom37: 'Now do you B-lieve me?'

Megan looked at Elizabeth and Elizabeth nodded. 'Say yes,' she said.

Skywatcher75: 'Yes'
T_Tom37: 'Then let's meet'
Skywatcher75: 'When and where?'

BLACK CAT RIDGE, TEXAS, 1999

That first Sunday we walked into church like a family, heads high, little hands in big hands. Willis holding Megan's, Bessie's little hand in mine. Graham walked next to his father, his body language suggesting he was almost as tense as his mom.

The foyer outside the sanctuary was crowded, as it was every Sunday morning. People were talking, catching up on each other's weeks, making plans for church activities and social events in the week to come. As we entered, the room slowly began to hush, like a concert hall when the maestro comes into the orchestra pit; not all at once, but little by little, until there was total silence. We were Moses and our church friends were the Red Sea parting silently before us as

142

we walked into the sanctuary.

Behind us I could hear conversations start up again. This time, however, I doubt it had anything to do with church activities or social events.

Those already seated in pews turned our way, then quickly turned back to hymnals, programs, anything to keep eyes off us. Rosemary Rush, the Right Reverend Rush's wife, already seated in the front row with her son, turned and saw us, gauged the reaction we were getting and stood, walking up to us and hugging me lightly. Part of me knew Rosemary Rush always knew exactly the right thing to do and was big on doing it; another part of me was never so glad to see anyone in my life.

'Why don't y'all come sit up front with Eric and me?' she said smiling, her arm hooked in mine, leading us to the front pew.

We sat, picking up our hymnals, studying the program, biding our time until the choir entered and the service began. I sat there, staring absently at the program in my hand, wondering why people were reacting in this way. *We* hadn't done anything wrong! When that thought entered my head, I realized that implied that someone *did* do something wrong. The Lesters? For getting killed? Shame on them! Part of me wanted to stand up and denounce everyone in the room for being the hypocritical bastards they were. And part of me knew if the shoe were on the other foot, maybe I too would be standing back, reticent, unable to put into words the mixed-up feelings such an event must bring.

Some of these people probably thought that their friend – our friend – Roy Lester had murdered his family. Some might have doubts. Some had read the Saturday paper and assumed old E.J. Pugh was being her controversial self – always trying to stir things up. Some, the really small and petty ones, would not want their pre-schoolers associating with Bessie because of what her daddy might have done.

I sighed. They were just people, with all the fears and hatreds that people have. I felt a hand on my shoulder and turned in the pew to look behind me. Marilou Tanner sat in the second pew. She had chaired a committee I'd been on the year before. Marilou put her cheek to mine and whispered in my ear, 'We've been out of town. I just heard. What can I do?'

Tears welled up in my eyes and threatened to spill over. I touched the hand still on my shoulder. 'Just be there,' I said. She hugged me from the back while her husband shook Willis's hand, whispering something to him, something positive I was sure, because Willis smiled.

Ruby Gale Mason came up and knelt in front of me (one of the advantages I'd never thought of about sitting in the front row). Ruby Gale was the substitute nursery supervisor and had known Megan and Bessie since they were in the crib area of the nursery. She patted my knee and took Bessie's hand in hers.

'Hey, darlin',' she said to Bessie. 'How you doing?'

Bessie just looked at her for a moment, then a small smile began to play at her lips and she

144

reached out and hugged Ruby Gale. Tears sprang to Ruby Gale's eyes as she hugged the child back. Patting my knee again, she said, 'Let me know if there's anything I can do.'

I smiled and nodded, not trusting myself to speak. Ruby Gale went back to her seat as the processional sounded and the choir began marching down the center aisle. Willis was sitting on the aisle seat and I noticed several choir members pat his arm, squeeze his shoulder, and one elderly lady we barely knew patted him gently on the top of his head as they proceeded toward the choir loft.

Berry Rush's sermon was as boring as usual. Rosemary sat rigidly next to me, her spine a study in military correctness, while Eric, her son, fidgeted next to her. Eric was the ultimate end product of a union like that of Berry and Rosemary Rush. Where the parents were stern, correct, earnest, and rigid, Eric was a nervous wreck.

He was a homely child of fourteen, his teeth in braces, his straw-colored haircut as short as a first-year Marine's, and even so, it managed to have a cowlick. His face was matted with oozing acne, and he wore glasses so thick his eyes appeared huge and froglike behind them. Eric had no friends at the church and rarely spoke to anyone. The Rushes' older child, a daughter, we'd never met. The story I heard was that she was born severely mentally retarded and had been in a private care facility since birth. She wasn't mentioned much.

After the service more people came up to us,

145

some hugging, some merely shaking hands, others just smiling and nodding their sympathy. No one said anything directly, not in front of Bessie, and I was grateful for that.

EIGHT

Damn, damn, damn!!!! I can't believe that stupid Myra screwed everything up! It wasn't time yet! She'd still been asleep when I went into the bathroom to take my shower and everything. I finish my shower and I'm standing at the sink shaving when she knocks and just walks in. I'm naked, but she notices the shaving first! Talk about stupid. I didn't know what I was doing – I just reached out. I always shave with a straight razor, my dad's and his dad's before him, honed to, well, a razor's edge. And I cut her, just on her arm, but she started screaming and dropped one of her crutches. But she just screamed and screamed. And I just started swiping at her, and there was blood everywhere. More blood than I've ever seen. And then she fell and her eyes were open, and there was blood on her face and a bloody line on her neck and other places. Places I can't even say. It was an accident. It was all Myra's fault.

Luna called me the next day. 'This guy's prints aren't in AFIS or any other listing.'

'I find that hard to believe.'

'I'm not saying he hasn't done bad deeds before,' she said, 'I'm just saying he wore gloves or wiped down the area when he did.'

'So we know nothing more about him than we did before we spent time working, playing, and having dinner with him,' I said, exasperated. 'So what do we do now?'

'*We* do nothing. My people and I will check out the day camp, go over the apartment again, see what we can find out. You don't happen to remember her license plate number, do you?'

I sighed. 'No. Didn't think I needed to make a note of it.'

'That's what you get for thinking,' Luna said and hung up.

I was worried about Bessie — Elizabeth, I mean. She'd been in her room for two days and I couldn't get her to come out. I've put lunch and dinner outside her door and the trays are mostly empty when I pick them up in the morning, but, truthfully, Graham could be eating it.

He seems relieved that day camp is over. I think Elizabeth and Megan aren't, however. They both were getting a lot out of it. Meanwhile, Graham has gone into Codderville to fill out job applications for every fast-food eatery in town – the six to twelve shift.

The doorbell rang and I went to answer it. Alicia stood there in front of me, Wednesday

Addams' clone.

'Is Elizabeth here?' she asked.

'Yes, honey, she is, but she's still in her room,' I told her.

'Oh,' Alicia said, more crestfallen than usual. 'Could I come in and talk to her through the door?' she asked. 'I have to tell her something important.'

I sighed. 'Sure, go on up.'

Things had progressed so far that I had absolutely no qualms about eavesdropping, which I did unabashedly from the bottom of the stairs.

Alicia knocked on the door. 'Elizabeth?' Two more knocks. 'Elizabeth it's me, Alicia.' Getting no response, she knocked again. 'It's important. It's about Ricky.'

Suddenly, on the third knock, the door finally opened. Alicia was pulled inside and the door was closed and locked behind her. Which meant I could no longer eavesdrop. Not good.

And then the thought struck me: Who's Ricky? Was there yet another Lothario after one of my daughters? Or, more likely, was my daughter after him? I could so easily remember myself at that age, all high drama and angst. His name was Larry, and he had long hair, about three chin whiskers, and the most gorgeous blue eyes. I would have done anything for him, if he would have just looked at me. But, alas, he was a normal eighth grade boy – five foot, seven or eight inches, whereas I had already reached my top height of five feet eleven. And, at that time (oh to be so again!) I weighed little more than one hundred pounds.

But, I reminded myself, Bessie wasn't me. She weighed about as much as I did at that age, but she was barely five foot, which meant those pounds were much better distributed. In fact, now that I really thought about it, she wasn't really a little girl any more. She had a nice shape – not the boobage my other daughter had, but, again, well distributed. I sighed. Both my girls were becoming beautiful young women, with all the heartache and horror that entailed. I surely didn't need to add a mad stalker to that mix.

I decided not to think about it and went into the kitchen to start dinner.

GRAHAM, THE PRESENT

I've got so much on my mind I can barely think. This was probably the first year since Myra came to work at the church that I haven't had wet dreams about her. I almost feel guilty about that, although I know her death had nothing to do with her not being featured nightly. And then there's Lotta. I'm pretty damn messed up about Myra, but how much do I let show to Lotta? I mean, the girl's jealous, ya know? And man, was I right about that ugly Christine! I shoulda figured the only way a girl could be that ugly was if she was a guy!

The girls, my sisters, are pretty torn up about Myra. And then there's the whole Christine thing for Liz. I mean she really got to like and trust that bitch – or should I say bastard, now that I know. It's just unfair what this guy is doing to her. If I could get my hands on him for five minutes, I'd let him know just how unfair *I* can be!

Lotta and I went out on her usual Wednesday night off, but neither of us felt like going to the movies. So we grabbed some burgers and Cokes and went out in the country to a back road to eat and talk. And whatever.

'How are you holding up?' she asked me, halfway through our burgers.

'Huh?' I said, mouth full of cheeseburger. I swallowed, then said, 'Fine, I guess.'

'You guess?' she said. 'I don't think so.'

'What's that supposed to mean?'

'It means if you have to put an "I guess" on the end, then you probably aren't "*fine*".' She hit me on the arm. 'You think I don't know you used to have a crush on Myra—'

'Crush? Hell no! Guys don't have crushes, for God's sake.'

'Oh, really? What do guys have?' she asked.

'The hots,' I answered immediately, without thinking it through.

'Oh. You had the hots for Myra?'

'Ah ... No, not really. Yeah, you're right, it was just a little crush, I guess.'

She leaned over and kissed me. 'You're so silly. It's OK if you had the hots for Myra. White guys do that—'

'White guys? Hey, now—'

'Don't get all huffy. Latino boys don't go for older women because that reminds them of their mothers, and Latino boys have a thing for their mothers—'

150

'God, you talk about white people stereo-typing Latinos—'

'Is it stereotyping if it's true?'

'Are you saying every single Latino boy in the world doesn't go for older women because they have a thing for their mothers—?'

'Hey!' she said, slapping my arm again. 'I didn't mean *a thing* for their mothers! I just meant they respect their mothers and would always think of an older woman like a moth-er—'

'Whoa now! Are you saying because I'm white I don't respect my mother?' I was getting hot. And not the good kind of hot.

Lotta was silent for a moment. Then she said, 'I guess I was stereotyping.' She leaned over and kissed me again. 'I'm sorry,' she said. 'All I really wanted to say when I started this conver-sation was that you have every right in the world to grieve about Myra. She was someone you'd known for years, someone you liked, in what-ever way that may be. Don't hide your feelings for her death because of me, OK?'

I pulled her closer to me. 'OK,' I said, and kissed the top of her head.

BLACK CAT RIDGE, TEXAS, 1999

After church, and after a quick lunch for the kids and Willis, I headed into Codderville. At first I didn't even think about the day before, I was so intent on my mission, but when I got on to the highway into Codderville, my body reacted before my mind did. My hands began to shake so hard I could barely hold the steering wheel, while my eyes were darting back and forth from the rearview mirror to the side mirrors, looking, I suppose, for black vans. None to be seen.

I took the first exit into Codderville and pulled into a service station, stopping the engine and sitting for a moment. The station was closed on Sunday so I was able to sit in absolute silence. Someone had tried to kill me yesterday. Me and my kids. Someone wanted us dead. Or someone wanted Bessie dead. And I had started that. Me. With my big mouth. I had set the wheels in motion that could cause the demise of Terry's only surviving child, and my kids and me to boot.

Somebody had killed the Lesters. Murdered them. If I'd had any doubt before, if somewhere in my being a nagging atom wanted to blame Roy for the deaths of his family, it was gone now. I was convinced. The black van was no coincidence. Definitely no accident. I hadn't cut anyone off, hadn't stolen a parking space, hadn't been driving too fast, too slow, or over the line. I hadn't committed any violations that would inflame a motorist to mayhem. It had been deliberate. Attempted murder. But the police didn't think so. Even if they did, even if I could convince Elena Luna that someone was out to get Bessie, I hadn't gotten a license number. There was no way to trace the black van. I wasn't even sure of the make and model. It could have been Japanese or domestic. It wasn't a Volkswagen, of that I was sure. But that was all I was sure of. Except that someone had tried to kill us.

I shuddered and looked around. Here I was at

an empty gas station right off the exit ramp of the highway, right next to the access road. There were no other businesses on that side of the highway. To get to Codderville, you had to go up a block, under the highway overpass, and then into town. I sat there, in a different car from that of the day before, but still – I started the engine and got the hell out of there.

The office supply store was open. I went in and looked at the binders and pads and forms. I wanted something to organize my pain. Put it in neat little piles. After ten minutes of looking I found it. The Office Organizer. It was eight and a half by eleven inches, had a brown leatherette binding and, when you opened it up, on one side, up in the corner, were 'while you were out' slips for messages, right next to a 'things to do' pad. Under these was a leatherette sleeve for catching loose pieces of paper – like receipts and bills. On the other side were two five-by-six-inch yellow-lined notepads. Under these was an address book and, next to that, a five-year calendar. It cost $13.95 and was worth twice that much to me. It would make everything better. I knew that. In my heart and in my soul.

ELIZABETH, THE PRESENT

I've been thinking about suicide for the past two days – not *doing* it, just the whole concept of suicide. For the first time in my life, I think I understand why people do it.

Guilt: it was my fault Myra was killed. If this
153

pervert wasn't stalking me, Myra would be alive.

Loss of Hope: I thought this guy was gone, then he comes back, and I know he'll be back yet again.

Betrayal: I thought Christine was my friend. I trusted her, relied on her. Cared about her.

So I can see, if one was so inclined, why one might off oneself. Not that I would, although the concept seems like a natural offshoot of what I've been through. I've done my birth family an injustice. I haven't really thought of them much since they were murdered ten years ago. I tell myself it was because I was so little and hardly remember them, but the truth is that the Pughs made me a part of their family so totally that it was easy to forget my true family. I'm not blaming Willis and E.J. (sorry, I can't bring myself to call them Mom and Dad anymore). I'm sure they did their best. But maybe it's time I moved on. I think I could be an emancipated minor, under these circumstances. I'll Google it.

E.J., THE PRESENT

Saturday morning, Luna's day off, she came over for a coffee klatch. As we've never done this in the ten years I've known her, I was slightly suspicious.

'What's up?' I said, starting a new pot of coffee and checking the freezer for any pastry-type nibbles I might have hidden up there. I found half of a coffee cake in the back, took it out, set it in a microwaveable dish, and offered Luna a chair.

'I just wanted to come over and see how the kids are,' Luna said.

I shrugged my shoulders then checked on the coffee. Still doing its thing. 'I haven't actually seen Elizabeth in three days,' I told her. 'She's hiding in her room. Graham and Megan are all right, I guess.'

The coffee was through, as was the coffee cake. I distributed coffee into cups, cake on to plates, found a slab of real butter in the back of the butter thingy in the fridge, put it all on the table, with paper towels as napkins, and felt a Martha Stewart flush come to my cheeks.

'Thanks,' Luna said as I placed her goodies in front of her. As I sat down, she said, 'Look. I know what you're going to say, but this has to be broached.'

'What?' I asked, feeling that not-good feeling in the pit of my stomach.

'My lieutenant is insistent that we put a guard on Bes— Elizabeth,' she said.

I didn't blow up. Couldn't imagine why I would. My child's welfare – her actual life – was at stake here. A guard sounded good to me. 'OK,' I said. 'When will this start?'

'Today,' she said. 'I'm moving in.'

'Excuse me?' OK, now I was indignant.

'You'll all get twenty-four-hour surveillance. I've told the boys to stay at school for a while, which they took very well, the little bastards. I'll spend the nights with you, and we'll have a uniform with you during the day.'

'Hey, a squad car coming by three or four times a day would be nice, but—'

'Sorry, no buts. This is what the higher-ups want. This is what the higher-ups get. You really don't have a voice in this, E.J.'

Well, shit, I thought.

ELIZABETH, APRIL, 2009

'You don't believe it's Aldon, do you?' Megan asked.

'Of course not,' Elizabeth said.

'I mean, you can't for a moment think Mom and Dad had anything to do with what happened to your family!' Megan said.

'Let's just drop it,' Elizabeth said, getting off the bed and turning the computer off at the box. 'No more IMs right now, thank you,' she said.

Megan stared at her sister. 'Mom and Dad loved your parents,' she said. 'We were all one big extended family, Mom said.'

'Let's drop it, Meg,' Liz said.

Megan stood up from the computer chair, looking hard at her sister. 'If you believe any of this, Liz...'

'No,' Elizabeth said, turning to Megan and staring hard at her. 'I don't believe it.'

Megan nodded her head slowly. 'OK, then. Well, we're on for tomorrow night, right?'

Elizabeth nodded. 'Sure,' she said.

Megan left her room and Elizabeth laid down on the bed, curled into a fetal position. *There's no way it's Aldon*, she told herself. *No way in hell. Aldon's dead. My mom and dad are dead.*

Monique's dead. They've all been dead for almost ten years. Dead and gone.

Her fingers reached out for the bejeweled silk drapes that passed for swags on her four-poster bed, the drapes that used to hang in the living room of their home next door. The drapes she'd used to pretend she was Princess Jasmine from Disney's *Aladdin*, the drapes she'd hide behind to sneak up on Aldon or to listen in on Monique's telephone conversations.

She'd only had them, her family, for four short years, and her memories were sporadic at best. Daddy laughing at something Aldon said, the huge sound of his laughter that shook his whole body and made everyone around him smile. Watching Monique put on make-up at her little dressing table, the care she'd take to cover every blemish, darken every lash. Sometimes she'd let Elizabeth try on some lipstick or eye shadow – once she even put the make-up on Elizabeth herself, and when Elizabeth looked in the mirror she thought her reflection was beautiful. She remembered her mother didn't think so, and Monique got in trouble. Oh, God, how she remembered her mother – holding her at night, reading her Dr Seuss or *Goodnight Moon*. She could still smell her – that scent of lemon and flowers, the cool touch of her fingers, the warmth of her lips on Elizabeth's cheek or forehead.

She tried to think of her time here, with Mama E.J. and Daddy Willis. They'd been good times. So many more years with them than with her real family – make that other family, birth

157

family, whatever. Real family didn't sound right. The Pughs were her *real* family – legally adopted. That made it real. And they loved her. That made it real.

She began to cry, the first time she'd cried for her forgotten family since she was a little girl.

BLACK CAT RIDGE, TEXAS, 1999

We got a name from a neighbor for a counselor for Bessie and she suggested, under the circumstances, that I come in to see her alone right away. Her name was Elaine Comstock and she was a five-foot-seven-inch blue-eyed blond. She definitely wasn't toothpaste-commercial pretty, but she had a face full of intelligence and strength. I liked her immediately. We went into her office and sat.

'Usually I like to give my clients a little breathing space, but I don't think we have time for that,' she said with a smile.

'I understand and I appreciate your seeing me on such short notice.'

'Dorothy said you're burying the child's family tomorrow?'

'Yes. I'm not sure at this point if Bessie even knows they're dead. She can't speak, as I said, so I have no idea what she knows or thinks or feels.'

'I wouldn't be surprised if she's suffering a little amnesia right now. A form of blocking. Usually, if a child is old enough, I feel they should go to the funerals of their loved ones. It's a closer, a way of saying goodbye. But under these circumstances, I'd say no, wait. The lack of speech is a fairly serious development. I'd like to work on that a while, letting her tell us finally what's going on. Do you understand?'

I nodded my head.

'Later, when she's ready, she can go to the cemetery and have her own goodbye ceremony with her new family.'

Again I nodded.

'Now, how are your other children handling her?'

I shook my head. 'I think Megan's mad because Bessie won't speak, but she won't say anything to me because I told her not to be mad. Dumb, huh?'

Elaine smiled. 'Not dumb,' she said, 'ill-informed. Megan is probably not reacting to Bessie as she normally would, and that's not helping Bessie. I understand your wanting Megan to be sensitive to Bessie's needs, but a four-year-old is not necessarily capable of that kind of compassion without getting a little bit miffed.'

Light dawned. Megan wasn't an unusually rotten child! She was normal!

Elaine stood up and I followed her out to the reception desk. To the receptionist, she said, 'Dorothy, set Bessie up for a play session as soon as possible.' To me she said, 'I'd like to set one up with Megan, too. These two are very connected, from what you tell me. They've been best friends forever and now they're going to be sharing a room. They're going to be sisters. We need to make sure there aren't any hidden problems that could backfire later.'

I nodded. I didn't want to ask, but I had to. 'How much?'

'Seventy-five dollars an hour.' Elaine smiled. 'But most insurance companies pay for it now. Check with yours.' She put her hand on my arm and squeezed. 'There's no charge for today, of course. And we'll defer any payments over the insurance coverage until after the estate is through probate.'

I almost burst into tears. 'Thanks,' I managed to get out.

'Dorothy will give you the times for Bessie and Megan's play sessions. Good luck.'

NINE

There's a squad car parked – **parked** *– outside Bessie's house. I thought at first it was just one of their older cars, just parked there to scare me – as if – but I used my binocs to look in the windows and I saw some asshole in uniform sitting at the old bitch's table filling his pie hole!! They think this is going to keep me from her??? They're crazy! All of them. Bessie is mine and she'll be with me while the others rot in hell!*

Having never lived with Elena Luna, there were things that I didn't know about her, even though

160

I've known her for ten years. Things like the fact that she actually wears rollers in her hair to sleep, plays with her toenails when she watches TV, and thinks atlases are great bedtime reading material. And, if anyone had asked me, I would have said without thinking and without a doubt that Elena Luna of the Codderville Police Department wore a T-shirt to sleep in. I would be wrong. To Willis's chagrin he discovered, as he headed to the kitchen for a midnight snack, that Luna, on her way to the kitchen for the same purpose, wore a black lace teddy to slumber land.

My first thought upon hearing this was that Luna, alone now for fifteen plus years while her husband whiled away his time in Leavenworth, was going after my husband. And who could blame her? Even in his mid-forties, my Willis was seriously hot. Shortly after Mr Hot Stuff left for work, I bounded – OK – I trudged up the stairs to Bessie's room, now designated the guest room, and burst in. Luna was awake, sitting up in bed, feet on the floor, and wearing the seductive teddy. Except it wasn't all that seductive. Except maybe to a man who never saw his own wife – EVER – in a black lace teddy. The one that adorned Luna was probably twenty years old or older, had rips in the lace and bleach stains on the faded black body, and was obviously entirely too tight for the good detective.

'Hey,' she said, looking up at my abrupt entrance to the room. 'Sorry about last night. Did Willis swear off women forever?'

'I think he thought you were hot,' I said, sitting down beside her on the bed.

She hooted with laughter. 'Why in God's name would he think that?'

I shrugged. 'I doubt he's ever seen a real live woman in a teddy before. I don't own one. Never have.'

'Hum,' she said, looking down at herself. 'Eddie bought this for me on our last anniversary before he was arrested. It was like a week before. When he got convicted, he asked me to wear it every night so he could go to sleep seeing me in it and knowing we were connected. I started to give it up when I started showing with Ernesto, but Eddie would comment on it and so I kept wearing it. I don't know now if he envisions me in it as I look now, or if he still sees me the way I looked when he gave it to me.' She shrugged. 'Leavenworth doesn't give conjugal visits, so he doesn't know.'

Impulsively I hugged her. 'I don't know how you do it,' I said. 'I think maybe you're a better wife than I could ever be.'

'Yeah? You think if Willis was away for twenty years you'd dump him? Start sleeping around?' She shook her head. 'You wouldn't. You'd just bitch about it.'

I laughed. 'Yeah, I would. I'd bitch about it a lot.'

BLACK CAT RIDGE, TEXAS, 1999

I called the church office. Instead of getting the secretary, Berry Rush himself answered the phone.

'Reverend Rush,' he said.

'Hi, this is E.J.'

'Hello, E.J. How are you holding up, dear? I was happy to see how the congregation rallied round yesterday.'

'Fine. I'm fine. And yes, they were wonderful. Look, I'm at a pay phone. I need to see your sermon before tomorrow.'

'I beg your pardon?' he said.

'I'll be by in a few minutes to get a copy. Bye.'

I hung up. I had my reasons. I didn't want any reference made to the erroneous assumption that Roy Lester had killed his family. I didn't feel I could trust Berry Rush not to do that. I stopped by the church on the way home and walked into Reverend Rush's office. He stood up upon seeing me, his hands outstretched. I shook one briefly.

'Do you have that copy for me?' I asked.

'E.J., please sit down,' he said, expansively waving toward a chair.

I shook my head. 'I really don't have time. I have a million things to do. Do you have that copy?'

'E.J., you must admit that's a rather unusual request. I don't believe in my twenty-one years of serving the Lord I have ever been asked by a member of my congregation to view any sermon I'm to give. Wedding vows some couples feel are open to interpretation, but of course, you know I don't allow that in weddings I perform. I certainly don't feel I need a critique on a sermon for a funeral. Even the most liberal of the clergy

163

don't allow their sermons to be rewritten by members of their congregation.'

Nothing to it but to do it, I thought. I sat down. 'Berry,' I said, too tired to play the little games he liked so well, 'let's cut to the chase.'

His response was total silence. I don't think that's ever happened before. He sat down in his large, throne-like chair.

I continued. 'I don't want any references at all to the general assumption that Roy killed his family. He didn't. It will soon be proven he didn't, and I don't want the family going to their final reward with gossip and innuendo at their funeral.'

'I see,' he said.

'I have no idea, of course, what you intend to say at the service, but I'd prefer it if you kept it to mostly Biblical readings and short personal remembrances. Willis has agreed to do the eulogy. At what point do you feel that should take place?'

'I'll discuss that with Willis.'

'When?'

'Tomorrow, right before the service.' He stood up. 'If that's all...'

Dismissal is a nasty thing, but I was ready to leave anyway. 'You understand about the sermon, Reverend Rush?'

'I had no intention of saying what a naughty boy Roy was for killing his family,' he said, sarcasm apparent and not a pretty sight on a preacher.

I'd hurt his feelings. 'I know that. I'm sorry if I've offended you. It's just that I don't want any references made to that...'

He nodded. 'I understand. Good day.'

He sat back down at his desk, his head bent toward the papers spread before him. Well, I wouldn't be winning any Member of the Year awards, that's for sure.

GRAHAM, THE PRESENT

Because of Lotta, I haven't been seeing a lot of my boys this summer, but all this shit going down made me think now would be the right time to let them know what's been going on. Together we could go after the pervert, find him, and come up with a clever idea of what to do to him. I called them all up and, because I'm the only one with my own wheels, went and picked them up. Hollister's dad, a half-assed alcoholic, always had a lot of beer in the fridge, so Hollister grabbed a six pack of cold ones and we headed to the stadium.

Surprisingly the high school stadium's fairly crowded in the summertime. Used to be a place where couples could sneak off and do the nasty without getting caught, but now so many kids hang out there, it's kinda not private anymore. Right now there were some guys playing drunken tackle down about the fifty-yard line, some girls drinking wine coolers at the top of the stands and laughing like idiots – or girls, same thing – a mixed bunch of boys and girls smoking pot under the bleachers, and a guy sitting by himself at the tip-top of the bleachers, looking like he was gonna jump. He reminded me of the

165

stalker. Not that I recognized anything specific, just the general demeanor. And, I hate to admit it, I kinda wished he *would* jump. That he was the stalker and he'd take himself out of the equation. Then one of the pot-smoker girls crawled up the stands, yelling, 'Gaaaarrrry! Come on, baby! I'm sorry!' After some mumbled words, he followed her back down the stands to the underbelly.

My guys and me took the stands opposite the girls with the wine coolers and at the opposite end of the field from the drunken football game. Hollister, of course, wanted to go meet the girls, but I told him and the rest of 'em how important this was so he shut up. I've known Hollister since freshman year and we've been running buddies since maybe the middle of sophomore year. He's a big guy with curly hair and when he laughs he sounds like a snake. Seriously. Tad, on the other hand, has a serious case of short-guy syndrome. It's not his fault, he says, it's society. Whatever. He's like five-five and skinny – like he's so skinny if he turned sideways and stuck out his tongue, he'd look like a zipper! I've got a million of 'em! His short-guy syndrome is responsible, I think, for him talking like and acting like an African-American most of the time. It's annoying to us and it seriously pisses off the black guys at school. Anyway, I've known him since junior high and been running with him about that long. The last guy was Leon, my best bud since first grade. Leon's not one to pull in the chicks, but he's a good wingman. He's a serious geek – keyboard for a brain, I swear to God – but he only hangs with the other geeks in school or extra-curricular, the rest of the time he hangs with us.

So I told them what had been going on. Tad went to the same church as me and knew about Myra, but not the details.

'Christ on a crutch, man!' Tad said. 'That was that guy? The one who stole Liz that time?'

'Yeah,' I said.

'Dressed like a girl?' Hollister said. 'Damn, that's some shit! What serious hetero stalker-dude dresses up like a girl?'

'Most transvestites are heterosexual,' Leon said.

Hollister gave him a look. 'TMI, geek-breath.'

'Why I'm bringing this up,' I said, giving them all a look, 'is this shit's got to stop. Liz is in her room in the fetal position and has been for days. Meg's roaming the house like a ghost, Mom's totally freaked and Dad, as usual, is out of town. So it's up to me, and, I hope, you guys. The police aren't doing shit. I wanna find this guy and turn him over.'

'After we beat the ever-lovin' shit out of him, right?' said Hollister, punching a fist into an open palm over and over.

I smiled. 'We might take a few minutes with him,' I said, liking the sound of it.

ELIZABETH, THE PRESENT

I don't know why this is happening to me. Haven't I had enough horror in my life? Oh, Jesus, Elizabeth, woman-up! Are you going to

167

just sit around feeling sorry for yourself? This asshole killed Myra! Killed her!!! Slit her throat! I heard Mom telling Dad on the phone that there was blood everywhere. And the person who did this wasn't my friend Christine. There never was a Christine. And that THING was never my friend! Why couldn't I see that it was that THING that grabbed me last spring? I don't know, maybe it was the make-up, the glasses, the wig. I don't know. I'm too trusting. I see a girl, I believe it's a girl! So shoot me! OK, never mind, I didn't say that. I have to do something! I have to find this THING!! But not by myself. I'm beginning to form a plan.

E.J., THE PRESENT

Well, Elizabeth came out of her room this morning. Surprise, surprise. And she hugged me. Out of nowhere. I'm suspicious but inclined at this moment to accept things at face value. I caught her and Megan in the living room whispering to each other, but they stopped when I walked by. Six months ago I would figure they were up to no good, but now I'm just happy to see them communicating again. If it's secrets they want to share, that's fine by me.

About noon, there was a knock on the front door. When I went to answer it I found Alicia standing there, mousy brown hair all but covering her face, wire-rimmed glasses the only thing keeping her eyes uncovered. Even in the heat of a Texas July, she was wearing long sleeves, a jumper, and tights. 'Hi, Alicia! Aren't you hot in that outfit?' I asked.

'Yes, ma'am. Is Elizabeth here?'

I sighed. 'Sure, honey, she's upstairs in her room.'

'Thank you, ma'am,' she said, and scurried in the house and up the stairs. Every time I saw that girl, she reminded me more and more of a mouse.

ELIZABETH, THE PRESENT

I called Alicia and went outside to find Megan. She, of course, was on the front porch, sucking face with skater-boy. He is *such* a geek-freak. I just can't understand what she sees in him. Megan's really pretty, I say grudgingly, and can do a lot better.

She looked up and saw me, her eyes wide. I guess it's because she hadn't seen me in a few days. My tan has faded some, but I know I didn't look bad enough for her to stare at me like she did. I motioned for her to come to me and she actually did, leaving her asshole boyfriend with his tongue literally hanging out. I was totally creeped.

'You OK?' she asked me.

'I called Alicia. She's on her way over. I've called a meeting in my room. I'd like you there.'
I turned to walk off and she grabbed my arm.

'What about?' she asked.

'What do you think?'

'Should we include Graham?'

I laughed bitterly. 'Why? Do you really think we need a *man* to help us?'

She looked over her shoulder at lover boy, who'd finally pulled in his tongue. So gross. 'No,' she said emphatically.

'OK then,' I said, again turning my back on her to go to the door. She grabbed my arm again.

'What about Lotta?' she said.

I thought about it. 'We have to make her promise not to tell Graham she's even coming over.'

'What about Mom? She'll see her,' Megan said.

I sighed. Then had an idea. Graham's birthday was coming up in mid-August. 'We'll tell Mom we're plotting a big birthday surprise for Graham and he can't know Lotta was here or he'd figure it out.'

'Cool!' Megan said. 'She'd go for that.'

'I'll call Lotta, you go tell Mom.'

And with that, we were on our way.

ELIZABETH, APRIL, 2009

Friday dragged on and on, the girls spending much of their time holed up in Elizabeth's room, going over scenarios of the following evening. Each scenario ended with Megan jumping out of the bushes and pulling a mask off Tommy/Aldon's face to reveal ... well, whoever they decided at that moment was the culprit – everyone from their brother Graham to Brandon Gregory, the cutest boy in school.

'Why would Brandon Gregory be doing this?' Elizabeth demanded.

'Because he's secretly in love with me,'

Megan said.

'Oh. So he's harassing *me*?' Elizabeth said, with a hint of sarcasm.

'Of course. He wouldn't harass me – he loves me. Secretly.'

'Which is why he's dating Heather McDonald, to further hide his desire for you?' Elizabeth inquired.

'Duh. Anyway, he's harassing you to get my attention. He knows I'm the kind of girl to proteck her sister—'

'Pro-tect me,' Elizabeth said slowly.

'Duh. And he knows I'll be there when you meet him. Then we'll get rid of you—'

'Do you mean that figuratively or permanently?' Elizabeth asked, raising an eyebrow.

'We'll let you drive Dad's car back—'

'Then you two will make out in the bushes?' Elizabeth asked.

'Of course not. We'll have a meaningful dialog, at which point he'll ask me to marry him. After we both graduate college, of course. Then we'll go together all the way through high school, both go to UT together, then get married, move to Houston where he'll go to med school and I'll support him as a fashion buyer for Neimans.'

Elizabeth looked at her sister with admiration. 'Wow,' she said, 'you don't mess around with your fantasies, do you?'

'Uh uh,' Megan said. 'You wanna know the color of our bedroom?'

'No,' Elizabeth said and sighed. 'I wanna know who this creep really is.' Sighing again,

171

and wrapping her arms around herself, she said, 'Half of me wants to believe it's Aldon. But that would mean that Mom and Dad have been lying to me all these years, and I don't want to believe that. The other half of me knows this creep is full of crap. That he's after something else.'

'And I know what that something else is,' Megan said.

'What?' Elizabeth asked.

'Your virtue,' she said.

BLACK CAT RIDGE, TEXAS, 1999

I had an hour before I needed to pick up the kids, starting with Bessie at Grandma Vera's house in Codderville. I went to the window and looked out at the lawn. Clouds were gathering in the east, big, black nasty-looking ones. Another spring storm. I looked past the lawn to the Lesters' house next door, sitting forlorn and abandoned. I hadn't been in there since Friday morning, when I'd gone to get Bessie's stuff. I should check on it, I thought. Make sure everything's OK. Somewhere deep in my being, I knew that wasn't the real reason. The house compelled me. Beckoned me.

I stepped out of my back door and crossed the side-by-side driveways, large drops of rain pelting my head and shoulders. Using my key, I unlocked the Lesters' back door, stepping inside the dark kitchen. My foot hit something grainy and I almost slipped, grabbing the kitchen counter for support. I flipped on the light switch.

The kitchen had been ransacked. Totally

trashed. All the cupboard doors stood open, plates and glasses smashed on the floor, staples and condiments – the only foodstuffs still there after I'd cleaned up on Friday – smeared the counters, floor and tabletop.

I stood still and listened. Not a sound. No one could be repeating this performance in other parts of the house without making quite a racket. A week ago I would have run like a jackrabbit on seeing this kind of mess. But I was tired of running and being afraid. Now I was pissed. That somebody could do this with me right next door! When had it happened? In the middle of the night, while we slept? Luna wanted something concrete? Well, by God, this was pretty damned concrete!

I went to the wall phone in the kitchen and dialed Luna for the second time in an hour.

'What?' she said, her voice clipping dangerously at the 't'.

'You want concrete?' I asked.

'What's happened?'

'I'm at the Lesters' house. It's been trashed. Totaled. You wanna come have a look?' I hung up the phone, almost grinning at my triumph.

TEN

I lull myself to sleep at night dreaming about Bessie. About the family we could be together. She just doesn't know how much she needs me, how alike we are, how we were fated to be together. Our lives are intertwined. It's God's will. None of this would have happened if God had not deemed it so. I'm ready for our life together to begin. And no one will be able to stop me this time.

E.J., THE PRESENT

About ten minutes after Alicia arrived, Lotta came walking up our block. I could see the bus pulling away from the corner. 'Hi, Mrs Pugh,' she said, smiling at me.

I returned the smile. I liked this girl in spite of the fact that she was trying to seduce my son. Get over it, Pugh, I told myself. It still didn't work. 'Hi, Lotta. Graham's not here...'

'I know,' she said. 'I'm here to see Liz.'

'Oh,' I said, taken aback. First Alicia, then Megan ran upstairs and into Elizabeth's room, and now Lotta. At least she was seeing people, I told myself. Somehow, that wasn't as reassuring as I thought it should be. 'She's in her room.'

174

'Thanks!' Lotta said, giving me a little wave as she headed up the stairs.

Megan had voluntarily come in from whatever she was doing on the front porch with skater-boy – excuse me, Cyril – and told me first that Lotta was coming, and second not to tell Graham because they were all getting together to plan a surprise for Graham's birthday. OK, I'm not stupid. The only person upstairs in Elizabeth's room who would give a damn about Graham's birthday was Lotta. In the past I've had to bribe the girls to get their brother something for his birthday. And as far as I can tell, Alicia has never spoken a word to Graham. So what was the big surprise for? It wasn't even a significant birthday – he was going to be seventeen. Eighteen maybe I'd buy, but seventeen? And coming immediately after Myra's untimely death? Like I said, I'm not stupid.

I went to the laundry room and stared at the dirty clothes.

ELIZABETH, THE PRESENT

Mom knocked on my door and opened it without me saying enter. I tried to ignore it.

'I have to go to the store,' she said. 'I'll be gone a while. I've got some serious shopping to do.'

'OK, Mom,' Megan and I said almost in unison. 'Don't worry,' Megan said on her own. 'We'll take care of the house.'

Mom smiled. I didn't like the smile. It didn't reach her eyes. 'See that you do!' She gave a finger wave – she never gives finger waves – and closed the door.

'Something's up!' I said as soon as she was gone.

'What?' asked Alicia.

'My mother never finger waves,' Megan said.

'And that smile *didn't reach her eyes*!' I said.

Lotta looked at the door then back at us. 'You think she knows?'

I said 'no' at the same time that Megan said 'yes'.

'She may not *know* know, but she knows something's up,' Megan said.

I shook my head. 'I don't care. This is the perfect opportunity to find this son of a bitch!' I said.

'You're not thinking this is maybe *too* perfect an opportunity? When was the last time you heard Mom say she was going shopping and might be gone *a while*? She never says that, even when she's gone for *hours*!' Megan said.

I stood up. 'I don't really care if she knows or not, if this opportunity is too perfect or not. I say we take off. We get Lotta's uncle's car and we cruise Codderville.'

'Just *Codderville*?' Megan said sarcastically. 'It's not a big city, grant you, but there's still a lot of ground to cover.'

'No, I'm looking for one place in particular.'

'Where, Liz?' Alicia asked.

'The one place in Codderville no self-respecting girls would ever be caught dead,' I said.

And in unison, they all answered: 'The bowling alley!'

'A cut-and-dried burglary,' Luna said.

'What?' I threw up my hands in disgust. Looking around the Lesters' living room, I said, 'You call yourself a detective? A three-year-old could tell this place's been searched!'

She glanced around at the knife-torn couches and chairs, upended with the bottoms also slashed; the potted plants uprooted and all the dirt poured out on the floor; the paintings ripped off the walls, their canvases slashed; the carpet ripped up at the corners and pulled to the center of the room. This was no 'cut-and-dried burglary'.

'Every room's like this,' I told her.

'You've gone through the whole house?'

I sighed. 'I had a while to wait for you, you know.'

'Thought maybe you'd prove your point?' Luna looked at me. I didn't like the look she was giving me.

'What?' I asked.

'I said not to call unless you had something concrete. Maybe you decided to manufacture something you considered concrete.'

'What?' My hands were on my hips and the look on my face must have matched hers in intensity.

Luna broke eye contact by taking out a small notebook from her purse. 'OK, when was the last time you were in here?' she asked.

'You mean before I started tearing up the place?' I asked.

She looked up from the notebook. 'When was the last time you were in the house before today?'

'Friday morning. I came over to get Bessie's stuff so she could leave the hospital.'

'Everything was OK then?'

I nodded. 'I cleaned out the refrigerator and took out the trash.'

'So sometime between Friday – when?'

'Midmorning – around nine or ten.'

'OK, so sometime between then and now, somebody broke in here and burglarized the place. Can you tell what's missing?'

I pointed at the almost brand-new forty-inch Sony TV in the living room. 'Seems funny to me they'd smash a thousand-dollar TV rather than take it, don't you think?'

'Maybe they just took smaller stuff like jewelry,' Luna said. 'Easier to carry than that huge TV. Smash-and-grab types.'

'Who systematically searched the whole house?' I whirled around, pointing at the destruction. 'This isn't smash-and-grab, Luna! Even if they did take a couple of things to make it look like a burglary! My God, how stupid are you?'

Boy, had I gone too far! Luna turned and looked at me and I wished I was anywhere but in the Lesters' living room at that moment. 'Not stupid enough to make myself a sitting duck for God knows what! Not stupid enough to put Bessie and my own kids in jeopardy by blabbing to the newspapers! And not stupid enough to try to alienate the only people on my side!'

'Are you on my side?' I asked. 'How the hell

178

can I tell that? By all the tremendous support?'

'By the fact that you're not in jail for obstructing justice!'

Then it hit me. 'You don't think Roy did it, do you?'

Luna sighed. 'I don't know.'

I stood up. 'I have to go pick up the kids.'

'I'll drive you.'

'You don't have to do that—'

'Shut up and get in the car,' she said. Luna walked toward the back door, heading for the driveway, where her cruiser was parked.

'You know, I'm getting really tired of you telling me to shut up,' I said to her back, following.

'Get in the car,' she said.

'Yes, sir.'

'Shut up, Pugh.'

We picked up the kids at Vera's house and I suggested Luna drop us off at Willis's office, which was just across the highway in Codderville. She nodded and I gave her directions. As I herded the kids out of the car, she said, 'E.J., listen.'

Turning back after the last child was safely on the steps to Willis's building, I said, 'What?'

'I'm sorry I got rough with you,' she said.

I shrugged.

She sighed and said, 'I'm scared for you and the kids.'

'We'll be OK.'

'Maybe. If you're full of shit. Unfortunately, if you're not – if you're right – things could go bad.'

I leaned against the car. 'Maybe I *am* full of

179

shit,' I said, wondering for the first time if that could be true. If Roy really did do everything everybody said he did and if I was just playing wishing games. Wishing my friend hadn't been a homicidal maniac.

Luna reached through the car window and squeezed my arm. 'Call me. Any time of the day or night.' She took out a card and scribbled her home phone number on the back. Handing it to me, she said, 'Be careful.'

I took the card. 'Yeah. More careful than I have been. You're right. I've been stupid.'

Luna grinned. 'Yeah, well, civilians some-times think life is a made-for-TV movie.' The grin faded. 'It's not.'

She put the car in gear and pulled away, while I gathered the kids and went into the building.

E.J., THE PRESENT

I hid the Volvo behind a large oak tree on a side street by the entrance to our section of Black Cat Ridge. And waited. We don't have large munici-pal-size buses like in Austin or other big cities; ours are small bus size, just not yellow. Half the reason for the system is to get service workers – maids, etc. – from Codderville to Black Cat Ridge and back again without the more affluent having to actually drive the help to and from home. The other half of the reason is so our children can sneak off to Codderville without us having to drive them.

I saw the girls coming – all four of them. They were talking so vehemently that they never noticed the Volvo. Of course, the dark green of the car fairly faded in with the spread of the oak tree and the green lawns. If I stretched my neck out the window, I could see them standing at the corner, waiting for the bus – still all talking a mile a minute. If I hadn't been terribly suspicious of what they were doing, I might have enjoyed watching my daughters unawares.

The bus came and I started the Volvo's engine. As the bus pulled away from the stop, I followed suit.

ELIZABETH, THE PRESENT

'Mom's behind us,' Megan said.

I sighed. 'Did we expect anything less?'

'No,' Megan said.

'Well, I love your mother,' Lotta said, 'but we should probably get rid of her.'

'What do we do?' I asked sarcastically. 'Ask the driver to lose the tail?'

'No,' Lotta said, drawing out the word. She obviously hadn't missed the sarcasm. 'I meant when we get the car in Codderville.'

'How do you know we can get it? What if your uncle says no? Or what if he's gone?' Alicia asked, literally wringing her hands. I've read that in romance novels but I always thought it was something women *used* to do. I've got to say it looked stupid.

Lotta pulled a key out of her handbag. 'I have a copy of his key. And he'll never notice it's gone. He's in court all day today and my aunt had to take him in her car because he's losing his

181

driver's license because of speeding tickets.'

We all smiled. 'Cool,' I said, and we did a multiple high five. It was on.

E.J., THE PRESENT

The bus dropped the girls off on a corner in a mostly middle-class, mostly Hispanic neighborhood. I watched as they walked down the side street – Chicon Lane – to a house five doors down on the left. There was a Virgin Mary in the front yard, her midsection a large vase with plastic flowers blooming capriciously, plastic being the only variety of flower that would survive a full Texas sun exposure. There was a mid-nineties Chevy sitting in the driveway. Dark blue with red and orange flames shooting down the sides, it was low to the ground and at first I wasn't sure if it was running, since it looked *too* low to the ground – like all four tires were flat. Then Lotta unlocked the doors and all four girls piled inside. The car started, a loud rumbling sound, and it slowly backed up. As Lotta went down the driveway to the street, the tailpipe hit the pavement and shot off sparks. My first thought was: 'Stop this now.' But I needed to know what they were up to, and I figured as long as I was right behind them, how much trouble could they get into? A mother should never think that.

ELIZABETH, THE PRESENT

Things weren't going well. Lotta couldn't figure

182

the car out and we were going about twenty miles an hour while the car went up and down and up and down. My mother was behind us, probably having a hard time trying to convince herself that she couldn't be seen by us. Megan and I were both in the front seat and she was down on the floorboard, trying to find a switch or something to turn the up and down thingy off. I mean, this is what low-riders do – go up and down and up and down – but not all the time. There had to be an on/off switch. We were all beginning to get sick when Megan pulled some wires and the car stopped going up and down and, since Lotta had the pedal to the metal trying to get the car to go over twenty, when Megan pulled the wire, we went blasting off so fast the car tilted upward like a cowboy on a horse. It was cool except it made me puke a little bit in my mouth.

Lotta doesn't have a license and has only driven Graham's Valiant and had no idea how to handle what she said was a V8. I thought it was a yucky juice but she said in this instance it had something to do with engines. When the car's front two wheels lifted from the ground, Lotta had no idea what to do and started steering like crazy, so that when the car's front wheels came back down, they were pointed in a weird direc-tion and we ended up going on to someone's lawn, knocking over some religious statues, running through a flowerbed, and almost hitting a cat. We all, including Lotta, started crying when we almost hit the cat, which made her overcompensate with the steering, which made us careen across the street and into another yard where we knocked down five pink flamingos and some laundry hung up in the *front* yard, which I think is just tacky, and they deserved it. But who am I to judge, ya know?

Lotta finally got out in the street again, stopped the car, and we just sat there for at least a full minute, not even worrying about Mom, who had tried to hide the Volvo in somebody's driveway. It wasn't working.

'OK,' Lotta said with a big sigh, 'I think every-thing's under control.' I doubted that but didn't say anything.

Megan got up from the floorboard and sat down on the bench seat between Lotta and me. I learned a lot about low-riders by just being in one. Lotta told us that nineties cars didn't come with bench seats, but that her uncle had the interior customized with tuck and roll, two-tone leather front and back, shag carpeting on the floorboards, and velvet headliner. There was a painting of Jesus on the headliner with the interior light sort of in the position where his navel would have been. It was cool.

'OK,' she said again, 'now to get rid of your mother.'

And then she took off.

ELIZABETH, APRIL, 2009

After making all their fearful plans to abscond with their father's car in the wee hours of the morning – well, eleven o'clock actually, but still – they discovered Dad was going to Austin to be with their mom at her convention and Grandma Vera was coming to stay.

'Oh my God!' Megan said, grabbing her sister's shoulders and jumping up and down. 'This is fabulous!'

Jumping up and down in unison with Megan, Elizabeth said, 'I know! I know! She goes to bed at eight-thirty!'

'She sleeps like the dead!' Megan said.

'She'll never know we're gone!' Elizabeth said.

Needless to say, the girls were happy about the change in plans.

The next night, Graham tried to leave early, but Grandma made him stay and eat supper. Elizabeth's good hygiene included eating right, and looking at the meal in front of her she knew it was all unhealthy. She also knew her grandmother made the best fried chicken in Texas. Hygiene be damned, she had seconds of the mashed potatoes and cream gravy.

Pushing herself away from the table, she and Megan did the dishes while Graham, whose turn it actually was, was allowed to leave the house with his friends. Grandma was like that: rather misogynistic, if a woman could be that. Elizabeth decided to look that up.

After the dishes, they sat in the family room and watched TV with their grandmother until, at eight o'clock, Grandma Vera announced, 'Well, it's been a long day. Gets that way when you're up at five-thirty like I am every morning.' To Elizabeth's ears it sounded like she was bragging, but Elizabeth couldn't figure out why anyone would be proud of that. It seemed silly to her. But, since it worked to her advantage, she just smiled and said, 'Good night, Grandma. Sleep tight.'

'Don't let the bedbugs bite,' Megan finished, which was the refrain Grandma used with them when they were little and spent the night with her.

Grandma Vera smiled and said, 'You girls lock up, OK?'

'No problem,' Megan said.

They sat in front of the TV until nine, then crept upstairs to make sure Grandma was asleep. Opening the door of Elizabeth's room, which Grandma was using, resulted in hearing the sounds of Grandma's snoring, snorting, and heavy breathing, an indication she was well into REM sleep. Her purse was on the dresser and Megan quietly crept in and lifted it, taking it into the hall. Finding the keys, she gingerly crept back in and put the purse back on the dresser.

It was show time.

BLACK CAT RIDGE, TEXAS, 1999

I watched TV with the kids until eight-thirty, then supervised baths and got them to bed by nine-thirty. There was nothing on TV, so I closed up the house, turning off lights, and started to go to bed. At the bottom of the stairs I stopped. I wasn't tired. I headed for my office under the stairs, turned on my computer, and shut the door behind me. I might need to print something, and as my computer printer was vintage, I was afraid the noise might wake the kids.

I hadn't worked in so long I couldn't remember what was happening with Lady Leslie and her hunk. I skipped back two chapters and began to read to get into the flow of it. At 10:03 by my watch, the electricity went off.

I sat stock still in the pitch-blackness of my office. There was no storm – why had the lights gone off? OK, it happens, I told myself. Somebody tripped a wire at the main switch place or something. I stood up and opened the door to my office. The kitchen was to my right, just a few steps. In there were flashlights and candles and matches. There was no moon that night and the street light, still shining, was at the end of the block. A light was on in an upstairs bedroom of the house across the street. It wasn't the block, I decided. Just my house. But the little bit of ambient light did little to illuminate my kitchen.

I closed my eyes to get used to the darkness. When I opened them I could see much better. And hear better, too. And what I could hear sent a shiver down my spine and turned the contents of my stomach into sulfuric acid.

The window in the dining room was opening. I could hear the scrape of aluminum against aluminum. I heard a voice whisper, 'Shit, man, you'll wake 'em up!'

There was a crude return comment. Then the thump of a foot on the carpeted floor, then another, and another, and another.

They were in my house. *They*, the ones who'd killed my friends, tried to run me off the road, vandalized the house next door. The ones who were going to kill my children and me. And I stood frozen in the little hall between the kitchen and the utility room, unable to move my eyelids, much less my body.

'You take care of the ones upstairs while I check out down here,' one whispered.

Upstairs, I thought. Oh my God, upstairs! The kids. I moved quietly, stealthily, into the kitchen. I was almost to the counter when I hit the bowl of milk on the floor for the new kittens. It skittered across the room, making a noise not unlike a cherry bomb in a toilet.

I whirled towards the opening from the kitchen into the dining room. A male form was standing there, his hand pointing at me. I fell to the floor as the bright flash of his gun blinded me and the muffled 'thump' of the report reverberated like thunder in the quiet house. I rolled toward the opening and kicked up as high and as hard as I could with my leg. By his guttural response and his bent-over position, I knew I'd connected with the groin, as I'd been hoping for.

I scrambled to my feet and ran toward the counter where I kept my knives. He grabbed my hair, pulling me backward. I twisted in his grasp, seeing the dim glint of the gun in his hand. With both hands clasped together, I hit his arm with all my might, sending the gun flying behind us, into the dining room.

'You bitch!' he spat, no longer whispering, his grasp on my hair tightening and twisting. Then, for a moment, I was free, his hand off my hair. Before I could react, it was around my throat. I now knew his choice of my demise: I would be strangled to death.

This was my kitchen. I had the advantage of knowing the territory. I reached behind me for the butcher-block slab that held my knives. I grabbed the handle of the largest knife and pulled. Instead of the knife coming out and stabbing my assailant, the entire butcher-block slab came with my hand, slamming against the side of his head. Stunned, his grasp on my throat lessened, but not enough. I hit him again. And again.

Finally he fell to his knees, his hands up to protect his bleeding head.

How many nights have I spent in front of the TV, watching the heroine in some dumb made-for-TV movie hit the bad guy and run? How many times have I heard my husband grunt and say, 'Jesus, finish him off, stupid.' Enough.

I hit him again and again and again, until his entire body fell to the floor. And then I hit him again. And again. Until the butcher block slab split in two in my hands, the matching hickory knives falling on the body on my kitchen floor. I stood up and looked down at the man. His face was so messed up I doubt if I'd recognize him if I knew him. I kicked him, mostly to see if he was conscious. He wasn't. I wondered if I'd killed him. But only for a moment.

There was someone else upstairs with my kids. I grabbed the flashlight out of the drawer and raced for the dining room where the gun had flown earlier. I picked it up and flashed the light on it.

My father had shown me a gun when I was a teenager. He'd bought it because two houses in the neighborhood had been burglarized. He showed me the safety and how to remove it. He showed me how to hold it and how to fire. Two days later, Mother made him sell it. But I remembered. *Thank you, Daddy*, I thought.

I put one of the smaller knives in the back pocket of my blue jeans and held the gun in both hands, the flashlight under my left arm, and headed for the front of the house and the stairs. I froze as the front door slowly began to open.

ELEVEN

She's alone now, except for those girls. But no big brother, no cops, no daddy-dearest to screw things up. I could pick her like a flower among those girls and they'd hardly notice. Our time has come, my darlin' Bessie.

E.J., THE PRESENT

I was hysterical. Partly from fright at what the girls were doing, and partly because it was a front seat viewing of the Keystone Cops. I laughed, suppressed a scream, and laughed again. Then I thought I might puke. While I was suppressing that, Lotta got the car under control and took off. She'd turned a corner before I even got myself together enough to follow her.

I floored the Volvo and shot around the corner,

just in time to catch her turning left on a busy street. I heard a screech of tires and got to the corner in time to see the low-rider taking off and a car from the south and one from the north both turned slightly sideways to get out of Lotta's way. While they were figuring out what to do, I shot between them and headed after the low-rider, which I'd seen taking a right-hand turn three blocks up.

I got to the street where they'd turned, took my own right, and couldn't see hide nor hair of them. I slowed and looked down side streets. The first was a dead end and I didn't see the low-rider parked anywhere, the second was too short to have done them any good, but the third led to another major street. I headed down that, getting my speed back up.

GRAHAM, THE PRESENT

'That one chick is really hot!' Hollister said, looking across the stadium at the girls drinking wine coolers.

'Hey man!' I said, as sternly as I could. 'We're supposed to be talking about how to get this stalker asshole! Not staring at chicks!'

Hollister shook his head. 'Sorry, man. Can't help it. If there are chicks, Hollister is going to stare at them.'

I turned to look at the other guys in my crew. 'When did he start the third-person crap?'

'About three weeks ago,' Leon said. 'He thinks it makes him sound cool.'

'It doesn't,' Tad said.

191

'I know,' Leon said.

'OK!' I said, or shouted, actually. This wasn't going as planned. 'Listen. All of you! I need your help.' I took a deep breath. 'This could be dangerous. Myra Morris is already dead. This guy is not above killing all of us.' I said it, even though I sorta doubted it. But this speech called for, well, drama. 'If any of you feel you can't handle this, then please say so now. And just walk away.' They all looked at each other, waiting for one to move so they all could. Nobody moved. I had them. 'Then you're with me.' I put my arms around the two guys nearest me, then they pulled in the third. We huddled like a slightly anemic football team. 'You guys are my crew,' I said in a soft voice. 'Now and forever!' I said loudly.

And my three best buds shouted, 'Now and forever!' at the tops of their voices. This shit was way cool.

ELIZABETH, THE PRESENT

Lotta got out of the car on the dead-end street where we were hiding, creeping to the back of the low-rider, and looked around it to see if the Volvo was in sight. It wasn't and she ran back to the car and backed it out of its hiding place behind a bright-yellow Hummer. We went back to the street and turned in the opposite direction of the way we'd been going.

'We lost her!' Megan shouted, holding up a hand for a high five. Alicia slapped her palm, but Lotta was too busy trying to keep control of the growling beast we were in, and I was too anxious.

'Now the bowling alley, right?' asked Lotta.

'Right!' I said, sitting back and trying to figure out where to go from there.

BLACK CAT RIDGE, TEXAS, 1999

Willis stuck his head around the door. 'E.J.?' he called softly.

I grabbed his arm and pulled him inside, slamming a hand over his mouth. 'They're here!' I whispered. 'One's upstairs and one's in the kitchen.'

He looked wide-eyed toward the kitchen. I shook my head. 'It's OK, I think I killed him.' I caught a giggle coming halfway out of me. I hoped to hell it was just nerves. The only other alternative was I was a secret homicidal maniac.

He removed my hand. 'Baby, are you OK?'

I nodded. He looked down at the gun in my hand. 'Where did that come from?'

I nodded toward the kitchen. 'Willis, one's upstairs with the kids.'

Slowly he looked toward the top of the stairs. 'Jesus,' he breathed. He took the gun from my hand. 'Does the phone work?'

I ran as quietly as I could into the living room and picked up the receiver. Dead. I ran back to Willis and shook my head.

With his mouth close to my ear, he said, 'Go next door and call Luna.'

I shook my head. 'I'm not leaving you.'

'Screw that! Just do it.' His voice was soft, but

his grip on my arm wasn't.

I moved quickly into the kitchen, skirting around the body on the floor, and grabbed the Lesters' house key off the ring inside the Tupperware cabinet. Skirting the body once again, I made it to the back door, gingerly flipped back the deadbolt, and slid out into the darkness.

I made a dash for the Lesters' back door, the key hitting everywhere but the keyhole as I fumbled in the dark. Finally it went in and I turned the key. The blow to my back shoved me through the door and on to the floor. I heard the door slam as I looked back. A man's outline stood in silhouette against the lightly curtained window of the door. Was this the man who'd been with my kids, or was this a third member of the group?

'You're a hard bitch to kill,' he said.

I sat up and scooted backwards, quickly blocked by the legs of the kitchen table.

He laughed. It wasn't a particularly friendly laugh. 'No place to run, baby, no place to hide. Come to daddy,' he cooed.

He'd taken his first step towards me when the door behind him crashed forward off its hinges, landing on the man with the gun. The gun skittered across the floor, but the bad guy wasn't going for it. He was under the door and Willis's two hundred and something pounds were standing on top of him.

Jumping to my feet, I asked Willis, 'Are the kids OK?'

He nodded. 'Sound asleep.'

'You sure they're asleep, not...'

Again he nodded. 'I used Graham's flashlight. They're OK.'

Willis leaned over from his stance on the broken door and switched on the kitchen light. I went for the gun where it lay on the floor, next to the refrigerator. I handed it to Willis, who got off the door. I flipped the broken wood and glass off our prisoner. 'Call the cops,' Willis said.

I ran to the wall phone and dialed Luna's home number, which I'd certainly had the time to memorize. A sleepy voice answered, 'Luna.'

'Hey, it's E.J.'

'Jesus. A body could get tired of you.'

'Two guys broke into my home tonight. I think I killed one of them. The other one we have. He was after our kids. Would you like to do something about this?'

'Where are you now?'

'At the Lesters' house.'

'What in the hell are you do— never mind. Who's with the kids?'

My heart began to race. 'Nobody,' I said as I dropped the phone and ran back to my house. I took the butcher knife out of my back pocket where I'd put it what seemed like hours before, and I ran up the stairs, the flashlight still in my hand. The kids were asleep. No one was in the house. Unless they were hiding in the attic crawl space. I checked. They weren't.

Going to the back door again, I met Willis and Mr X coming in. Willis flipped on the kitchen light. 'They'd turned off the main switch at the breaker. I turned it back on.'

I didn't look behind me at the mess I'd made on the kitchen floor. Instead I said, 'Should I get the kids up?'

Willis thought a moment. 'No. Just check on them again.'

I nodded and went back upstairs, turning on the overhead lights this time to make absolutely sure. Still they slept, no bloodstains or bullet holes, all three little chests moving up and down in a natural sleep rhythm.

By the time I got back downstairs, I could hear the sirens turning on to our street. I went to the front door and opened it. Luna's private car, an antique Chevy Malibu, pulled in first, followed by two patrol cars and an ambulance. Well, I thought, I finally got somebody's attention. That's when I sat down on the first step of the stairs and started bawling. And that's how Luna found me, crying my eyes out, holding a butcher knife in one hand and a flashlight in the other.

She knelt down in front of me. 'The kids...' she started.

I nodded. 'They're OK,' I got out. I pointed towards the kitchen. 'They're in there. The dead one. And the live one. With Willis.'

She left me, leading her troops towards the kitchen. I sat on the step for only a few minutes when it dawned on me that the live one might tell Luna something. Something important. I asked myself if I could stand being in the same room with the body I'd created. I answered myself that I could.

I went into the kitchen. Luna was supervising the cuffing of the live one. I got my first look at him in the light. He was a scrawny guy in his late twenties, with a weasely face – a face I'd never seen before.

The paramedics knelt by the other intruder, who suddenly moaned. I leaned up against the wall and felt my body relax. I hadn't killed him. Thank God. I hadn't killed the son of a bitch. Gingerly, I took a peek over the counter at the mess I'd created on my sparkling clean tile. I was right. I wouldn't be able to recognize this one if I knew him. I suppressed an urge to gag and leaned back against the wall. At least he was alive. There was that.

One of the uniforms handed Luna a wallet he'd taken from the guy when he'd frisked and cuffed him. Luna opened it. 'Larry Douglas.' She smiled. 'Well, Larry, looks like you two picked the wrong family to mess with this time.'

E.J., THE PRESENT

I hit Main Street going forty miles an hour, taking a fast left, anxious to find the girls. That's when I heard the 'woop-woop' of the cop car behind me. Cursing a blue streak, I pulled over and waited for the officer to get to me.

Just as he did, the dark blue streaked with flames Chevy made a left in front of me on to Main Street, heading south. I lowered my window quickly. 'I've got to catch that Chevy!' I yelled at him. 'Call Elena Luna! I'm her neighbor! She'll know!' I called to him as I hit the accelerator and took off.

I was hot on their trail when I realized the

197

officer I'd talked to only moments before either hadn't heard my last comment, or didn't care. I was cut off from the front by a police car, penned in at the back by a police car, and had one a couple of inches from the driver's door of the Volvo. Guns were pointed at me. 'Well, shit,' I said to myself.

ELIZABETH, THE PRESENT

'The cops got Mom!' Megan yelled from the back seat.

I turned around from my shotgun seat in time to see the officers drawing their weapons. I wasn't too worried about it. Mom seemed to have a get-out-of-jail-free pass by having Elena Luna as a friend. I mean as far as minor infractions go. Which got me to thinking: If we killed this stalker guy, would we all get off? I thought on that for a while until Lotta pulled into the parking lot. I checked my watch. Six-thirty. Daylight savings time meant it wouldn't get dark until well after eight. We'd have daylight to do some searching around here – and the cover of darkness for any real clandestine searching. Things were working out well.

Lotta pulled into a parking spot fairly close to the front of the bowling alley and cut the engine. We all sat there for a quiet minute staring at the entrance. Then Lotta rolled her window down and we all followed suit. It was getting 'don't leave your dog in the car' hot in there. With the windows down we could all breathe a little better. 'Now what?' Lotta asked.

198

I looked around the parking lot. I didn't see any motorcycles in the lot. 'We go in?' I said, not liking the question mark sound that came out of my mouth. I would have liked to have been a little more assertive.

BLACK CAT RIDGE, TEXAS, APRIL 2009

On this particular Saturday night in April, Graham Pugh found himself in rather dire circumstances. After a fiasco at the bowling alley that had led him to run for his life through the back alleys of Codderville, he had found himself the guest – at gunpoint – of a car full of young Hispanic men taking a leisurely low-rider spin through town. They had stopped only twice, once to get some soda and snacks from the Stop N Go, and once to get their cousin Lotta from her job at the KFC. As the car was crowded with way too many people, Graham happily found himself with Lotta on his lap. As he was falling in love, the low-rider cruised by a local hangout, the Pizza Garden, where Graham saw something out of the corner of his eye. When he registered what it was, he yelled, 'Stop!'

The low-rider came to a shuddering halt.

'Back up!' Graham yelled.

Graham's new friend Manny's brother Eddie, the driver of the car, muttered an obscenity, but Manny said, 'Back up, man!' so Eddie did.

'Whoa!' Manny said, upon seeing what had gotten Graham's attention. 'She'd be hot if she wasn't crying,' he said.

'Shut up, man!' Graham said through clenched

teeth. 'That's my fourteen-year-old sister! Let me out!'

Graham opened the door and Lotta moved to let him out. He ran to Megan who threw her arms around him, sobbing.

'He got her! He got her!' Megan screamed.

'Who?' Graham demanded. 'What's happened?'

'In Grandma's car! Hurry!' Megan ran to the low-rider and jumped in, Graham and Lotta following. Megan straddled the hump in the middle of the back seat, leaning over the back of the front bench seat. The cousin riding in the middle of the front seat had been shoved to the side so Manny could 'help' the newest arrival.

'Go fast!' Megan wailed. 'They got like a three-minute lead!'

'Megan, what in the hell's going on?' Graham demanded, trying to pull her back from the front seat, either to get her attention so she'd tell him her story, or to get her away from Manny. Not even Graham was sure of his actual motive.

'First make him go fast!' Megan shouted. 'Then I'll tell you what's going on!'

'For God's sake, *culo*!' Lotta said. 'Make this piece of crap move!'

Eddie stopped the car, did something under the dash, and the low-rider moved upward, into the position of a normal car.

Hitting the accelerator, the Chevy pulled several Gs, knocking those in the back seat against the tuck-and-rolled leather upholstery.

Graham grabbed his sister's arm. 'What's going on?'

'He kidnapped Liz!' she said.

'Who did?' Graham demanded.

Megan looked at her brother for a long moment. Then, sighing, she said, 'Aldon.'

E.J., THE PRESENT

'Get Elena Luna!' I said for the umpteenth time. Still no one listened. 'She knows who I am.'

The officer who had arrested me clung harder to my right arm. I'm going to bruise, I thought. Get pictures, I told myself. For the lawsuit.

He roughly pushed me up to a fenced-off area with a window-like hole in it. A uniformed woman in her fifties was looking down at papers in front of her when I hit the shelf in front of her.

She looked up, frowning. 'Watch it!' she said.

'He did it!' I told her. She ignored me. I wondered for a moment if my vocal cords had weakened. No one seemed to hear me.

'Whatjagot, Ralphie?' she said, elbows on the counter, looking beyond me to the man holding my handcuffed arms behind my back. Like I was going to miraculously break through the cuffs if he hadn't been holding my arms!

'I told you, Velma, no Ralphie. Just Ralph, OK?'

She smiled at him, showing two rows of yellowed, crooked teeth. 'Sure, OK, Ralphie,' she said.

He sighed and shoved me at the counter – again. 'Book her on resisting arrest, speeding, reckless endangerment, and anything else you got back there, 'K, Velma?'

'You got it, Ralphie, I'll throw the book at her, as they say.' And she giggled. It was amazing.

Out of the corner of my eye, I saw a familiar sight. I turned roughly in Ralphie's arms. 'Luna!' I shouted.

There was something wrong with my vocal cords, all right. Luna didn't seem to hear me at all.

GRAHAM, THE PRESENT

'So what do we do?' Leon asked.

'This guy's not in Black Cat,' Graham said. 'It's too small. He knows we'd find him here. I say we go into Codderville—'

'Not the bowling alley again!' Leon said.

Graham shuddered. 'God no! If I never see that place again it'll be too soon.'

'Huh?' Hollister said.

Graham shook his head. 'Never mind. No, I think we look for low-rent places he could—'

'Nothin's lower rent than the bowling alley,' Tad said.

'I'm talking for him to stay at. Like sleazebag motels, trailer parks, pay-by-the-week places,' Graham said.

'Makes sense,' Leon said.

'So how do we find places like that?' Hollister asked.

Graham took a sheet of folded paper out of his back pocket and shook it open. 'I Googled them,' he said.

202

It looked benign enough. There weren't that many people inside the bowling alley and most of them looked like employees. One group of old people was bowling at the end on the right, but that was it. They certainly didn't look like bikers. They were making some noise, laughing and cutting up like teenagers – very lame, if you ask me – and there was a jukebox playing oldies really loud, but mostly it was quiet, even if that does sound weird.

There was a little restaurant thing at the front and I thought that would be a good place to sit and watch as people came in. I knew I'd recognize him this time, even if the last time I saw him he was dressed as a girl.

I pointed my head towards the restaurant. 'Y'all want something to drink?'

Confused faces turned knowing after just a moment. After we'd sat down and all ordered drinks, I asked Lotta, 'Don't you have to be at work soon?'

'I was supposed to be there half an hour ago.' She shrugged. 'I've never not shown up before. It should be OK.'

'Why don't you call?' Megan asked.

'I don't want to go to the bathroom here. That's where I saw the sign for a phone,' Lotta said.

'Here, use my cell phone,' Megan said.

'Cool!' Lotta said, taking the phone. 'Do you all have cell phones? I know Graham always has one.'

'Yeah,' I said. 'Our parents want to be able to get hold of us at any time.'

'Do they have those GPS things in them?' Alicia asked, eyes huge. 'I saw that on TV.'

Megan smiled. 'No. Ours are old. No GPS.'

'Cool,' Lotta said, and began dialing the KFC.

E.J., THE PRESENT

'I swear to God, Luna, you keep ignoring me and I'm going to sic the neighborhood association on you!' I yelled.

'Did she just threaten a police officer?' Velma asked Ralphie.

'Believe she did,' Ralphie answered.

Luna sighed and came over. 'What did she do?' she asked Ralphie.

'What *didn't* she do is more like it,' Ralphie answered.

'I was going after the girls!' I shouted. 'They've gone after the stalker! Myra's killer! Four of them out there in a low-rider cruising Codderville looking for trouble! I was following them!'

'Guess who found trouble first,' Luna said.

'I tried to explain to this—'

'Watch it,' Luna said.

'Officer what was going on and to call you but...' I faltered.

Turning to Officer Ralphie, Luna asked, 'What do you have on her?'

'Speeding, resisting arrest, leaving the scene, and vehicular menace,' Ralphie said.

'Leaving what scene?' Luna asked.

'The scene of me giving her a ticket, that's what scene!' Ralphie said indignantly.

'Ralph, there's no such thing as vehicular menace,' she said.

Ralphie grumbled, 'Well there should be.'

'At what point did she resist arrest?'

'She just took off in the middle of me giving her a ticket!' Ralphie said.

Ralphie was getting pissed and I was delighted. Luna had my back!

'Give her an extra ten on the speeding ticket. That work for you, Ralph?' Luna asked.

'Ten what?' I demanded.

'Ten miles over,' Luna said. 'Ralph?'

'Make it twenty,' he countered.

'I'll go fifteen,' Luna said.

'Hey!' I said and was generally ignored.

'Fifteen,' Ralphie agreed.

'Wait now!' I said as Ralphie leaned down to undo the handcuffs. 'That's like twenty-five over the speed limit! That's a lot of money!'

'You know how much resisting arrest is?' she asked me.

'No,' I admitted.

'It can't even be counted in money. Actually, it's counted in months. Sometimes years. Do you still want to bitch?'

I sighed. 'Not at all. Thank you, Officer Ralphie—'

'Burgess!' he all but shouted. 'Ralph Burgess!'

'Sorry, Officer Burgess. And Detective Luna, I thank you—'

'Where's your purse?' she asked, grabbing me by the arm.

'I got it,' Velma said, handing my purse through the window area of her fence-wall.

Luna grabbed the purse and hauled me away. 'Where are we going?' I asked.

'To my car. I'm off duty. We're going to go look for the girls.'

And with that, we were off.

BLACK CAT RIDGE, TEXAS, 1999

Willis and I stood in the small observation room next to the interrogation room. We watched with Luna's boss while she interviewed Larry Douglas, the man who had gone upstairs after our kids. The man who'd accosted me at the Lesters' house.

Luna moved so quickly I jumped. She lunged at Douglas, her face only inches from his. 'Who paid you to off the Lesters? Who paid you to hit the house last night?' She knocked the cigarette from Douglas's mouth. 'Who?'

'Swear to God I don't know shit about Lester. Whoever the hell he is. I just come along last night with Clyde, see. Me and Clyde were in the joint together. I seen him at Scooters yesterday and he says he got a job for me. Pay me five hundred bucks to go to this house and rough up some people. He didn't say nothing about offin' nobody. I swear to God.'

Luna sat down in the chair opposite Larry Douglas. 'You know something, Larry?' she said. 'I believe you. 'Cause I don't think even Clyde would be stupid enough to tell you anything important.'

'Fuck you, bitch!' he said.

Luna laughed. 'Jeez, with a vocabulary like that, maybe you should become a jailhouse lawyer, Lare. Whatcha think?'

Luna left the interrogation room and we met her at her desk. The first thing I asked her was, 'How's Clyde? Is he going to be able to talk anytime soon?'

Luna snorted. 'His jaw's wired shut. He has a concussion, a lacerated left eye, had to have twelve stitches in his forehead, and three in his scalp, his nose is busted, and his left ear had to be partially sewn back on. But other than that...'

'What's wrong with his jaw?' Willis asked.

Pointing a thumb my direction, Luna said, 'She broke it.'

TWELVE

Why would she go in the bowling alley? That's so dangerous! It's those other girls! They're a bad influence on my Bessie! I have to get her away from them! Correction: I have to get them *away from* her. *That I can do. No sweat.*

ELIZABETH, THE PRESENT

We sat and watched as people started arriving. Lotta knew a couple of guys who came in. They waved to her, said, 'Hey, Lotta! Where's Graham?'

'He'll be here in a minute,' she said smiling.

They moved on. Alicia said, 'Graham's coming?'

Lotta shook her head. 'No. But if I didn't say that, those two would be over here in a flash trying to hit on all of us.'

'Me too?' Alicia said, her eyes huge.

Lotta looked at her. 'Yeah, hon, you too. What? You think guys don't look at you? They do.'

Alicia shook her head, making her long hair cover her face even more.

Lotta said, 'Megan, get a brush and a hair fixer out of my purse,' as she turned Alicia's chair around and began pulling back her hair.

'No, that's all right...' Alicia began.

'Hush,' Lotta said, taking the brush from Megan and using it on Alicia's hair.

'No, really...' Alicia said.

That's when I saw it. I'd never known it was there. A scar on Alicia's face that ran from her hairline to the corner of her eye. It was thick and red and ugly.

'You got some make-up in that purse?' I asked Lotta.

'Yeah,' she said with difficulty, the hair fixer firmly between her teeth. 'Meg?'

Megan rummaged through Lotta's large bag until she came up with a smaller bag full of make-up. I opened it, found some concealer and foundation and went to work on the scar. And while I was there, I just kept on going. By the time Lotta and I were through, there was a different girl sitting in the chair. A girl with a pretty face and striking eyes, a strong chin, and a turned-up nose. Who knew?

'My God, Alicia,' Megan said. 'You're hot!'

The skin under the foundation make-up turned red, but you could barely tell with all the goop I had on her.

'You're gorgeous!' Lotta said.

'You should wear your hair back all the time!' Megan said.

'I can't,' Alicia said, her voice soft.

'Oh! You mean that scar?' Megan said. 'That's nothing! Look at these freckles! Some as big as a dime!'

'No one asks you where you got the freckles,' Alicia said, head down and voice soft. 'But everyone asks me where I got the scar. That's why I wear my hair like this.'

'Is that why you wear those jumpers and sweaters all the time? Do you have more scars?' Lotta asked her quietly.

Alicia shook her head. 'No. They're just all the clothes I got,' she said. 'It's an outfit that goes together. I know it's hot out, but it goes together.'

I could feel tears springing to my eyes. I'd known Alicia for months and never knew about the scar, or about the lack of clothes. She didn't just have a lot of those jumpers and sweaters, she just had the one 'outfit'. And washed it over and over. I turned away to get myself back together, and said, 'Well, you need to mix and match. Specially in the summer months,' I said,

209

trying to find that inner spunk my mother had. 'Tomorrow we'll go through my closet and see what goes with that jumper. And maybe add some shorts.'

'I've got a whole bag of clothes that don't fit me anymore,' Lotta said, 'and I don't have any little sisters or cousins to hand them down to. I'm the only girl. So, we'll pretend you're my little sister, OK?'

Alicia smiled. Then we heard a low voice say, 'Hey, gorgeous.'

We all looked up to see a grown man towering over us, staring straight at Alicia. Her smile faded and she grabbed my hand. Looking around us, we noticed that while we were playing make-over, the bikers had invaded the bowling alley.

'Wanna go for a ride?' he said. He was at least as tall as my dad, but a lot bigger. Like maybe twice as big, and he was only wearing a leather vest on his top half. He had a do-rag on his head, a drooping mustache like Hulk Hogan, faded jeans stuck into knee-high black leather boots. He had chains hanging from his waist somehow, a studded belt with a silver skull with ruby eyes for a belt buckle. He was scary as shit, excuse my French.

'We're waiting for our boyfriends,' Lotta said.

'Good, I can eat 'em for an appetizer,' he said, then laughed like he was channeling the voice of Optimus Prime

Then a woman came up and grabbed his arm. 'Jail bait, baby,' she said, and hauled him away. He blew a kiss at Alicia and let the woman, wearing exactly the same thing he was –

including just a leather vest covering her ample breasts – drag him away.

Alicia pulled the hair fixer out of her hair. 'Can we leave now?' she asked.

Unfortunately she asked too late. The door to the bowling alley opened and a man walked in. Young, not too tall, fair skinned with light brown hair. Someone I recognized immediately. I barely got out the words 'It's him!' before he lifted an assault rifle and began to fire.

BLACK CAT RIDGE, TEXAS, 1999

Clyde Hayden, the bad guy I'd almost killed, was under guard on the top floor, the locked floor, of the hospital. A cop sat in a chair outside the door and another sat inside. The Codderville Police Department was finally paying some attention to what was going on around them.

Clyde looked terrible. The guilt attack I got just looking at him could have felled a lesser woman. His head was swathed in bandages, as was his nose, his left ear, and his left eye – on which he wore a rather snazzy pirate patch, over the bandages. His jaw was indeed wired shut with a tube stuck in one side for breathing and another in the other side for liquids. An IV was plugged in one arm. His good eye looked at us as we came in, finally settling on me, where it stayed, following me as I moved around the room. It wasn't the most benevolent of eyes.

'Hey, Clyde, how you doing?' Luna greeted, sitting down in the chair next to his good side and patting his arm gently. 'I'm Detective Luna

211

and these are Mr and Mrs Pugh, the people you tried to kill.'

A sound came out of his mouth – not words, just sounds. Luna handed him a blackboard and some chalk. 'Here you go, fella. Make life a little easier for you. Can you read and write?'

He gave her the look he'd been giving me and scratched out 'eat shit and die' on the blackboard.

Luna smiled broadly at us. 'Well, see now, I told you old Clyde wasn't an illiterate.' Turning back to Hayden, she said, 'Now, Clyde, honey, I want you to write down on that blackboard the name of the person who paid you and old Larry to off this nice family.' She patted his arm again. 'You gonna do that for me, darlin'?'

'Fuck you' was scratched on the board.

'Tsk, tsk,' Luna said. 'Such language. Well, I guess I'll tell the prosecutor to go ahead with the death penalty he's talking 'bout for you two.'

Clyde's eye got wide and pointed at Willis and me. 'Their alive!' he scratched.

Luna laughed. 'You're right, they sure are.' Pointing at the blackboard, she said, 'And that should be t-h-e-y apostrophe r-e. It's a contraction, as in "they are". But a lot of people get those mixed up – they're, their, and there. It's a common mistake. Doesn't make you stupid. Well, that doesn't, anyway.' She shook her head. 'I'm not talking about the death penalty for these two,' she said, indicating Willis and me. 'They are pretty obviously alive, like you tried to say. I'm talking about the Lester family. You remember? The mama and papa and the little boy you got on the stairs and that pretty little teenaged girl?'

Clyde shook his head so hard one of the bandages loosened. Luna reached up and stuck it, not so gently, back to Clyde's skin. 'There you go. Now don't you go thrashing around like that. We want you nice and healthy for when the State sticks you with that old needle, now don't we?'

Frantically Clyde scratched out 'don't know no Lesters!!!!'

'You don't? Well, maybe you didn't catch their names when you were doing them. It happens.'

Luna looked at Willis and me. 'Well, you know, whoever hired the hit on you may have hired a separate team to hit the Lesters. But the bad thing is, whoever did, Clyde and Larry are going to go down for it.' She shrugged and held up her hands in a helpless gesture.

'We don't have any other names...' she started.

The scratching sound of chalk on blackboard stopped Luna. She looked toward the board outstretched in Clyde's hands. 'Billy Dave Petrie – Birdsong Road – outside of Brenham.'

Luna smiled and took the blackboard out of Clyde's hands. 'Thanks, Clyde. We'll go talk to Billy Dave. You get well now, you hear?'

As we walked out, I turned toward Clyde. 'Sorry,' I said and shrugged. He didn't look pleased.

GRAHAM, THE PRESENT

I got Hollister, Tad and Leon into the car, Leon

213

having yelled 'shotgun' first, sitting in the front seat with me.

'Where we going first?' Leon asked, rubbing his hands together like this was some sort of high adventure. He hadn't been there last time – none of them had. I could tell them for sure this wasn't high adventure.

'I'm gonna call Lotta at work, see if she can get off,' I said.

I saw Leon roll his eyes and heard groans from the back seat. 'Shit, OK? I'll just say hi. Damn, y'all.'

I hit the speed dial on my phone for the KFC. Lotta usually picks it up, but this time Tamara, the manager, answered.

'Hey, Tamara,' I said, 'it's Graham. Lotta there?'

'No she not. And I'm telling you right now that girl better get her butt in here tomorrow or her ass is grass, you know what I mean?'

'She's sick?' I asked.

'So she say,' Tamara said. 'But I ain't buying it. That girl don't sound sick, you know what I mean?'

'OK, thanks, Tamara.'

'You tell her—' she started but I hung up and used speed dial to Lotta's home number, hoping like hell neither of her parents answered. They didn't like me.

'Hello.' It was Manny, my friend and Lotta's cousin who lived with her family in Black Cat Ridge so he could go to our high school. He'd gotten in a little trouble at the Codderville High School and the principal, counselors, teachers and his parents all decided it was in the boy's best interest to go to school elsewhere.

'Hey, Manny!' I said. 'Lotta home? She sick?'

'What? No, man, she's at work!' Manny said.

'Hey, don't talk so loud. Don't let her parents hear. She's not at work,' I said.

'Shit, man,' Manny said, voice a whisper. 'Where is she? She with you?'

'Would I be calling if she was with me?'

'Hum, well, probably not. But she ain't at work, ain't home, and ain't with you, where is—Holy shit!' he almost shouted.

'Shhhhhhhhh. What?'

'Oh, shit, oh shit, oh man!'

'What?' I almost shouted into the phone.

'My brother Eddie called a while ago saying somebody took his car, man! Somebody who knew where he kept the extra key, man! You don't think Lotta woulda done that, do you?'

'Shit! The low-rider?' I said, thinking about Lotta behind the wheel of that beast. 'Man, she only has a learner's permit, and she's not that good!'

'Why would she take it?' Manny all but wailed. 'Man, like Eddie's having a shit fit. He's gonna kill her, man!'

'If she lives through driving that damn thing!' I said. 'Look, Manny, I gotta go. I'm heading to Codderville and I'll keep an eye out for her. Believe me!'

'Man, you find her, let me know! Tia Anita's asleep and I can use her car to meet you.'

'Don't you think there's been enough car stealing for one night?'

215

'Hey, I ain't gonna steal it, man. Just borrow it, ya know?'

At that I hung up and looked at my guys. 'Lotta's missing,' I said, as we crossed the bridge into Codderville.

We started driving around and I found myself going by the infamous bowling alley. And then I saw it. Big as shit. Eddie's low-rider, flames and all. Sitting there in the front row at the bowling alley. I pulled in a couple of rows behind, as far away from all the bikes as possible, and the four of us piled out.

BLACK CAT RIDGE, TEXAS, APRIL 2009

'Who's Alton?' Manny asked from the front seat, not taking his eyes off Megan.

'Aldon,' Graham corrected. 'Nobody really,' he said, also staring at his sister. 'Used to be my best friend when I was a kid. That was before he died, though.'

'Huh?' Manny said, finally turning to Graham. All eyes and ears in the car were on Graham, except Megan, who looked to her lap.

'Where the hell am I going?' Eddie, the driver, asked.

'Straight ahead. It's an 'eighty-four Dodge Valiant. Blue. Vanity plates that say "Granof4",' Megan said.

'That's a dumb ride to kidnap somebody in,' Uncle Ernesto said, honestly disgusted at the ineptitude of some people.

'He stole our car,' Megan said.

'Grandma's car!' corrected Graham, letting

216

himself get off track. Shaking his head, he said, 'Tell me. Who the hell is this guy?'

'Can you go faster?' Megan pleaded to Eddie as his ride began to pick up speed.

'Sure, *chica*. Calm down,' Eddie said.

'Megan! What is going on?' Graham insisted.

So she told him – about Tommy, about the Internet, about him suddenly changing his tune and saying he was Aldon. About the accusations against their mother and Elena Luna.

'And Liz believed this shit?' Graham said, incensed.

'No, of course not. I mean, not really,' Megan said.

'You mean she did!' Graham accused.

'No! She was so confused, Graham,' Megan said, tears stinging her eyes. 'Someone claiming to be a part of her *real* family—'

'We're her *real* family!' Graham said.

Megan turned to the driver. 'Do you see it?' she asked.

'No, *chica*. No blue Valiant. I don't think I've seen one of those in a hundred years!'

'Well, it *is* a blue Valiant! Trust me!' Megan said, letting her temper show.

Manny patted her hand. 'It's OK, Megan,' he said. 'We'll find her.'

Graham removed Manny's hand from his sister's. 'Fourteen!' he said, glaring at Manny.

'So who's this chick we're looking for?' Manny asked, keeping his hand on the back of the seat, just inches from Megan's.

'My sister,' Graham said.

'I thought *she* was your sister?' Manny said,

217

pointing at Megan.

'She is, dumb ass! I have two.'

'How old is the one we're looking for?' Manny asked.

'Fourteen!' Graham said, shooting Manny a look.

Manny turned around in his seat. 'Well, somebody's got an attitude!' he said under his breath.

'And you two thought you'd just come confront this guy, right?' Graham said, glaring at his sister.

Sinking back on to Uncle Ernesto's lap, Megan said, 'It seemed like a good idea at the time.'

'Graham, I think you're missing the big picture here,' Lotta said from his lap.

'You know, I really don't need y'all's help here—' he started, but Lotta interrupted.

'You need *somebody's* help, buster,' she said, glaring down at him. 'First off, Megan, are you OK?'

Megan shook her head. 'No, not really. But thank you for asking,' she said, shooting a look at her brother.

'Did he hurt you?' Graham demanded, moving forward so fast Lotta fell between his feet and the back of Manny's seat.

'Hey, *pendejo*!' she yelled. 'Pick me up!'

'Sorry,' Graham said, pulling her back on to his lap. To Megan he asked, 'Did he?'

'Not really. He threw me on the ground and I might have scraped my hands.' She looked at them and they were indeed scraped. Manny grabbed one while Uncle Ernesto grabbed the other.

'Oh, poor *chica*!' Uncle Ernesto said. 'We need to get these cleaned out!'

Graham hit both men's hands away from Megan's.

'But mostly I'm just scared for Elizabeth,' Megan told Lotta. 'She's not real strong,' Megan said, as tears began to fall down her cheeks. 'She's little. A lot smaller than me. If I'd seen him, maybe...'

Lotta reached over and put her arms around Megan. 'Honey, you did what you could! The guy blindsided you!' She held Megan's face up and with a finger wiped away her tears. 'But we're going to find her. And when we do, with all these macho guys we got here, the asshole's not gonna know what hit him!'

Megan smiled for the first time in an hour.

E.J., THE PRESENT

We'd barely gotten in Luna's car when her phone rang. She said, 'What?' then listened, then said, 'Shit.' Then she listened again. Finally she said, 'Thanks,' and hung up. She started the car, took her little dome light thingy from under my feet on the passenger side and put it on top of her car, and then started her siren.

'What's going on?' I asked, beginning to panic.

'There's been an incident at the bowling alley. A bunch of underage girls...' She faltered. Finally she said, 'Shots fired.'

I just looked at her as she took the streets of Codderville at eighty miles an hour. We got to the bowling alley in record time, only to find two ambulances, a couple of squad cars, and a fire truck blocking the way. Scores of motor-cycles were lying on their sides, and I could see the dark blue Chevy with the flames on the side pushed up against the building by the fire truck. And then I saw Graham's Valiant and thought I was going to vomit. All my children, all of them, at a place where shots were fired. Before Luna could even stop the car, I had my door open and was puking out the side.

'Hold on, Pugh. Nobody said anybody was hurt or anything...'

'Yeah, yeah. Just stop the car.' All I could think of was how I was going to tell Willis, who was in Houston yet again, that one or all of his children were hurt and/or dead. Just the thought made me woozy and Luna grabbed my arm.

'Don't panic until we get inside,' she said.

I looked at her. 'Then I have your permission to panic?'

'Sure. Go for it.'

There was a uniformed cop standing by the entrance to the bowling alley. Seeing Luna he opened the door without question. Since Luna was holding my arm, the invitation seemed to include me.

We walked inside to be met with bedlam. The first thing I saw was a stretcher with a child-sized person on it. I pulled away from Luna and ran to the stretcher. The little face showing from under the sheet was covered with so much blood I didn't recognize her. Her eyes were closed.

Then I heard a sound that almost ruptured my

heart. 'Mom!'

I whirled around to see all three of my kids standing with a uniformed officer. My girls ran to me and I pulled them to me, hugging them so hard it hurt all three of us. 'Who—?' I said, pointing my head in the direction of the stretcher.

Elizabeth was crying. 'Alicia!' she said.

'Oh, my God!' I said, letting go of my girls to turn back to the stretcher. The EMTs were still administering to her. 'How bad is it?' I asked.

'Are you her parent?' the female EMT asked.

Elizabeth grabbed my hand and I looked at her. She was nodding her head like crazy.

'Yes,' I said to the EMT.

'It was a head wound,' she said. 'They bleed like crazy. I think she just passed out from the sheer fright of it all. Her vitals are good – hey, Mac, hand me some smelling salts.'

She waved the smelling salts under Alicia's nose and she shook her head and then her eyes popped open and she said, 'My head hurts.'

I bent down and kissed her on the cheek. 'It's OK, honey,' I said. 'You just got hurt a little. You're going to be fine.'

'Mrs Pugh?' she said, looking at me.

I looked at the EMT. 'She's delirious,' I said.

'Are Elizabeth and the others OK?' she asked.

'I'm right here,' Bessie said, coming to hold Alicia's other hand.

'And the others?'

Elizabeth looked up at me and then over to her siblings. 'Megan got winged in the arm...' she started, at which time I let go of Alicia's hand

and turned to my other daughter, who, I noticed for the first time, had a bandage on her arm.

Before I could say a word, Megan piped up, 'It's fine, Mom. It barely hurts.'

'What about Lotta?' Alicia asked.

At which point I looked around. I didn't see Lotta anywhere. 'Where *is* Lotta?' I asked.

Looking at Graham I could tell something was wrong. His face was pale and drawn, and his hands were fisted. When I asked where Lotta was, I saw his friends, Hollister, Tad, and Leon, come up behind him, hands on Graham's shoulders, as if holding him back.

'What happened?' I asked.

The front doors of the bowling alley opened and another officer came in, his hand gently on the arm of Lotta Hernandez. Graham, my big brave boy, burst into tears and ran to her, throwing his arms around her. Lotta started to cry, too, and they clung to each other, making me tear up, and I didn't even know what was going on.

Finally, I got the story...

BLACK CAT RIDGE, TEXAS, 1999

Luna said it would be OK if Willis and I went with her to check out Billy Dave Petrie, the man Clyde Hayden said had paid him five hundred dollars to take care of my family and me. It was a fairly nice drive from Codderville to the outskirts of Brenham. It took us forty-five minutes to find the sign saying Washington County, and another twenty minutes to find Birdsong Road and the mailbox that said 'Petrie'.

The mailbox itself should have told us something. The door to the box was hanging open from all the circulars and junk mail shoved inside. We drove up the rutted dirt drive, splashing mud on the clean city car from the puddles left by a recent rain.

Four vehicles sat in the yard of the dilapidated trailer house, only two of them serviceable. The front door of the trailer stood open and as we got out of the car and walked towards the door, the odor almost knocked me over. Willis grabbed my arm and pulled me back.

Luna said, 'Shit,' under her breath. Turning, she said to Willis, 'You know how to work a two-way radio?' He nodded his head. 'I think we're still in range. Get the station and have them call the Washington County sheriff's office. I need backup on this thing.'

Willis ran to the car while I stood where I was, watching Luna pull a hanky out of her purse to cover her mouth, her gun ready in her right hand. With her foot, she opened the door wide and stepped inside.

THIRTEEN

I hate them all so much! Hate them hate them hate them hate them!!!! I'm going to kill them all! And I'm going to enjoy it!

ELIZABETH, THE PRESENT

The door to the bowling alley opened and a man walked in. Young, not too tall, fair skinned with light brown hair. Someone I recognized immediately. I barely got out the words 'It's him!' before he lifted an assault rifle and began to fire.

And he was firing at us. We all hit the floor. Everything felt like it was in slo-mo. Like a Quentin Tarantino movie. Except these bullets were real. Alicia was the last one down. On her back – dead. Blood all over her face. I started screaming and couldn't stop. Megan, on the other side of Alicia, got up to run to me and got hit, falling to the floor. Lotta, next to me, grabbed for Megan, but Megan said, 'It's OK, it's OK.' Her right hand was pressed against the wound, blood oozing between her fingers.

Alicia dead, Megan wounded – I looked up and saw the bikers heading toward my stalker. 'Get him!' I said. 'Kill him!' I wanted them to smash his head in, pulverize him. I wanted to personally stomp on his exposed lungs! But he turned the rifle on them and then seven or eight handguns came out and everyone started firing. Lotta grabbed me to pull me down, pushing me to the floor on the other side of her, just as the stalker lunged for me. He grabbed Lotta instead and dragged her out the door, firing his weapon as he went, and mostly hitting the ceiling.

When he was gone, the waitress in the little café said, 'The cops are on their way.' She ran to Alicia and felt for a pulse. 'She's alive,' she said.

The biker chick who'd been with the big Hulk Hogan-mustache guy rushed over to check on Alicia and Megan.

I just stood there, staring at all the blood, knowing neither Alicia nor Megan would be hurt now if not for me. And Lotta – I couldn't think about it. It was truly all my fault. Every bit of it. 'I'm sorry,' I said, then realized I'd been saying it for a long time.

'You guys OK?' Megan asked the biker chick.

'Yeah, couple of wing shots like you, honey, but the fucker couldn't shoot worth shit.'

'That's good,' Megan said.

'Damn skippy,' the biker chick said.

That's when the first police officer arrived and, with him, the first ambulance.

When I got through with my part of the story, Mom said, 'Well thank God Alicia's OK. And Meggy,' she said, pulling my sister to her and making Megan say 'ouch!' I hadn't heard Mom call Megan 'Meggy' in a hundred years. It sounded nice.

Everyone looked at Lotta, who was still firmly

in Graham's arms. 'He just dragged me to his car...'

'What was the make and model?' Mrs Luna asked.

'It was a Toyota Celica, newish, dark blue with a gray cloth interior,' she said as Mrs Luna wrote furiously. 'But I don't think it was his,' Lotta continued. 'There was a baby seat in the back. I think maybe he stole it.'

'OK,' Mrs Luna said. 'What happened after he put you in the car?'

'He drove toward Black Cat Ridge, but then he stopped at the bridge over the river and yanked me out. He tried to shove me over the bridge, but I kicked him in the balls and started running. I heard him start the car up, but when I turned to look, he was going over the bridge the other way so I stopped running.' Looking over her shoulder, her gaze landed on this really cute policeman. 'Then Officer Martinez came by and picked me up,' she said, smiling at him. 'And the rest, as they say, is history.'

I think Graham wasn't sure whether to thank Officer Martinez or slug him, although I think thanking him would be the safer route.

'Did he say anything to you in the car?' Mrs Luna asked.

'Not to me, really. He just kept saying, "I'll kill them, I'll kill them" over and over. It was really scary,' Lotta said.

Mom went up to her and got between Lotta and Graham and hugged her. 'I'm so sorry this happened to you,' she said. Then slapped Lotta's hand. 'But that's what you get for taking the

226

girls out in that low-rider!'

'Hey, it wasn't my idea!' Lotta said, pointing at me.

My mom turned to look at me. 'It seemed to be a good idea at the time,' I said.

Mom stared at me for a full half-minute, then started laughing. She hugged me and said, 'You are soooooooooooo grounded.'

E.J., THE PRESENT

The upshot of the whole thing was three bikers got arrested for possession of unlicensed concealed weapons and discharging firearms within the city limits, and just being butt-ugly I think, while the real criminal, Elizabeth's stalker, got away yet again.

I took the girls to Vera's house while Graham took his boys home then was going to take Lotta home and explain to her parents what happened. I should have gone with him, but I had someone else to notify.

I went with Luna in her car back to Black Cat Ridge to notify Alicia's foster parents that she was in the hospital.

The house where Alicia lived was just outside Black Cat Ridge. The houses inside Black Cat Ridge are all homogenized builders' homes, each little village inside the 'city' a certain price range. Each little village having its own pool and rec center. This way the kids at the high school just had to ask each other which village they lived in to find out whether or not the other was good enough to befriend. OK, I had some problems with the set-up.

The foster home was in the country outside the city limits of Black Cat Ridge. When we found the right dirt road to go down, it took a while at night to find the right mailbox. I knew the name of the foster parents was 'Rampy', George and Inez, which helped us find the mailbox, which stood next to a rutted drive between clumps of brush and trees. Luna turned into the drive and within seconds we could see the house, all lit up like a Christmas tree, but not nearly as merry.

There were several vehicles in the drive, on the grass, and further out in the acreage. We could hear someone cursing and banging on what sounded like yet another vehicle behind the house. Most of the vehicles we saw appeared to be non-working.

The house itself was very large, three storeys, and leaned haphazardly to the left. The front porch, which ran the length of the house, listed to the right. The wooden steps leading to the porch numbered four, but only two of them weren't broken through. Since the house was so lit up one could readily tell that what paint had once been on this house was so far gone the color was unknown.

Luna knocked on the door and we waited. Finally it was opened and a child stood there staring at us. He was about five, maybe six years old, hair sticking out every which way, nose running. He had on only underwear shorts, so old and dingy they looked gray.

'Is your mother home?' Luna asked the child.

'Huh?' he said.

'Are either Mr or Mrs Rampy home?' she asked again.

'Huh?' he said.

Then we heard a woman's voice. 'Don't be stupid, Jarred!' The boy was roughly pushed away from the door and then a woman was standing in front of us.

'What?' she demanded. She was maybe in her forties, with bleached blond hair, wearing lots of make-up and a halter-top that was failing to hold up enormous breasts. A muffin top of extreme proportions was exposed between the halter-top and the short-shorts, themselves exposing thighs like beef hindquarters. 'Who are you?'

Luna showed her badge and identified herself. Then said, 'Are you the legal guardian of Alicia Donnelly?'

The woman, Inez Rampy one could only assume, seemed to think about it for a moment, then said, 'Yeah. What's she done?'

'She was hurt this evening at the bowling alley in Codderville,' Luna said.

The woman took a stance, one hand on her hip, the other hip sticking out, a frown on her face. 'What in the hell was she doing in Codderville?' she demanded. 'She was supposed to be over at some friend's house in Black Cat.'

'Do you know what friend she was visiting?' Luna asked, her hand pressing against me as I'd started to answer.

The woman shrugged. 'I dunno. Some kid from school. She's over there all the time. Who can keep up?' As she said that a child about three ran up and hugged her leg. Inez Rampy shook the child off and yelled, 'Gretchen! Get your ass down here and take this brat upstairs like I tole you!' To Luna she said, 'God, kids! Whatja gonna do? Law says you can't kill 'em!' She laughed.

I already had a grip on Luna's waistband, which got tighter as the woman spoke. I couldn't help it. I whispered, 'Luna!'

She elbowed me in the gut.

'So what's Alicia gotten herself into?' Inez Rampy asked.

'Like I said, she's been hurt,' Luna said, speaking slowly, her words clipped. 'As her legal guardian I thought you should be notified.'

'Well, I ain't paying for it! Shit, they don't pay me enough to do that! You need to contact Children's Services,' she said. 'They'll take care of the hospital bill.'

'Don't you want to know what happened to her?' I demanded. 'Don't you want to go visit her?'

For the first time the woman looked at me. 'Who are you?' she demanded.

'That doesn't matter,' Luna said. 'You might want to contact the hospital and see when you'll be able to bring her home.'

'Well now, somebody's gonna have to bring her back here. I don't got a car in the daytime, my man has to work, ya know. And if she's gonna need special care, they're gonna have to put her someplace else. I don't have time to be taking care of a special needs kid, know what I mean? I got four kids in diapers here and then five others. Who's got the time for changing bandages and shit?'

'Thank you for your time, ma'am,' Luna said, and pushed me down the broken steps and over to her car.

As we drove back down the dirt road, I said, 'Boy, Willis is going to be surprised when he gets home to find another girl living there.'

BLACK CAT RIDGE, TEXAS, 1999

There were three bodies inside the trailer, those of two men and a woman. One had been identified as Billy Dave Petrie, the other two were man and wife, and they'd all been dead for several days.

After Luna answered the questions of the Washington County sheriff's department personnel, we headed home, Luna dropping us off at our house where we gathered the kittens and their paraphernalia, packed a suitcase for ourselves, and dropped the kittens off at the nearest boarding facility. Then Luna took us to a motel on the outskirts of town.

'I'm getting sick and tired of unsolved cases,' she said, once we were safely inside our 'no-tell-motel' room. 'We're at a standstill. Larry took us to Clyde who took us to Billy Dave, who, frankly, ain't taking us nowhere no how. And this isn't even my only whodunnit.'

'You're working on another case?' I asked, stretching out on the bed.

'Yeah. Remember that school counselor, Mrs Olson, who died in the car wreck last week?'

'Yeah, I read about it in the paper,' I said,

almost too tired to make my mouth move with the words.

'Turns out it wasn't an accident. Somebody cut her brake line.' She shook herself and stood up from the bed. 'I gotta get out of here before I take your lead, Pugh, and fall asleep.'

'I'm not asleep,' I said, at least I thought I did.

I heard the TV go on. 'Pugh, wake up. You have a husband right here,' Luna said, 'and they got that special TV here! Bye, y'all.' And she was out the door.

Willis pulled me down on the bed. 'You sleepy?'

We cuddled while we watched the picture on the TV. It was entirely too bizarre even to try to describe. Willis turned his head sideways, staring at the screen. Then the other way. Finally, he nibbled my ear. 'You wanna try that?'

I pulled at his T-shirt. 'Is our Blue Cross paid up?'

We were half undressed and pursuing a rather unusual line of foreplay when I sat bolt upright in the bed, knocking Willis to the floor.

'What the hell?' he said, rubbing his head.

'Mrs Olson!' I said loudly. Willis turned off the TV. 'She was Monique's sponsor in the PAL program!'

'The what?' he asked, crawling back up on the bed where he began nibbling on parts of me.

I pushed him away. 'Peer Assistance and Leadership! At the high school! The juniors and seniors counseled the freshmen and sopho-mores!'

'OK,' Willis said. 'Now the big question: So?'

'So ... I don't know! But there's got to be a connection. We thought all this time somebody was after Roy! But don't you see? It didn't have to be Roy. It could have been Terry, or Aldon ... or Monique! Monique is murdered and then her counselor is murdered! That's a coincidence?'

Willis shrugged as he leaned towards my neck, his tongue searching out that particular spot. 'Could be...'

I jumped off the bed and pulled the sheet up to cover my body. It's not what it used to be, but Willis still seems to have a one-track mind when it's bared to him.

Willis moaned. 'Jeez, Eeg! Enough! We're in a motel room. The kids are fifty miles away – safe. We've got a dirty movie on the TV. Relax, damn it!'

I picked up the phone and dialed Luna's home number, giving her the information I'd given Willis.

'Hum,' she said.

'Hum? *Hum?* That's all you've got to say?'

'What? OK, it's a coincidence!'

'It can't be!' I yelled. I took a deep breath and plunged ahead. 'All I'm saying is we may have been looking in the wrong place. It doesn't have to have been Roy who was the target. It could have been Monique.'

'Monique and Mrs Olson were running drugs through the school? Jesus, E.J.'

'No! Luna, listen to me! Something they had in common – something to do with the PAL program.'

Luna sighed. 'Fourteen-year-old kids griping

233

because their mothers make them take out the garbage? I've got one of those. Believe me, it's not worth killing over.'

'Check the school!' I insisted.

'I've checked the school! Fifty times! Everybody loved Mrs Olson. Nobody wanted to off her.'

'But you said somebody did!' I insisted.

There was a long silence on the line. 'E.J., go screw your husband,' she said, and hung up on me.

With nothing better to do, I took her advice.

GRAHAM, THE PRESENT

Didn't do things exactly as my mother had ordered me to. We drove Lotta home first. I did go inside, but Manny said Lotta's parents were both asleep, so I left without having my big discussion with them. Her mother would have just started crying and her father would have taken out his gun and shot me, and I thought there'd been enough of that already. I kissed her goodbye then went back outside to the Valiant where my buds awaited.

And then we headed in search of the stalker. Lotta said he'd gone over the bridge into Black Cat after he'd tried to dump her in the river, but I knew there was no place for him to hide in Black Cat. All there is here are people's homes, and lots of them. But there was a lot of country around Black Cat and he could be hidden out in a cabin, like when he first took Liz back in April, or just laying low in the trees like a homeless person. I still wasn't exactly sure what he looked like, but I knew what he didn't look like – a homeless person. I was going to find him, and then, well, it wasn't going to be pretty.

ELIZABETH, APRIL, 2009

'Let me out!' Elizabeth yelled for what felt like the millionth time. She was on the floor of the back seat of Grandma's old Valiant, her hands and feet bound with duct tape. He hadn't taped her mouth, and she was glad for that. She never saw his face. He'd shoved Megan down and grabbed Elizabeth's head, burying it in the seat, and holding it there as he got in the driver's seat and spun out of the Pizza Garden parking lot. They were several miles down the road before he stopped the car and bound her hands and feet with the duct tape and threw her in the back of the car, the entire time keeping her face turned away from him. He also hadn't said a word.

He was driving moderately, probably the speed limit, Elizabeth thought, not wanting to draw the attention of the police. If she'd been in the trunk, she thought, she could kick out one of the tail lights like she saw on 'Oprah' that time, and get the police to stop them. But lying on the floor of the back seat, she had no options.

Finally she decided to try some finesse. 'Aldon?' He didn't answer. 'Why are you doing this?' Still no answer. 'I want to see you. I want to talk to you about what's happening. I don't understand why you've thrown me back here! I'm your sister!'

It was as if the car was driving itself. There was no sound, no movement from the front seat. Elizabeth tried again. 'Is it because I brought Megan with me? I'm sorry about that, but I don't drive. She had to drive me here. Is that what you're mad about?' Still only silence met her words. 'She doesn't know, if that's what you're worried about. She thinks I was meeting a boy. I mean, you know, like a boyfriend. I didn't say a word about you, Aldon! You told me not to. And I've always done what you told me to do, haven't I, big brother?'

Softly, from the front seat, he said, 'You were a good baby sister.'

Elizabeth felt her skin crawl. Was it better having him answer her? At this point she wasn't sure. 'And you were a good big brother,' she said.

'I tried,' he said. 'I saved you that night.'

Mama E.J. had told her that her real mother, Terry, had fallen on her when she was shot, keeping her safe with her dead body. She said Aldon had been found on the stairs, trying to run away. 'Yes, I know,' Elizabeth said. 'I always knew it was you who saved me.'

'I've changed, Bessie,' he said. 'Physically and emotionally. I'm not the same Aldon you knew.'

'How could you be?' Elizabeth said. 'After what you've been through.'

'I've had work done to hide my appearance,' he said. 'That picture I sent you on email was taken right before I had everything done.'

'Oh,' she said. And she knew in that moment,

although she'd thought she'd known all along, at this point she really knew: This was not Aldon. Aldon had been dead for the past ten years, just as she'd always been told. Tears sprang to her eyes as the half-hope left her. She really hadn't known which to hope for – that her brother Aldon was alive and that her adoptive mother and father were evil, or that her world was just as she'd always thought it was, and still without Aldon.

Something in her tone must have alerted the driver. He said, 'You don't believe me.'

Trying to control her thoughts and tears, Elizabeth said, 'Of course I do, Aldon.'

There was a laugh from the front seat. 'No you don't. But that's OK. I don't really care. You ever see *Aliens*?' he asked. 'The second one. Where that Marine gets scared and he yells, "Game over, man, game over." You ever see that?'

'Yes, I saw that,' Elizabeth said, remembering parts of that movie that had scared her so badly she had nightmares.

'Well, Bessie,' he said, pulling Grandma's Valiant to a stop. 'Game over.'

ELIZABETH, THE PRESENT

Mom called earlier in the evening and said she'd pick us up in the morning to take us to Codderville Memorial Hospital, where Alicia was. I was too ... everything, I guess, to go to sleep. I just paced the room that Megan and I shared at Grandma's and worried. Everything was my fault. Everything. Even the guy stalking me in the first place was my fault. I don't know what I did to him, but I did something that started this whole thing. And now look what had happened. Alicia had been shot, Megan had been shot, Lotta had been kidnapped, Mom had almost been arrested, and Myra Morris – oh, yeah, don't forget Myra Morris! – was dead. D-E-A-D dead. Like, she wasn't coming back. Like her whole life was ahead of her and now it was no more. Gone. *Fini!*

I'm not being melodramatic. I'm just telling it like it is: It was all my fault. Maybe my birth parents dying was my fault, too! Who knew? I know I was only four, but four-year-olds are people, too, ya know? I had to *do* something! *Fix* something! But the only thing I could think to do at this moment was go to the hospital and see Alicia. My mother had been up there, said Alicia had been given a pain pill and was resting. But that didn't mean I couldn't just go up there and sit beside her. Yes, I know. There were rules, like visiting hours, and crap like that, but under the current circumstances who could possible argue my point? And if someone tried to, well, then, I'd just sneak in there and hide.

I got dressed while Megan slept, ready to quietly sneak out of the house.

E.J., THE PRESENT

Luna and I sat in my living room with a bottle of wine. I needed it. I was glad we didn't have scotch in the house, or bourbon, or heroin. Just kidding. It had been a rough evening. I left the girls at Vera's where I knew they'd be safe. Vera had so many dogs that there wasn't much of a chance anybody could sneak in.

'I've been thinking,' I said to Luna.

'Always a bad sign,' she said, helping herself liberally to my $9.95 bottle of white.

'No. Really. We've been assuming all along that this stalker is some stranger who fixated on Bessie for some unknown reason. What if he's not? What if it's someone she knows? Or someone we – the family – know?'

'Happens,' Luna said.

'Of course it happens!' I snapped. I mean, really. 'But who? Have you thought about that?' I said, accusingly this time.

'Yes, as a matter of fact I have. I talked to Elizabeth about any boys who've been bothering her at school, or boys who just look at her funny—'

'This isn't a boy at school. He's too old,' I interjected.

'We didn't know this in April when I talked to her about it!' All right, now she was getting testy.

I apologized in an unconvincing manner and she went on. 'You don't have any youngish men in your circle of friends that I'm aware of...'

She looked at me. 'No, we don't,' I answered.

'How about at church? I asked Elizabeth that but she couldn't think of anybody,' Luna said.

'At church? The youth group director is a guy, but he's like six-four, so he's not the one. There are a few eighteen-year-olds in the youth group, but they're girls.' Then I thought about someone. It made me feel horrible to think of him, but I did. 'Ah, there might be someone,' I said.

'Who?'

My shoulders slumped and I felt like crying. I didn't want to accuse him, to sic the cops on this young man, but... 'There is a young man at church. He's mildly retarded. He used to come with his elderly mother every Sunday, but she passed away recently.'

'When?' Luna demanded.

'Let me think. March? Yes, I believe her service was right after St Patrick's Day because there were still some green decorations in the Sunday school wing when I went to her service.'

'The stressor!' Luna declared.

'The huh?' I asked.

'The stressor. His mom dies in March, Bessie is kidnapped in April. Where is he living now?'

'I think he's still in his mom's house. He's only mildly retarded, but very shy—'

'Has he been around the girls? How tall is he? Does he have the smarts to do the computer crap?'

'Whoa,' I said. 'Give me a minute. Oh, God! Yes, he knows computers! That's how he earns his living! I remember Mrs Marsh told me when he got this job – working from home with his computer! She was thrilled.'

'That's his mother?' Luna asked. I nodded. 'What's his name?'

'Thomas Marsh. They live in Sherwood Forest,' I said, naming the most expensive village in Black Cat Ridge. 'I mean, he lives there.'

'Has he been around the girls?' she asked.
'Only when I would speak to his mother after church. Oh, and now I speak to him and the girls are usually with me.'
'How tall is he?' Luna asked.
'Shorter than me by a few inches.' I felt slightly sick as I said it. 'Just about the right height.'
'We'll ask Elizabeth in the morning. She said she recognized the stalker when he came in shooting, so she'll know if it was this Thomas character or not.'
'You're right. She did recognize him. Which means it can't be Thomas because she knows him.'
'We'll ask,' Luna repeated.

BLACK CAT RIDGE, TEXAS, 1999

The next morning we went to LaGrange to pick up the kids. I was eating some of Aunt Louise's wonderful baked goods and she was in the middle of a story about a friend of hers whose son was murdered by a guy wielding a hacksaw. It took a while but the guy obviously got the job done. I was half-listening, the other part of my mind was thinking about how much Monique would have loved the story. Pretty, tiny Monique with her penchant for Freddy Krueger movies and heavy metal music. Monique, at sixteen a senior, was such a dichotomy of the teenager: silly and serious, childlike and grown-up. Would Megan and Bessie be like that when they were sixteen? Would they apply their mascara remembering exactly how Barbie dressed for the 'big

241

date'? Would they switch from MTV to the Disney Channel with such abandon? Would they hide their secrets with grown-up next-door-neighbors?

I sat up straight on the horsehair sofa. My God, I thought. Oh my God!

'What is it?' Willis asked.

'We have to go home.'

'Honey, we can't go home—'

I stood up. 'Willis! We have to go home now!'

I ran for the front door, turning to Aunt Louise. 'You'll keep the kids?'

She was standing, her short, pudgy body all aquiver from the excitement she knew was there but didn't understand. 'Of course!'

In my mind, as I ran for the car, I could hear Aunt Louise say, 'Run! Run like the wind!'

I did.

FOURTEEN

I have to think, think, think! This is wrong! All of it! Wrong, wrong, wrong!! Why can't she see I'm doing the right thing here? If she keeps resisting me like this, I may have to just let her go. But she needs to be with her real family, her birth family, and I can definitely make that happen!

242

It was dark out. No moon. The only light came from the headlights of my Valiant as it roared through the night and the dark woods, heading in search of the stalker. He had been heading toward Black Cat when he'd tried to throw Lotta in the river, so that's where I was going. My theory was that he wouldn't – couldn't stay in Black Cat, but would be somewhere close. Black Cat was a lopsided circle in the middle of the woods north of Codderville. We'd follow that circle, check out roads leading off the main road, check for cabins. Do whatever we could do until we found him.

'I don't get it,' Leon said.

'Don't get what?' I asked, not caring what he did or did not get.

'We're just gonna drive around? What are the chances we're going to find this guy doing that?' Leon asked.

'About a thousand to one!' Tad said from the back seat.

'More like a million to one,' Hollister said.

I slammed on the brakes. There was no one behind us – no one in front of us – hell, no one anywhere. 'Y'all don't wanna do this, fine. Get out. I'll go on my own.'

'Hey, man, don't be like that,' Leon said.

'Shit, Graham, this is a dumb idea!' Hollister said. 'I wanna catch this asshole just about as much as you do. Hell, you don't mess with our Black Cat women, know what I mean? But, shit, man, this is *not* the way to do it!'

'Then what the hell do you propose we do?' I asked, whirling around in my seat to stare at the two in back.

Hollister and Tad looked at each other, then looked at Leon, who was turned to the back seat, too.

Leon said, 'Let's figure out where we've seen him. Where he's been spotted. Figure out the distances one from the other. Calculate—'

Hollister threw his head back on the cushioned backseat. 'Ah, shit, man. He's gonna make us do homework!'

'No, no, no!' Leon said. 'This could work! Graham, let's go back to your house, order a pizza, get on the computer and figure it out.'

'Pizza!' Hollister said. 'Now there's an idea!'

GRAHAM, APRIL, 2009

They were in the country now, having left Codderville behind. Still no sign of the Valiant. Giant oaks and pine lined the sides of the two-lane blacktop, no shoulder for emergencies. The asphalt was still wet from the earlier storm, slick and dangerous, with potholes hidden by pools of black water. The Chevy rolled along at a fairly fast clip, all eyes out the windows, searching for Grandma Vera's car. As they made a sharp turn they saw tail lights up ahead.

'Is that it?' Megan asked, leaning into the front seat.

Manny patted her shoulder. 'Let's get closer, Eddie,' he said. To Megan, he added, 'We'll find out.'

Eddie hit the accelerator, and Megan could feel the 'G's pulling at her face. Eddie shined his brights and they could see the car ahead. An antique Valiant. There could be only one in the Codderville area.

The car in front put on their brake lights, slowing. 'I think he wants you to go around,' Graham said from the back seat. Thinking fast, he said, 'Do it. Pass him. Everybody down,' he said, pushing Megan's head toward the floor.

They could feel the Chevy accelerate once again, could feel the wheel turn slightly as they moved into the oncoming lane, then back.

'Stay low,' Graham ordered, 'but you guys try to keep an eye out.'

'You got it, *el jeffe*,' Uncle Ernesto said.

'Slow down,' Graham told the driver, 'we need to keep 'em in sight.'

'Got it,' Eddie said, taking his foot off the accelerator and slowly letting the speed lessen.

They were approximately four car lengths ahead of the Valiant when there came another tight corner. Eddie applied the brake, slowing the Chevy down even more to make the turn. A straightaway was ahead and he coasted into it, keeping his eye on the rearview mirror.

All eyes were staring out the back window of the Chevy. Nothing happened. Eddie let the car slow more. Finally Graham said, 'Stop. We lost 'em.'

'No, man, they turned off!' Manny said. 'Eddie, back up! We gotta see where they turned off, man!'

Eddie put the car in reverse.

245

'Jesus, Mary, and Joseph!' Lotta said from Graham's lap. 'Don't back up, you idiot! Turn around! What if somebody else decides to use this public road? Gawd!' she said, leaning back against Graham. Turning to him, she said, 'You see where I come from? You see the adversity I've had to overcome? A family of complete idiots!'

'You're a strong woman,' Graham said, his hand on her tiny nipped-in waist.

'Graham!' Megan said, turning his attention back to the problem at hand.

Driving down the correct lane in the correct direction, Eddie eased the Chevy around the bend. There they saw an almost invisible dirt road, leading off to the left.

'Cut the lights!' Lotta ordered.

'I'm gonna hit something!' Eddie protested.

'So we hit something! Get over it!' Lotta ordered.

'But my Chevy...' Eddie wailed.

'Just do it, man,' Manny said. 'Or you know she's gonna hurt you.'

Eddie turned off the Chevy's headlights and turned on to the dirt road. All could feel the Chevy slipping and sliding in the mud caused by the heavy rain.

'We're gonna get stuck!' Eddie protested.

'Try to drive like you know what you're doing!' Lotta ordered.

'There it is!' Megan yelled, pointing at the tail end of the Valiant peeking out of some bushes to the right of the road. In front of where the Valiant had pulled off was a mud puddle the size of Dallas.

Eddie put on the brakes. 'I ain't driving through that!' he said, arms across his chest. Eddie had taken a stand.

'Everybody out,' Graham said, 'and be quiet!'

ELIZABETH, THE PRESENT

I had decided not to walk to the hospital. It was too far and it was too dark outside and, frankly, I was too scared. I'm woman enough to admit that. I was going to take Grandma's new car instead. I know what you're thinking: that that was an irresponsible thing to do, that I was showing my immaturity, that I wasn't thinking straight. Well, all of those things might be true, but I needed to see Alicia, make sure she was OK, and tell her how sorry I was. None of that could wait until morning.

My grandma has four dogs – two shelties, a German Shepherd, and a pound puppy named Ingrid. Ingrid weighs about two hundred pounds and likes to sit on people. Ingrid, thank God, was kept outside at night because she liked to jump on Grandma in the middle of the night – all two hundred pounds of her. Since Grandma might weigh as much as me, around one hundred pounds, the chances of Ingrid killing Grandma in the middle of the night are pretty good. So she stays outside. At least I didn't have to worry about being sat upon as I tried to sneak out. Dobie and Dufus, the shelties, are always happy to see anyone at any time, and they tend to bark, squeal and jump around banging into things

247

when they see someone. Mary Margaret, the German Shepherd, growls. And it's very scary. So I had to find a way to get out of the house that meant not getting out of the bedroom wing by either the door into the rest of the house or the window in the room I shared with Megan that went into the backyard, where Ingrid, the two-hundred-pound pound puppy, resided.

I knew a way. I snuck out of the bedroom through the door to the hall, being as quiet as possible, and snuck into Grandma's sewing room. That room had two windows – one into the backyard, the other just a few inches on the freedom side of the fence. I crawled over boxes and bags of scraps and beads and bangles and made it to the window, which, it turns out, was painted shut.

I sighed. But I wasn't through trying. I had a mission and planned on completing it. I had Grandma's room, which had a freedom window on the other side of the house, or the bathroom, which had a high, small window that actually balanced the fence on that side. I figured the worst that could happen was that Ingrid would lean on my leg, which wouldn't be pleasant, but was something I could handle.

So I headed to the bathroom. I used the facilities, then closed the lid to the toilet and climbed on top of it to reach the window. It was not painted shut. It was smaller than I remembered but still doable. I moved the shampoos, conditioners, moisturizers, lotions, and so on off the windowsill, opened the window and managed to get my head through. I maneuvered my shoulders through and was balanced on my stomach shoving mightily when I realized my hips were stuck. Jeez, I thought, when did I get hips? I was delighted and stymied at the same time. Then fear and frustration took over.

I tried going in, I tried going out, nothing worked. After a particularly painful forward thrust, I opened my eyes to see Ingrid staring up at me. Her tongue was lolling and she was smiling at me. 'Go away!' I whispered.

I tried twisting. It didn't work. I tried bouncing. It didn't work. I thought longingly of the lotions I'd moved to get to the window. None were in reach. I could have lotioned up my womanly hips and slid right out. I was very close to tears – of frustration – when the light came on in the bathroom. I froze. Of course, there wasn't much else I could do.

'Well, you're certainly in a pickle,' Grandma Vera said.

'Hi, Grandma,' I said from outside.

'You wanna come in, honey, 'cause you're not going out.'

'Yes, ma'am, I'd like to come in, but I'm stuck.'

'Hum,' she said. 'It does serve you right, don't you think?'

'Yes, ma'am,' I said.

'Well, just hold on while I do my business, then we'll see about getting you out,' she said.

'Yes, ma'am,' I said, and balanced myself on the sill.

She did her business and then said, 'I'm gonna go get Megan.'

'Oh no, Grandma, please don't!' I pleaded.

'Why not?'

'Because she'll give me hell about this for the rest of my life!'

Grandma laughed. 'Why do you think I'm going to get her?'

And that's when I saw him: a man walking down the street carrying an assault rifle. Headed for Grandma's house.

I started kicking my feet wildly and whispering, 'Grandma! Wait!'

'What?'

'He's here! He's coming to the house!'

All of a sudden I could feel Grandma's hands trying to push me aside so she could see out the window. Not only was there not enough room for her to do that, she wasn't tall enough to look out the window without standing on something.

'You sure it's him?' she asked.

'Yes!'

'Sic Ingrid on him! You can reach the gate, right?'

Since I was practically straddling the fence – well, the top part of me anyway – if I stretched myself way out I could reach the gate. I did so and unlatched it. Ingrid had already seen her quarry and shot like a bullet from the gate to the sidewalk where the man was lurking. As I was stretched out trying to see what was going on, I fell to the ground on my face.

BLACK CAT RIDGE, TEXAS, 1999

We broke all the speeding laws and several other

moving violations, making the fifty miles from LaGrange to Codderville in less than forty-five minutes.

'We can't go back to the house!' Willis said as he drove in that direction.

'We have to!' I said.

'Why?' he demanded.

'Because I think there's something there that could explain what's going on.'

'Then let's stop right now and call Luna and have her meet us there.'

'No! What if I'm wrong? I couldn't stand that again with Luna. She gets so uppity!'

'Well, I couldn't stand it if one of us got killed!' He sighed. 'What do you think's there?'

I sighed right back. 'You know when I told you last year that Monique was getting letters at our house from that boyfriend of hers who joined the Marines?'

'Yeah, and I told you that was a total betrayal of your friendship with Terry and you said you'd tell Monique not to do it!' he said.

'Well, I didn't have to. They broke up and the letters stopped.'

'OK...' He motioned with his hand for me to go on – and be quick about it.

'A few days before ... before it happened, Monique brought me a manila envelope.'

'What?' Willis said, looking at me and not the road he was taking at close to ninety miles an hour.

I pointed at the road and he turned his eyes back to driving. 'She asked me not to look in it but to hide it.'

'Jesus, E.J.! It could be drugs, or some other contraband for all you know!' Eyes darting back to me. I pointed ahead again.

'I thought it was boy stuff! It could still be! I thought it was just Monique stuff. You know how dramatic she gets— got,' I said, tears springing to my eyes. I wiped them with the back of my hand. 'And that's probably what it is, I don't know. But Willis, that school counselor...'

'Mrs Olson,' he said.

'Hurry,' I said.

E.J., THE PRESENT

'Can you think of anybody else?' Luna asked me as she slouched down in the couch with her second glass of wine.

'Most of the guys the age of the stalker are young marrieds. I mean, we don't have a lot of single guys in their twenties hanging around the church.'

'What about people who work there?' she asked.

'OK, we've got two clergy, the music director, the youth director, the children's director, the church secretary—'

'Could that be our guy dressed up again?' Luna asked.

I shook my head. 'No. I've known Candy since we started going there. She's my age. Her kids go to youth group with my kids.'

'Anybody else?' she asked.

'Just maintenance. A cleaning lady and a

maintenance man.'

'What about the maintenance man?'

I shook my head. 'He's new, but he's Hispanic and about sixty. Don't think he's our guy.'

'What about anybody involved in any of the cases you've helped me with?'

'Helped you with? You mean *solved* for you?' I said.

'Actually, no I don't. I mean *helped*. Don't get full of yourself, Pugh. Any ideas?'

I shrugged my shoulders. 'Not that I can think of.'

'This is getting us nowhere,' Luna said as she put her empty glass down on the coffee table and picked up the bottle of white. She left the glass where it was and upended the bottle, taking three big gulps before it was empty. 'Got any more? I prefer red,' she said.

GRAHAM, THE PRESENT

When we got home, Mom was in the living room with Mrs Luna from next door, a couple of empty bottles of wine in front of them.

'Where have you been?' Mom asked.

'Out,' I said as we headed for the stairs.

'Out where?' she said, her head lolling to one side.

'Just riding around,' I answered, almost to the top.

'With who?' she asked, then seeing my buds trailing me said, 'Oh. Never mind.' Then she giggled, I shook my head, and we were in my room.

253

Once in my room, Leon said, 'I thought your mother was a writer! It should be "with whom" not "who".'

'Are you sure about that?' I said skeptically.

Leon frowned. 'Well, I'll admit that's a hard one.'

I gave him the eye, just grateful I could come to my mother's defense about *something*, after having walked in with my buds to her drunken debauchery with another woman.

'Where's the computer?' Leon said, changing the subject lest I pull out an English book and prove him wrong – like I could.

I showed him the computer and he sat down and demanded paper and pen. 'Hell, you've got my computer.'

'Shut up and give me dates, times, and places!' Leon said.

And so we began.

ELIZABETH, THE PRESENT

I was scrambling to get back into the bathroom, the stalker was screaming on the sidewalk, and Grandma was not responding to my pleas of help.

I shouted for her one more time then saw my sister's head. 'What the crap are you doing?' she demanded.

'Help me get back in! Ingrid's sitting on the stalker! Call the police!'

'You want me to pull you in first or call the police first?' Megan demanded, reaching down to grab my arms. 'And what the you-know-what are you doing outside anyway?'

Then Grandma was in the room. 'I called the cops,' she said. 'They're on the way. You need help, Megan?' she asked.

'No, thanks, Grandma. I think I can handle this,' she said as she pulled my top half into the bathroom. With one jerk I was on the cold linoleum of Grandma's bathroom floor, the breath knocked out of me.

'Is Ingrid still sitting on him?' Grandma asked, she and Megan both ignoring my struggle to breathe.

I could feel Megan walking over me, not being at all gentle about it. 'Yeah, she's still got him. And seems to be enjoying it.'

'She always does,' Grandma said.

I felt Megan's foot on my head as she and Grandma left the bathroom. I gingerly got to my knees, wondering what was broken, and finally managed to get up and look out the window myself. It was a pleasant sight. The man was wiggling and kicking his legs, his arms flailing, as he screamed for help. Unfortunately, lights in the neighborhood were coming on and I was afraid someone would come out and help him. I ran into the living room to Grandma's coat closet to get the baseball bat. Grandma and Megan were on the front porch, watching him.

'Where are you going, young lady?' Grandma asked as I ran past her with the baseball bat.

'To make sure nobody lets him up!' I shouted.

'Good thinking!' Grandma said and I could hear her and Megan running behind me.

I got to him just as the first squad car pulled up.

'Mr Chang?' Grandma said.

I looked at the man lying on the ground under Ingrid. He was definitely Asian. 'Well, shit,' I thought. I couldn't figure out a way the stalker could fake what appeared to be a middle-aged, five-foot-two-inch Asian man.

'Ingrid! Off!' Grandma said, pulling at the two-hundred-pound dog's collar. Megan and I helped by pushing from Ingrid's bottom. She got the idea and began to move as Grandma led her by her collar to the back gate.

The police officer helped Mr Chang to his feet. Mr Chang turned to Megan and me, as I suppose Grandma's emissaries at this particular time. 'What in the cornbread hell was that all about? Cain't y'all keep that beast locked up?'

'Mr Chang!' Grandma said as she scurried back to the ... well ... scene of the crime. 'I'm terribly sorry about what happened, but I'll insist that you do not speak to my granddaughters in such a manner!'

Yeah, Grandma to the rescue!

'You mind telling me what's going on?' the police officer asked. 'You Mrs Pugh?'

'Yes, Officer, I am and I'm the one who called y'all. Unfortunately it was a misunderstanding.'

'You called the cops on *me*?' Mr Chang yelled. 'Why'd you do such a thing? A man can't walk down his own street—'

'In the middle of the night!' Grandma yelled.

'Yes, ma'am, in the middle of the night!' Mr Chang yelled back. ''Sides, its only half-past

256

midnight! How's that the middle of the night, I ask you?'

'OK, OK, you two. Ma'am, that your house?' the cop said, pointing at Grandma's house.

'Yes, Officer, it is.'

'Why don't we all go in there to discuss this and let the neighborhood get back to sleep?' the cop suggested.

That's when I looked around and saw a sea of people in PJs and robes watching us. There was a slew of ten to twelve-year-old boys hanging to the side where my sister stood in her shorty PJs and no bra. Men, I swear!

So we all trooped inside, two police officers, Mr Chang and his bag that really *did* look like that assault rifle the stalker had when he shot at us, and Grandma, Megan and me.

'Please let me explain,' I said, when everyone was sitting in the living room and a pot of coffee was brewing in the kitchen.

And I did, leaving out the part where I was actually trying to escape the house when I saw him.

'Coffee's ready,' Grandma said when I'd finished, and led everyone into the kitchen where we sat at her large kitchen table with coffee and fixin's (as Grandma says) and some microwaved frozen coffee cake. Megan and I had coffee – well, half coffee, half milk, like we'd been getting at Grandma's house since we were six (don't tell Mom).

'May I ask, Mr Chang,' I said, 'what's in the bag?'

He put down his coffee cup and picked up the

bag, unzipping it. Out came a beautiful mahogany-like stick, the pointy end carved with Asian figures, the tip a gold cap.

'It's beautiful!' I said.

'Man o' man,' said one of the officers. 'Can I hold it?'

'Sure, just be careful,' Mr Chang said.

The officer put the thing in position, at which point I realized it was a pool cue. The prettiest one I'd ever seen.

'Where'd you get this?' the officer asked.

'It was my grandfather's. His father had it special made for him when he left China. He paid for his passage with his pool winnings, got to San Francisco, ended up marrying and buying a house from his winnings there. Then somebody figured out he was a shark, and luckily he had enough stashed to get Grandma and my dad and his siblings out of San Francisco to Texas.'

'You a shark?' the cop asked with a grin.

Mr Chang grinned back. 'I play for money occasionally, but mostly I like to enter tournaments and show up the kids. They get so pissed!'

'Hell, man,' the other officer said. 'If I saw that cue coming at me, I'd figure shark and crap out.'

At that point, everyone thanked Grandma for the coffee and cake and got up to leave.

'No hard feelings, Mr Chang?' Grandma asked, holding out her hand.

'You make a darn fine cup of coffee, Mrs Pugh. Can't hold a grudge against a woman who can do that,' he said, taking her hand and bowing slightly over it.

Grandma walked her company to the door. 'Come back any time for a cup, Mr Chang,' she said.

'Thank you kindly, ma'am,' he said, tipped an imaginary hat and followed the cops out the door.

FIFTEEN

I'm itching all over, but there's nothing there. My skin is crawling. I can't stand it! If Bessie were here this wouldn't be happening! It's all her fault! Everything is her fault! If she won't come to me I'll destroy her! Yes. Destroy her. That's exactly what I'm going to do.

E.J., THE PRESENT

I woke up the next morning hungover. It had been a while since I'd drunk that much, and I felt sick as a dog. I crawled into the bathroom and splashed water on my face. It hurt. I went back in the bedroom and looked at the clock. Correction: I woke up the next *afternoon*. It was after twelve. I hadn't slept this late since before Graham was born! Speaking of Graham, I thought, panic setting in, where were my kids? Then I remembered: the girls were at Vera's, but Graham was here – hopefully.

I bolted out of my room on the first floor – in

my mind I bolted, in actuality I walked gingerly – to find Graham in the family room, playing games on TV, the volume blessedly turned low.

'Morning,' I said, my first utterance that day. I sounded like a frog.

'You and Mrs Luna have fun last night?' Graham asked, looking at me with what appeared to be pity in his green eyes.

'No!' I said defensively. 'We were trying to figure out who this stalker is that's after your sister! It is no time to be having fun.' I sat down gently on the couch. That long a speech made me queasy.

Graham stopped his game and turned to me. 'So, did y'all figure anything out?'

'Yes. It's not the new janitor at the church.'

Graham turned away from me with disgust. 'Jeez, Mom, great work! Mr Garcia's son Robbie's in my AP algebra class. Like the stalker has a robot son or something?' He shook his head, again in disgust, and turned on his game. And upped the volume.

'We think it's Thomas Marsh!' I shouted over the noise of the game. Then thought I might pass out from the effort.

Graham turned off the TV, looked at me and said, 'Jeez, Mom, get some coffee or something. You look like sh— Ah, you don't look so good.' He went in the kitchen and came back with a Coke. 'Try this. At least it's got caffeine. Who's Thomas Marsh?'

'What?' I said, gratefully swigging the Coke. Nothing ever tasted so good. All that fizz, and the caffeine, and the sugar. Oh, my God.

'Is that who you said? Tom Marsh?' Graham repeated.

'Um,' I said, having consumed at least half of the can of Coke. 'Thomas. But I don't think it's him.'

Graham let out a long-suffering sigh. 'You just said you and Mrs Luna thought it *was* him.'

'Well, until Bess – Elizabeth – rules him out.'

'Who is he?'

'You know, Mrs Marsh's son,' I said, holding the still chilly can of Coke to my forehead.

'Oh. *That* Thomas Marsh,' he said. 'I thought you meant Mrs Somebody Else's son!'

'Don't get sarcastic with me, young man,' I said.

'Hey, Mom, I'll talk to you later, 'K?'

'Where are you going?'

'Out.'

'Pick up the girls at Grandma's house and bring them home first, OK?'

'Mom!' It was that 'mom' that has three syllables.

'Please don't argue with me, Graham, or I may have to kill you,' I said, lying down on the couch.

'Great! Put me out of my misery!' he said, heading for the door.

'Thanks, honey,' I said to his retreating back.

'Whatever,' he said.

ELIZABETH, APRIL, 2009

It was so dark Elizabeth could barely see her hands in front of her face; that is, if she could

261

have *gotten* her hands in front of her face. But since they were duct-taped behind her back, that was pretty much an impossibility.

Tommy/Aldon had stopped the car and come to the back, pulling her up on the seat and un-taping her feet. 'We walk from here,' he said. 'We're almost home, Bessie.'

Now she followed him, or tried to. She could barely see him in the dark, could barely hear his footfalls for the sound of the cicadas coming from the woods, louder than she'd ever heard them.

'Wait, Aldon,' she said, forcing herself to use that name. 'I can barely see you!'

He stopped and she bumped into him. 'Please untie my hands!' Elizabeth pleaded. 'I can't get my balance with them tied behind me.'

She could see him now. Definitely not Aldon. No amount of plastic surgery could have changed the shape of his head, the texture of his hair. She may have only been four years old when her brother had been murdered, but she remembered him. She remembered all her family, everything about them. The touch of her mother's skin, the way her father's early-morning beard had tickled her cheek when he kissed her, the sound of Monique's laugh, the feel of Aldon's hand in hers. Aldon had been a tease, loving to play jokes on his sisters and his parents. Some had been in bad taste, as only a ten-year-old boy could conceive. Others had been just plain funny. Elizabeth had loved to follow him around, take his toys and hide them, elicit his ire, which usually led to running, to laughing, to tickling, to fun.

This brown-eyed blond was not Aldon. Aldon had looked like their father and would have grown to look even more like him. His build had been a miniature of their father's – short and stocky with slightly bowed legs. This guy was thin and reedy and, if anything, was knock-kneed. Not Aldon. Aldon's hand had felt safe and welcoming when she held it; when this guy grabbed her hand to lead her further into the woods, it felt anything but.

This was not Aldon. Tears sprang to her eyes. This was not Aldon.

GRAHAM, THE PRESENT

I'd never before seen my mother drunk or hungover and I have to say, I hope I never do again. It's not a pleasant sight. I really had no plan other than to get out of the house, so going to get the girls at least gave me a reason. And I thought maybe I should take them to the hospital to check on that chick, what's her name, the orphan, to see how she was doing after having been shot and all.

When I got to Grandma's house they were eating lunch.

'You hungry?' Grandma asked me.

Never one to turn down one of Grandma Vera's meals, I admitted I was. Since this was just *lunch*, Grandma had out a ham, potato salad, a green salad, deviled eggs, and a fruit salad for dessert. While we ate, they told me about the night before.

'And then it turns out,' Megan said with delight, 'that it's this Chinese guy – with a Southern accent, mind you – carrying a really fancy pool cue in a bag, not the stalker with an assault rifle!' Which made Megan laugh out loud.

'It wasn't that funny at the time!' Liz said, shooting daggers at Meg.

Grandma said, 'I thought it was a *little* funny when you fell out of the window, honey.'

I nudged Liz with my elbow. 'Come on, kid,' I said, 'that's kinda funny. Admit it, the whole thing's kinda funny.'

'Well, it wasn't when I thought it was him!' Liz insisted, frowning. Then she grinned. 'But one good thing came out of it,' she said. 'Grandma has a boyfriend.'

Megan jumped on that bandwagon, which got the attention off of Liz and on to Grandma Vera.

'Now don't you two start!' Grandma said, blushing. 'That man's young enough to be my ... nephew by a much older sister.'

Which got the girls to laughing.

That's when I suggested they help Grandma clean up – which she of course refused (I knew she would) and they grabbed their stuff and we headed for the hospital to see what's her face, the orphan.

BLACK CAT RIDGE, TEXAS, 1999

We drove to our house, not slowing down as we passed it, peering at it and the Lesters' house, then circled the block. Twice more and we figured we could pull into the driveway. Once in the house I went directly to the utility room. There on the shelf was the envelope. I reached up and pulled it down and opened it. Inside was the imitation leather diary with the faux gold lettering spelling out 'Journal'. I opened the front page. On it, in bright red Magic Marker, were the words 'PAL PROGRAM'. Willis leaned over my shoulder and we both read.

Twenty minutes later we parked at the police station and rushed inside to Luna's desk. I held out the journal. 'Read this,' I said. She took the book and read.

Ten minutes later, she looked up. 'Jesus,' she said.

Willis and I just stared at her. She turned to a uniform at the desk behind her. 'Get me an arrest warrant. Make it out in the name of Berry Rush.'

ELIZABETH, THE PRESENT

Graham drove us to the hospital to see Alicia. Her head was bandaged and her ear on the left was heavily taped up with gauze and tape.

'Hey,' she said as we all marched in. She smiled and said, 'My first visitors!'

'Your foster mom hasn't been here yet?' I asked, a little stunned.

Alicia shook her head. 'Oh no. I doubt she'll be able to get here. She has the younger kids, ya know.'

Behind me, Megan grabbed my hand and squeezed. I knew just how she felt. But what did one say?

'So how you feeling, kid?' Graham asked, pulling up a chair next to her bed and sitting down.

Alicia blushed when he spoke to her. Who knew? Alicia had a thing for my brother. Yuck.

'I'm OK,' she said, her voice barely audible.

'They treating you OK here?' he asked.

She nodded her head.

'Where were you shot?' he asked.

Alicia looked to me as if for help. 'She was shot in the head, dumb-butt. Can't you see?' Turning to Alicia, I asked, 'What did the doctors say? Mom said they took you to surgery.'

She nodded again. 'Yeah,' she said, facing me, away from my brother. 'It blew off part of my ear—'

'Gross!' Megan said, while I said, 'Oh, my God!' and Graham threw in 'Cool!'

'One of the bikers found the piece and brought it to the hospital so that's what the surgery was for last night – to sew my ear back on,' she explained, pointing to the heavily bandaged ear.

'Well, Mom'll come and find out all about it and get your instructions to take home and all that,' I said as soothingly as possible, patting Alicia's hand as I did so.

'But probably not today,' Graham said. When Megan and I looked at him, he said, 'Mom and Mrs Luna got skunked last night, and she's so hungover today she can barely move.'

'Who *haven't* you told?' said someone from the doorway. We turned. It was Mom.

'Sorry, Mom,' Graham said, getting up from the chair. 'Need to sit down a minute?'

She walked over and slapped him on the back of the head. 'Thank you, son,' she said, taking his seat. 'How are you, Alicia?'

'Just fine, Mrs Pugh,' Alicia said.

'Well, I doubt that, but OK.'

We spent another half hour with Alicia then headed out. Passing one of those rooms called a 'family room' where the doctors tell families bad news, Mom said, 'Let's go in here for a minute.'

I panicked, thinking there was something seriously wrong with Alicia. 'Oh my God, what is it?'

'No, sweetie,' Mom said, taking my hand, 'Alicia's OK. The doctor said the bullet grazed her skull and took off a hunk of her ear, which they found and have sewn back on. They don't think there should be a problem with that, and if it comes out looking bad, they can always do plastic surgery. Alicia's going to be fine.'

Then she changed the subject. 'Mrs Luna and I paid a visit to Alicia's foster mother last night, to tell her what happened.' Mom seemed uncomfortable, like she didn't know how to say what she wanted to say. I wasn't sure if it was the hangover Graham had mentioned or something else.

'The thing is,' she said, then stopped. Finally she sighed. 'I don't know how to say this other than to just say it. Luna is going to call CPS and turn the woman in. She's got way too many children there and they're certainly not being cared for...'

That's when Megan broke in. 'Mom! Alicia

only has that one outfit! She washes it every night! It's the only clothes she has!'

Mom shook her head. 'I guess that's not surprising, having met that woman, but still, I'm shocked.' Again, she took a deep breath. 'The thing is, God only knows where they'll put Alicia the next time. So, your Dad and I talked it over, and, if y'all agree, we'd like to submit the forms to become Alicia's foster family.'

We all just sat there, stunned. Then Graham groaned. 'Not another damned sister? Can't you find a boy, for God's sake?'

Megan and I both hit him. 'I can't wait to go buy her new clothes!' Megan said. 'And make-up! Nobody at school's gonna believe it when they see her!'

'And we've got to get her to the pool!' I said. 'Did you see how pale she was?'

'I take it this is OK?' Mom said.

'Sure!' Megan and I said together and Graham said, 'Whatever. What's one more girl?'

'Can Meg and I go tell her?' I asked.

'We haven't filled out the papers yet,' Mom warned.

'Yeah, OK,' I said. 'But she needs to know she's wanted, Mom. Know what I mean?'

Mom said, 'Yeah, honey, I know what you mean.'

E.J., THE PRESENT

Elizabeth, when asked, denied that her stalker was Thomas Marsh, which brought us back to zilch. Willis came home that evening and we spent the better part of it discussing what had been going on, including Graham (with what I'm sure Elizabeth felt was his big mouth) telling us the story of the girls' sleepover with Grandma Vera.

Willis, of course, missed the humor of the thing. 'Where in the hell did you think you were going, young lady?' he demanded of Elizabeth.

She turned red, hung her head, and said, 'I dunno. The hospital?'

'You couldn't wait until morning?' he demanded.

I watched as my daughter squared her shoulders and looked her father in the eye. 'It was my fault that Alicia got shot, Dad. I just wanted to be with her, to make sure she was OK.'

Willis just sat there for a moment, his whole body still, then he nodded. 'OK. But it was a dumb idea.'

'Yes, sir,' she said.

'Don't call me sir,' Willis said. He had a thing about that, and the kids knew it. They only used it when they wanted to irritate him. I lowered my head and smiled.

'But you should have seen Grandma and Mr Chang!' Megan said. 'I think there's something going on there!'

Something else Willis didn't find amusing. Usually a man with an acute sense of humor, Willis didn't find anything funny that involved his daughters or his mother. Some men are like that.

Later that night, as we lay in bed with our arms around each other, he asked, 'So, any ideas about who's after our child?'

'No,' I admitted. 'I've run out of ideas. And so has Luna. She's got a patrol car coming by here every half hour, which she says is excessive, but that's all she can do, and she can't do that for long.'

'What about our new daughter? The one in the hospital? What's her name?'

'Alicia,' I told him.

'Yeah. Her. Should she be under guard?' he asked.

I picked up the phone on the bedside table and dialed Luna next door.

'What?' she said upon answering. 'It's after midnight, Pugh!'

'Should we have a guard on Alicia?' I asked her. 'He did shoot her. Maybe he'll think she'd be good leverage to kidnap.'

'Shit,' Luna said. 'You're right. I'll set up a guard.'

'Thanks,' I said and hung up. Turning to my husband, I snapped my fingers. 'Done!' I said and giggled.

That appeared to be Willis's signal for fun and games.

SIXTEEN

There are cops everywhere. At Bessie's house, at the hospital where that stupid friend of hers is. I wanted to be a family – just the two of us – but she'd rather stay with them. They're not her family! I'm more her family than they are. I could be Aldon. I could! I could be anybody she wanted me to be! Doesn't she know how much I need her? Why doesn't she know? Why? She's going to die for that!!!

VERA PUGH, APRIL, 2009

Vera Pugh woke up, slightly disoriented. She had to go to the bathroom, that much was for sure. But where was she? Then she remembered: In Willis and E.J.'s bed. Which meant the bathroom was right here in the room. She found it, used it, then decided to go upstairs and check on the kids, wondering what time it was and whether Graham was home yet.

Leaving the bedroom she passed through the family room, noting the time on the digital clock of the cable box. Twelve-thirty. Graham should be home. She pulled herself up the stairs, wondering why anyone in their right mind would buy a two-storey house. First you had to climb

271

stairs, and then you had to vacuum them. Vera, who vacuumed every day, thought having stairs was an excessive waste of time and energy.

She got to the upstairs landing and turned left toward Graham's room. The door was shut, but Vera opened it to peek in. Her night vision was still very good, thank you very much, and she had no need for a nightlight. She could see quite well that Graham was not in his bed. Had she given him a curfew? She wondered. She didn't remember doing it. Which meant he thought he could come in whenever he wanted, forgetting what his parents usually told him. She smiled. Such a willful boy, that one. Just like both her boys had been.

Deciding to check on the girls to make sure they were covered properly, she went back down the hall, stopping first at Elizabeth's room. Opening the door, she discovered Elizabeth was not in her bed. Hoping her granddaughters had decided to sleep together this night, she hurried to Megan's room. Through the piles of clothes on the floor, Vera could see the bed, stacked high with something. Was it the girls, she wondered. Flipping on the overhead light, she discovered that it was just more clothes. Neither Megan nor Elizabeth was here.

Vera went back downstairs to the front door and opened it. Sure enough, her Valiant was not in the driveway. She went to the family room and grabbed the cordless phone. She didn't really care what time it was; an emergency was an emergency, period. She dialed Elena Luna's number.

It was Wednesday and Lotta had the night off. We went to an early movie and then headed to the boonies.

'I can't believe your parents are taking that girl in! I mean she's sweet and all, but she's not, you know, family,' Lotta said.

'Yeah, well, technically, neither was Liz—'

'What?' she said, her eyes wide.

'Liz is adopted. I thought you knew,' I said.

'Why would your parents do that? They had you. And Megan. Couldn't your mom have more babies?'

'No, that wasn't it,' I said, shaking my head. 'See, what happened was...' And I told her the whole story, or as much of it as I knew. I've never been sure my parents have told us the whole thing, but I've always figured we knew as much as we needed to know.

And then she was full of questions. All I wanted to do was start making out, but when Lotta had questions, you had to answer them.

'So Liz's whole family was murdered? Oh my God! That poor thing! She must be devastated!'

'Honey, that was a long time ago,' I said. 'She's been through counseling and had ten years of us—'

'You called me honey,' she said, a smile on her face.

'Ah...' I said. Shit! What did that mean? Did saying honey mean we had to get engaged or something? What had I done?

'I liked that you called me honey,' she said,

273

and kissed me. OK, so the Liz discussion was over. And maybe I was engaged. Whatever.

We were making out like crazy and I was headed to a base I'd never been to before when a loud noise and the tinkling of glass brought me up. As I sat up there was another loud noise and a hole appeared in the driver's side window.

'Shit!' I yelled, pushing Lotta back down on the seat. 'Stay down!'

She was saying something but the words were muffled by her face being slammed into the front seat by my hand. With the other hand I turned the key in the ignition, just as another explosion took out the back window. The car started and I hit the accelerator, my head bent down as far as I could and still see out the windshield a little.

Then I saw him. Standing right in my way. Aiming the assault rifle straight at the car. I floored it! I wanted to run over the son of a bitch! Cream him! Grind him into the ground!

He jumped out of the way. I started to turn around and go for him again, but he was up and aiming the rifle at us again. I headed toward Black Cat. Next time, I told myself. Next time your ass is grass and I'm the lawn mower!

E.J., THE PRESENT

For someone who never thought she wanted kids, I seem to collect them like some people collect stamps. I've found out over the years, though, that I kind of like them, at times. Sort of. We spent the next morning shopping, the girls and I. We went to Wal-Mart and got a package of bikini panties, cotton, extra-small, in patterns and bright colors. We bought two bras, one white, one black with multicolored polka-dots (Elizabeth's idea), a pair of bright orange flip-flops with tassels, a pair of blue jean shorts, and a vivid green, ruffled, cotton, short-sleeved shirt, and assorted scrunchies and other hair-fixers in a rainbow of colors. With that, Alicia would be able to leave the hospital.

Carrying our booty, we emerged in Alicia's room at the hospital just as the doctor came in.

'Mrs Pugh,' he said, extending his hand. We shook and he said, 'Alicia is doing great. Her ear is healing nicely and there appear to be no complications. The nurse will give you a sheet of paper that will have things to watch out for from this type of injury, and reasons to call.' He shook my hand again, patted Alicia's shoulder and was gone.

'All right!' I said cheerfully, wondering how in the hell I got myself into these things. 'Girls, you want to show her the loot?'

'What?' Alicia said, eyes big when she saw the Wal-Mart bag.

'I'll wait outside,' I said, letting the girls have fun playing dress-up.

In about five minutes, Megan stuck her head out the door. 'It's OK, Mom.'

I went in. It was an entirely different girl. The large bandage had been removed from her head, and all that was left was the one on her ear. Her hair was pulled back in a ponytail, showing a pretty face, and the shorts revealed very long, very nice legs. Wednesday was gone; in her

275

place was Alicia, the girl she should have been all along.

We grabbed everything – which included a balloon the girls had brought her and the clothes she was wearing when she got shot. As we started to drive home, Alicia yelled, 'Stop!' and I slammed on the brakes.

'What's wrong?' I said, turning in my seat.

'Ah, sorry,' she said, blushing. 'Could you back up to that dumpster please?'

I did as she asked, and she scooted past Elizabeth and out the door, her bag of belongings in her hand. With a wind-up worthy of a major-leaguer, Alicia tossed the bag into the dumpster. Without a word she climbed back in the car, while both my *other* girls slapped her on the back.

BLACK CAT RIDGE, TEXAS, 1999

We found Berry Rush in his church office. He looked up as we burst into the room. Luna slapped the warrant on his desktop.

'Reverend Rush, you have the right to remain silent, anything you say can be used against you. You have the right to an attorney. If you cannot afford an attorney, one will be appointed—'

'What in the world?' He looked at Willis and me. 'Willis, E.J., what's going on here?'

Luna finished reading him his rights. 'Do you understand these rights as I have outlined them to you?'

'Of course, Officer,' he said. 'I'm not an idiot! What in the world are you arresting me for, if I may be so bold?'

'For the murders of Roy Lester, Terry Lester, Monique Lester, and Aldon Lester.'

Reverend Rush, who'd been lifting himself from his chair, sank back down. 'My God,' he said.

'Do you wish to waive your right to an attorney?' Luna asked.

Reverend Rush shook his head, his hand reaching out for the phone. 'May I call the church attorney now?' he asked.

Luna nodded and he picked up the phone.

Willis and I drove back to our house, calling Aunt Louise to let her know all was well and to ask if she'd keep the kids another night.

'Of course, honey. They're such a joy.' She sighed. 'I just can't believe it. A man of God! Doing such a thing!'

'I know,' I said. 'It's unbelievable. But it's happened before.'

I hung up and sat down on the couch with my husband who was reading the copy of the journal Luna had given us. I read over his shoulder for what seemed like the thousandth time. There was a lot to take in.

ELIZABETH, THE PRESENT

Mom decided to let us work out the room situation. Personally I thought the most efficient and fair thing would be for Mom to give up her office upstairs, go back to the one on the first floor (the closet under the stairs), and let Alicia have that room as hers. Any way you look at it –

277

Alicia gets her own room and I move in with Meg, or Meg keeps her own room and Alicia moves in with me – somebody is going to feel left out. I mentioned my idea about Mom's office out loud.

'Liz, that's a great idea!' Megan said. 'We could fix up her room so cute!'

'Oh no!' Alicia said. 'I can't take your mother's office! That would be awful!'

Megan brushed aside Alicia's reservations. 'She had her office under the stairs for years! And she loved it! I bet she'd really *like* to go back down there! We make too much noise upstairs while she's trying to work, anyway, huh, Liz?'

'Elizabeth,' I said succinctly. 'I'm really tired of both you and Graham calling me Liz! My name is Elizabeth. And yes, we do make too much noise up here while she's trying to work. Good point, Megs.'

'Don't call me Megs,' Megan said.

Alicia giggled. 'Y'all can call *me* anything you want!'

So we headed downstairs to take on our mother. She was in the kitchen, sitting at the table, reading a magazine. When she could have been upstairs working. See what we mean?

'Mom, may we talk to you?' I asked.

She put down the magazine and smiled. 'Sure, girls. Have a seat.'

I pulled up an extra chair from the dining room, and we all sat down. 'Well,' Megan started, then looked at me.

'We were talking about the room situation...' I

started.

'And, well, the thing is...' Megan continued.

'What we thought might work best is if...'

'Alicia took your office!' Megan said loudly and in a rush.

Mom looked at all of us and then said, 'You know, I was thinking the same thing. I can't hear myself think in my present office when y'all are home, what with your music and you two screaming at each other from room to room. And I sort of miss my old closet – I mean office.' She grinned.

Both Megan and I turned on Alicia as one and said, 'I told you!'

Alicia stood up. 'Mrs Pugh, thank you but I can't do that.'

Mom looked up at Alicia as she stood above us all. 'First of all, please call me E.J. and never Mrs Pugh. And second of all, I've been thinking about moving my office back downstairs for a while now, honey. You are not putting me out.'

Alicia sat back down and hung her head. There's an expression I've heard that I think applied to Alicia at that moment – she looked like she was waiting for the other shoe to drop. That means – well, I guess you know what that means. Anyway, I don't think she was used to people being nice to her and it broke my heart to think of what she must have been through. And then to think that I could have been in the same boat if not for Mom and Dad – E.J. and Willis, I mean. It made me sort of sick to my stomach.

Mom reached over and patted Alicia's hand. 'It's OK, honey. You'll get used to us. I'm pretty sure we're the good guys, so please don't be afraid. If anything bothers you, let's talk about it, OK? At the moment it happens, or the next day, or ten months later, I don't care. Talking. It's what we Pughs do.'

'Oh, yeah,' Megan said. 'We can talk. Talk your head off and spit in the hole, as Grandma Vera says.'

GRAHAM, APRIL, 2009

'Be quiet!' Graham hissed.

Everyone stopped talking. 'Just listen to me, OK?'

All eyes turned to Graham. 'Eddie, you and Uncle Ernesto stay with the car, in case they double back.'

Eddie and Uncle Ernesto nodded.

'Lotta, you take these two,' he said, indicating cousins whose names he'd forgotten, 'and fan out,' he said, pointing to the right. 'Manny, you and Megan come with me. We're taking the path.'

'You'd do better taking me than Manny!' Lotta said, hands on hips.

'Somebody's gotta control these guys,' Graham pointed out in a whisper.

Lotta thought for a moment then nodded her head. 'You're right. Without a babysitter they'll end up driving back to down for tacos!'

'Listen for me,' he told them. 'I'll holler out if I need you.'

They all nodded and he, Megan and Manny hit the trail.

Tommy/Aldon led her to the door of a shack in the middle of the woods. A poor excuse for a driveway led up to it, but she couldn't imagine anything but a four-wheel drive making it. The shack was just a black outline to Elizabeth, but she could smell mildew and dust and old. Inside was pitch black until Tommy/Aldon lit a candle, then she could see a bit of her surroundings, but mostly she could see him. His hair wasn't really blond so much as light brown, or what they called dirty blond. More like beige, really. All of him. His skin, his hair, his eyes, even his clothes, various shades of beige. His eyes were like glass doll's eyes. No spark of spirit or soul. His lips were thin and his nose pointed. She noted all this, memorizing it, ready for the sketch artist she would describe him to. Because Elizabeth knew she would get away from this man, knew that she would live to tell her tale. And hopefully live to beat the living shit out of him!

'Sit down, Bessie,' he said, indicating a neatly made-up cot in the corner. She moved to it, gingerly sitting down. The bedding was new; it didn't smell like the rest of the room; it smelled like Downy, the smell of home. This brought tears to her eyes that she willed away. *Don't break down*, she told herself. *Don't give him the satisfaction!*

'What now, Aldon?' she asked.

He looked at her for a long moment, a look on his face that scared Elizabeth. It wasn't a mean look, a dangerous look; it was a blank look. A look that said he had not thought beyond this point. From now on, Elizabeth knew, he would be playing it by ear. Which meant her living through the next few hours could be totally up to her – up to what she said, how she reacted, how she played his game.

Memories were flooding her, of playing Candy Land with Aldon, with his made-up rules that always let him win; of throwing the gingerbread men from the Candy Land game at her brother, hearing him laugh, hearing Mom say, 'You make a mess, you clean it up!' Same thing Mama E.J. said.

Mama E.J.! God, how she wanted her now. If she'd been here, this wouldn't have happened, Elizabeth thought. Nobody could have gotten to her if Mama had been here. Tears threatened again, and she pushed away the thoughts.

Tommy/Aldon had turned, moving into the small kitchen area, such as it was: a camp stove on a counter by a sink, and an ice chest next to it.

'You hungry?' he asked.

Elizabeth said, 'Yes.' Keep him busy, she thought. She was totally untaped now, both her hands and feet. With his back to her, she looked around the small cabin, looking for something heavy she could use to bash his skull in – some kind of weapon, anything.

She saw the door opening before the creaking of its hinges sounded, making Tommy/Aldon swing around, a sharp knife in his hand. Graham stood in the doorway.

SEVENTEEN

*If she doesn't want me, truly doesn't want me,
then my life is over. But I'm not going alone. I'll
take her with me to Heaven – where we'll be
together for eternity. She'll be mine forever.*

GRAHAM, THE PRESENT

I stayed in bed until I heard Mom and the girls
take off. I knew Thursdays were Mrs Luna's day
off, so I grabbed some jeans and a T-shirt and
headed next door. I rang the bell and waited,
then rang it again. She came to the door in her
bathrobe, her hair all Medusa-like around her
head. Scary.

'What?' she said, her voice louder than necessary.

'Sorry, Mrs Luna. Did I wake you up?' I said.

'Yes. What do you want?'

'Ah, well, I guess I can talk to you about it
later,' I said, turning to go. 'It's just that me and
Lotta got shot at by the stalker last night.'

She grabbed my arm and swung me around.
'Get in the house,' she said.

I sat in her living room for about ten minutes,
then heard her coming down the stairs. She had
on jeans and a sweatshirt and her hair was

combed. I was thankful for all of it.

'Did he hit either of you?' she demanded, once she was in the living room.

'No, ma'am,' I said, standing up.

'Your car?'

'Oh, yeah!' I said. 'It's parked in the garage so Mom and the girls can't see it.'

'Why?' she asked.

'Well.' I shrugged. 'They're all, you know, pumped about fixing up that girl, Alice—'

'Alicia,' she corrected.

'Right. Alicia. They went shopping this morning for her. I gotta admit it'll be nice seeing her in something other than that dress thing and that sweater thing.'

'The stalker!'

'Yeah, right. You wanna see it? My car?'

'Yes!' The woman was getting tense and I didn't know why. Maybe that time of the month or something. You know how they get.

Anyway, we left her house and crossed over the twin driveways to our garage. It's hardly ever used for cars and I had a hell of a time getting the Valiant in there, but I managed. I'd brought the clicker with me, in my back pocket, and pulled it out and opened the garage door. The gaping hole that used to be my back window loomed at us.

'Shit,' Luna said.

'Tell me about it!' I confirmed.

She shot me a look. Why? I don't know. She started walking around the car, checking out the damage.

'You got more than liability on this thing?'

284

That thought had already occurred to me. 'No,' I said, shaking my head sadly.

'Check out the county victims' assistance program. They may be able to cut you a check. Not much, mind you, but every penny counts, right?'

'Yeah, it sure does,' I said, smiling at Mrs Luna. Who knew? 'Thanks.'

She nodded and headed back to her house. As I shut the garage door and headed back to my house, she said, 'I need coffee. Get your ass over here.'

'Yes, ma'am,' I said and scurried after her. I know, not manly, but under the circumstances I think I can be excused.

Once back in her living room, she demanded details of the night before. I told her everything I could remember and she said, 'What about your girlfriend? What's her name?'

'Carlotta Hernandez,' I said.

'I need to interview her, too. And I'm not going into the station today, no way, no how. Call her and have her come over here,' she demanded.

'Yes, ma'am,' I said, and headed back to my house. I had no way to go get Lotta and she had no way to get here except walk, which was several miles and she had to work tonight. So, having a brain storm, I called Mom and asked her to pick up Lotta on her way back from shopping, cutting her off before she could ask why I couldn't pick her up, then called Lotta and told her, asking her not to mention a word about last night to my mom. Not until I could tell her

285

myself. Then I went upstairs and spent some quality time on my computer with Zombie Nazis from Outer Space.

E.J., THE PRESENT

I'm not saying any of this is my son's fault, I'm just saying that even if you wrapped Graham in foam rubber and put him in a rubber room, somehow he'd get bruised. He's just got that kind of luck.

When I saw his car I nearly fainted. The back window blown out, the driver's side window blown out, bullet holes in the back door, one back fin shot completely off. I was trying to control my breathing when my son said, 'See? It's not so bad. All I really need to fix are the windows—'

That's when I whacked him in the back of the head. 'What did you do that for?' he demanded, gingerly touching his 'wound'.

'Because you could have been killed!' I said, tears welling and spilling over. I grabbed Lotta and hugged her.

'She gets a hug? How about the guy that got us the hell out of there?' Graham demanded. 'Me!'

So I hugged him. And he of course squirmed.

'Mom!' he said.

'Hug me back!' I demanded.

He sighed and did so, and I held him for a minute. Maybe two.

Luna came out her side door on to our connected driveways. 'Graham, I told you I wanted to interview the girl.'

Since, including myself, there were five girls standing on the driveway, all of us turned to look at her.

Graham took Lotta by the hand to lead her to Luna. Graham whispered something to her, and I saw Lotta pull back. 'Cop?' she whispered, but much louder than Graham's whisper. 'I'm not talking to any cop! Are you crazy?'

I followed the two as they walked – Graham walked, Lotta was pulled – to where Luna stood.

'Mrs Luna, this is my girlfriend, Lotta Hernandez. Lotta, this is Mrs Luna,' he said.

Behind them I smiled proudly, thinking, 'He's so grown up! Introducing them like a little gentleman!' Then I tried to control myself.

'Nice to meet you,' Lotta said, stopping just short of a curtsy.

'Come on in the house.' Although I did not hesitate to follow, Luna added, 'You, too, Pugh.'

My God, the manners going around here were amazing. I turned to tell the girls to go on into our house, but they were already unloading the car and totally unaware of anything but their bounty.

I followed Graham and Lotta into Luna's kitchen and into the living room. I took a seat on one end of the couch, with Lotta in the middle and Graham on the other end. Luna sat in an easy chair opposite the three of us.

'Carlotta, could you tell me what happened last night?' Luna asked.

'It's Lotta,' she said. Then she looked at Graham, and he nodded his head. 'OK,' she said, 'so we were parking...' Then looking at me, she said, 'Just talking, you know? So anyway, I hear this noise, sounded like a firecracker, but then Graham grabbed me and pushed me to the floor, and I was thinking...' Again she looked at me. 'Anyway, then the glass blows out of his – Graham's – window, and I scream, and Graham...' At this point she smiles and clasps my son's hand. 'He's half lying on the seat but he starts the car and whirls it around and heads straight for the guy but he – the stalker – jumps out of the way and then the guy, the stalker, he blows out the back window, but we're out of there.' Her smile got even bigger. 'He's my hero,' she said.

Graham's smile couldn't have been removed with a butcher knife.

'Where exactly was this?' Luna asked.

Graham gave her explicit, long-winded directions, playing the hero to the hilt, then Luna said, 'I'm calling this in. I'll get our forensic guy and a uniform out there to check it out. See if he left anything. Like some blood or a billfold. That would be nice.'

She went to the phone while I sat on the couch pretending my son wasn't having carnal thoughts about the girl sitting next to me.

ELIZABETH, THE PRESENT

I sat on the bed watching Megan and Alicia unload the crap. Bed, Bath & Beyond bags full of bedding and towels and curtains that matched the bedding, and Wal-Mart bags full of make-up and cleaners and underwear and night clothes, and Gap bags full of shorts and jeans and tops and a swim suit, and Payless bags full of sandals and a beach bag. It was a serious haul.

But I couldn't stop thinking about Graham's car. Because of me Graham and Lotta could have been killed. At least injured. Already I had Myra Morris's death and Alicia's injuries on my conscience, and Megan's nick on her arm – although the way she played it up I was not all that sorry for her. She seemed to be having fun. I was just glad school wasn't in session: Megan would be hauled around school on someone's shoulders while poor Alicia carried her books. Ugh!

Alicia was lighting up, beaming at all the new stuff. Megan and I talked about it and decided not to ask her about her past, about her mom, or the horrible foster mom, or anything else. If she wanted to talk to us, one or both, then she would.

Meanwhile, nothing much had changed on the stalker front. He was still out there, he was still a threat, and we still didn't have a clue. Was this someone who just picked me out of a crowd? Who stumbled upon the clippings of my birth family's murders? Someone who thought it would be fun to terrorize me? Or some – excuse the expression – poor soul who fixated on me for some reason? Or was this someone I knew? Or someone connected to my birth parents?

I felt as if I couldn't really move, like I could do nothing more than mimic the appropriate response to things: Smile while Alicia showed off another outfit; nod when Megan asked what I thought; come to dinner; brush my teeth; go to bed; get up and do it all over again. I was glad school wasn't in session; I doubted if I could do any work right now. My 3.9 GPA would dwindle down to failure if this kept up.

Whoever he was, he was winning. I was giving up. Even my anger was gone. How could I stay mad at a ghost? Fight a phantom? He was going to kill someone else, probably me or a member of my family. And I was unable to stop it.

BLACK CAT RIDGE, TEXAS, 1999

Although the journal started at the beginning of the school year, the stuff of interest didn't start until the beginning of the second semester:

January 14—

Met w/ Eric Rush today. I feel so sorry for him. He doesn't have any friends, and all the girls treat him like a leper. If he'd do something about those zits it might help. But I think it's more than that. It's like he's got the weight of the world on his shoulders. We're meeting after school today at the Dairy Queen for a Coke. I just hope nobody thinks I'm dating him. Boy, is that an uncool thing to say, or what?

January 15—

I met w/ Eric at the Dairy Queen yesterday. He started crying right there and it was really embarrassing. Sometimes I think I'm not cut out for this counseling shit. Need to talk to Mrs Olson about that. Anyway, we left the Dairy Queen and started walking. We took the trail by the railroad tracks and then walked down the tracks. He didn't say much, but I think he's beginning to trust me because I don't let on how gross I think he is. But he's sweet, too. Really.

January 18—
  Spent my lunch hour w/ Eric today. Got him to smile. But that's about all.

The journal went on in that vein until early March. That's when things began to get interesting:

March 3—
  Oh, God. Now what do I do? Met w/ Eric today. I never thought doing this PAL thing would lead to people telling me crap like he did! I've got to talk to Mrs Olson. I'm also going to write all this down so I don't get any of the facts screwed up. This is soooooooooooooo awful!!!!!!!!

  When they lived in Houston, before Eric's dad got our church here, Eric's sister got in trouble. Rev. Rush is always talking about how abortion is wrong and he wants the whole church to back him in that Right to Life stuff. Nobody much listens to him at our church. You know a woman has a right to her own body! Anyway, Rev. and Mrs Rush were really big in the Right to Life movement back in Houston and had a lot of followers. Anyway, when Eric's sister got knocked up, she was only sixteen (and a preacher's daughter – but I've always heard preacher's kids are the wildest!) and her parents took her to Mexico for an abortion! Anyway, it got botched

291

up and they had to give her a hysterectomy. When they came home, his sister just cried and cried. And she told Eric what their parents had done! When he confronted his parents, they got really angry and told him it wasn't true. The next day his sister was gone. He found out two years later they'd put her in a mental institution! Can you believe it? That poor kid's been holding this in all those years! They threatened him once that he'd go there too if he kept talking about 'something that never happened', so he hasn't mentioned it since. Except to me. Oh, joy! I need Mrs Olson's help on this one!

March 18—
I haven't seen Eric to talk to in two weeks, until today. He's obviously been avoiding me. I told him I had to go to Mrs Olson with this. He got really upset. I tried to calm him down but he just ran away. Now what the hell do I do?

March 27—
Finally got up the nerve to speak to Mrs Olson. Haven't seen Eric since the last time I talked to him. He hasn't been in school. Mrs Olson was very upset, even though she tried to cover it up. She said for me to forget about it and she'd take care of it. Thank God it's off my shoulders.

March 31—
Eric's back in school. He came up to me at my locker and said for me to watch out. Said he'd told his parents he told me! Gross! How can I ever go back to church? He seemed really scared

and it sort of scared me a little. I'm going to hide these papers for insurance.

That was Monique's last entry in her journal. Three days later she was dead.

ELIZABETH, APRIL, 2009

Elizabeth saw him smile at her abductor. 'Hey, Aldon,' Graham said, 'remember me, man? It's Graham! Your best friend! Remember?'

Tommy/Aldon just stared at him, the knife pointed in his direction.

'God, I couldn't believe it when Megan told me you were alive!' Graham said. 'Man, I'm so glad! I really missed you, man! Hey, Liz...' he started, turning toward his sister.

Tommy/Aldon said, 'Bessie. Her name is Bessie.'

Graham nodded. 'Yeah, right, man. Bessie. You OK, kiddo?' Graham asked her.

Elizabeth nodded.

'She's better than OK,' Tommy/Aldon said. 'She's with me now, so she's where she belongs.'

'Man, that's cool,' Graham said, keeping the smile plastered on his face, trying to keep his demeanor non-threatening, his hands at his side. 'She's really missed you.'

'You were part of it!' Tommy/Aldon said, taking a threatening step toward Graham.

'Part of the conspiracy?' Graham asked. 'Man, how could I be? I was like only six at the time, remember?'

293

'Six?' Tommy/Aldon said, confusion on his face. 'But I was ten.'

'Yeah,' Graham said, smiling bigger now. 'You were my hero.'

'Yeah,' Tommy/Aldon said. 'Yeah, I remember. You followed me around.'

'Sure did,' Graham said. 'Went everywhere you went. Our moms called me "the shadow".' Graham forced a laugh.

'The Shadow,' Tommy/Aldon repeated. 'You were the shadow. Not me.'

'That's right, Aldon,' Graham said. 'I was the shadow.'

EIGHTEEN

I want them all dead! They've ruined my life and they keep trying to do it over and over and over and over! I want Monique back! I mean Bessie. She looks so much like her sister, her beautiful, wonderful sister. I'm sorry, Monique, so sorry!

E.J., THE PRESENT

They found nothing at the scene of the last stalker attack. Not even shells. 'He had time to pick up his casings,' Luna said. 'After Graham took off, he had all the time in the world.'

I, of course, turned on my son. 'Why in the hell didn't you call the police immediately?' I demanded. 'You had your cell phone, right?'

'Yeah,' he said, squirming in his seat. 'I ... well, I thought ... I dunno,' he finally said.

Luna was staring at my son with sympathy in her eyes. Where she got off being sympathetic to my son I'll never know. 'What?' I said to her, or shouted maybe.

'Out necking with his girlfriend, maybe doing something he thought he shouldn't be doing...'

'Were you having sex?' I demanded.

'Gawd, Mom!'

'Before they could even get to thinking that part through, someone starts shooting at them. In his head he knows it's the stalker, in his gut he's thinking it's everyone who doesn't want them even thinking about having sex,' Luna said.

Graham just stared at Luna for a long minute, then said, 'Get out of my head.'

'Sorry, son, but I'm a cop *and* a mom. I seem to stay there,' she said. 'That's why you didn't call it in. You felt guilty. Like you'd done something wrong. A good night's sleep, and it all worked itself out and you knew what you had to do.'

'Ma'am, *please* get out of my head,' Graham said.

Just then the front door opened and my husband walked in. I recognized him, but just barely.

'What's going on?' he asked immediately.

'Hey, Dad,' Graham said sheepishly.

'What did you do?' Willis demanded.

'Nothing!' Graham shouted. 'Jeez!'

So the three of us told Willis about the night before, with Luna explicitly laying out her theory as to why Graham didn't call it in. Somehow I didn't expect Willis's response.

'Leave the boy alone,' he said, standing from his sitting position. 'Y'all don't even know.' Turning to our son, he said, 'Let's go for a walk.'

BLACK CAT RIDGE, TEXAS, 1999

Willis and I went to sleep that night, huddled in each other's arms, feeling safe for the first time since I'd walked into the house next door. Sometime in the middle of the night I woke up coughing. I hadn't smoked since graduating college – why was I coughing like I'd just smoked a pack? Then I woke all the way up.

The house was on fire. I grabbed Willis and shook him. 'Wake up!' I screamed.

'We're on fire!'

I grabbed the telephone next to the bed and dialed 911. Nothing happened. I depressed the button and listened. No dial tone. Willis was still asleep next to me. I hit him and hit him, finally kicking him to the floor where there was air to breathe. He woke up on impact, groggy but awake.

'The house is on fire!' I yelled. I grabbed the journal still sitting on my bedside table and crawled down to where my husband was on the floor.

Finally awake, Willis yelled, 'The kids!'

I grabbed him. 'They're at your aunt's house – remember?'

He nodded and we crawled towards the window. We opened it and kicked out the screen, crawling on to the roof over the breakfast room. Smoke billowed out of our open window. We heard a crash from below and flames leaped out of the living-room window.

Willis said, 'I'll jump first then catch you.'

'No,' I said flatly.

'Honey, just do it! Which are you most scared of? Breaking a leg or burning to death?' With those as his last words, he jumped on the grass in the backyard, landing hard on his left leg. Struggling, he stood up, holding out his hands for me.

'Jump, baby!' he yelled.

I looked at him and beyond – at Rosemary Rush coming up behind my husband with a five-gallon metal gasoline can. I'd barely begun to scream when she hit him on the back of the head.

GRAHAM, THE PRESENT

Instead of a walk, Dad and I drove to the basket-ball court next to the community swimming pool. The girls were already at the pool, and when they saw Dad they came running over to the court, all wet with way too much skin showing. Except the new girl, what's-her-name. She had on a one-piece and I was amazed that there was an actual body under that stuff she usually wore. Not a bad little bod, either.

The new kid hung back as the other two jumped all over Dad, making complete asses of themselves.

'Well,' Dad said, straightening up, hands on

297

hips. 'I'll see y'all back at the house. Why don't you head back to the pool?'

'OK!' Megan said, jumping up on Dad to hug him again. Serious PDA. And finally they were gone.

Dad threw me the ball, and I dribbled down the court and made a basket from mid-line.

'Ha! Think you're a smart ass, huh, boy?' Dad said, grabbing the ball, bouncing it once and hitting the basket.

I grabbed the ball and he started his defense, blocking my every move. The dude's like Elastic Man, arms everywhere. Finally I got a clear field and fired. And missed the basket.

'So, about last night,' Dad said, grabbing the ball. I went into defensive mode, but I'm not Elastic Man. He made a basket and I grabbed the ball.

He was all over me. 'What about it?' I asked, breathing hard.

'You gotta watch where you go, son,' he said, managing to grab the ball the one time I tried to dribble it.

'Shit!' I said, then apologized.

'Just you and me, no problem.'

'What do you mean, watch where I go?' I asked.

'A deserted stretch of road at night? Great for necking, son, but not when there's a stalker on the loose,' Dad said.

'Yeah. I didn't think he was after me or Lotta. Thought he was after just Liz,' I said, distracting him enough to get the ball back without him scoring.

He laughed. 'Good one, kid,' he said as he lunged for the ball. I got my back to him, circled him and threw it. Score!

'What you did was right on. You should have probably called the cops at that moment, but the chances of them catching this guy were pretty remote,' he said. He'd captured the ball and was holding it under his arm. 'Don't let the women intimidate you, son. You did good, whatever the reasons. You got Lotta and yourself out of there, and the only injuries were to the Valiant.'

'About that, Dad,' I said. 'Mrs Luna said the county victims' assistance program might pick up part of the price to fix her up.'

'Daddy!' Megan called from the front of the pool. 'Can we get a ride home? We're pooped!'

'Be right there!' Dad called back. He put his arm around my neck. 'Don't worry about it, son. What they don't pay for I'll pick up. We'll get that heap primo in no time.'

We walked together to the car. I was feeling pretty good.

E.J., THE PRESENT

'So how long are you home for?' I asked my husband as we snuggled in bed. The snuggling was my idea. I was gonna make him beg.

He leaned up on one elbow and smiled down at me. 'It's done,' he said.

I figured that was enough begging.

Later as we lay in bed, he said, 'No more Houston, thank God. One more dinner with your parents and I would have killed either your father or me.'

'Don't be mean. My dad's getting old. It makes him mean.'

Willis laughed. 'Honey, you forget. He's always been mean.'

'Well, to do him justice, he's only been mean to the husbands, well, shall we say spouses.' The correction was due to one of my sisters who decided, after twenty-odd years of marriage and two children, that she was a lesbian.

'I'm just glad you're home for good,' I said. 'It's been scary here without you.'

He hugged me to him. 'Really bad timing, huh?' he said. 'This stalker guy must be terrifying for you.'

I sat up in bed. 'Oh, hell, honey, it's not him! It's Lotta! I think she's going to deflower our son.'

I fell asleep before Willis stopped laughing.

ELIZABETH, APRIL, 2009

Behind Tommy/Aldon was a window and Elizabeth could see someone at it. She had no idea who it was, a Hispanic boy she didn't recognize. Who was he? Was he with Graham or with this man who held them both at knifepoint? She looked to Graham, who smiled and nodded at her. She hoped he meant the guy at the window was with him. But she wasn't sure what good it was going to do. The window was closed and it looked as if it had been painted over a thousand times. No way was that window coming open. The face disappeared from the window and seconds later a heavy branch crashed through the glass. Tommy/Aldon whirled around and, when he did, Graham jumped forward, yelling, 'Liz, run!' as he did so.

She ran through the door, but stopped on the shallow porch, unable to move further as she watched through the open door as Graham tried to wrestle the knife from Tommy/Aldon. Someone grabbed her from behind. Elizabeth swung around, ready to take on whoever it was, but found Megan pulling at her. She threw her arms around her sister.

Just as she did, Tommy/Aldon came running out the open door, almost knocking over both girls.

'I got him!' yelled the Hispanic kid who took off after him. Megan and Elizabeth ran into the shack.

Graham lay on the floor. Elizabeth could see no blood. 'Are you all right?' she demanded, kneeling by him. 'Did he cut you?'

Graham lifted his head. 'Naw. Just knocked the wind out of me. Where is he?'

'Manny ran after him,' Megan said.

'Who's Manny?' Elizabeth asked.

'Long story,' Graham said. To Megan, he said, 'Go shout for the others.'

Megan got up and ran out of the cabin while Elizabeth asked, 'What others?'

'Come here,' Graham said.

Elizabeth moved to him and he took her in his arms. 'You OK?' he asked, kissing her on the forehead.

'Yeah,' she said, curling up in his arms. 'But I

think you saved my life.'

'Yeah, well, we superheroes are like that, ya know,' her brother answered.

Megan came back in with a limping Manny, his arm around her shoulder.

'You better be injured, bro,' Graham said, 'or I'm cutting your arm off.'

'Hey, man, I fell down. Think I broke my foot!' Manny said.

'It's probably a sprain,' Megan said.

Graham stood up, pulling Elizabeth to her feet. 'Let's get out of here,' he said.

Once outside, as Manny limped toward his cousins who were coming up the trail, Graham pulled both girls into his arms, hugging them to him. After a few seconds, Megan touched the top of her head, bringing back moisture on her hand.

Looking up at her brother, she said, 'Are you crying?'

Graham pushed both girls away, holding them at arm's length. 'If you ever mention this to anyone, I'll kill you both. Severely.'

'Mention what?' Elizabeth said.

Graham smiled at her, holding up his hand for a high five. Elizabeth reached up, slapping his hand with hers.

Megan said, 'I know what. Graham cri—'

Elizabeth elbowed her sister in the ribs. 'Ow! Jeez, can't a girl have any fun?' Megan wailed.

Putting his arms around the shoulders of his sisters, Graham led them down the trail and out of the woods. 'I think we've had enough fun for one night,' he said.

ELIZABETH, THE PRESENT

I'm glad Dad's home. It just feels better to have the whole family together, plus one. Until Mom gets the furniture for Alicia's room, she'll be taking turns sleeping in my room and then Megan's. That way nobody is left out and Alicia seems OK with it. Of course, Alicia would seem OK if one of us said, 'Alicia, we need another hand here. Would you please cut yours off?'

I think she's afraid to disagree with anything or anyone. Afraid we'll send her away. I guess I was too young to think like that when Mom and Dad took me in. Or maybe just too traumatized to actually *think* anything. I don't know why, but having Alicia here makes me feel more a part of the family, maybe because she's the new kid now. Is that unfair? Probably.

There was a lot more hidden under that baggy jumper Alicia always wore than just a cute figure. And there's more to her story than just a junky birth mom and a bad foster mom. Or maybe that's enough. I just hope someday she'll open up to me – just open up period. I was hurting for her – OK, and maybe a bit embarrassed – when she seemed so afraid of my dad. I've seen TV movies where foster girls and runaways and girls like that have reason to be afraid of foster fathers and other men in authority, but I always figured that was exaggerated.

And maybe, to be honest, maybe I'm not really all that worried about Alicia; maybe I'm using her so as not to think about the craziness around me. Like this stalker guy. Why? I mean, why is he doing this to me? What have I ever done to him? And it's not just me! It's my whole family, and anyone who gets close to me! Like Myra, and one of those biker dudes who got shot, and Alicia, and even Megan! And now Graham and Lotta! I really can't stand it, ya know? I really can't. And I can only think of two ways to stop this: kill myself, or go with him. Well, maybe a third: kill *him*.

NINETEEN

I have a new plan. This one is going to work. Bessie will be with me forever. The others – some will go to Heaven, others will go to Hell, where they belong!

E.J., THE PRESENT

It's funny how life goes on. We had this new plague hanging over our heads, this stalker out to hurt Elizabeth and possibly the rest of us, and yet we settled in. With Willis back there was a butt-load of laundry, suits and dress shirts to the dry cleaners, and it was going to be necessary to fix real meals, instead of sandwiches or take-out. OK, if I sound like Suzy-Homemaker, I'm not. It's just that Willis and I made a deal a long time ago. If I wanted to stay home and write, then I would be in charge of kids and house, while he held up the manly end by bringing home the bacon and mowing the lawn. Unfortunately I put in no proviso to change things when and if I brought home more bacon sitting at my computer under the stairs than he did in his big old office. And there have been years where that proved to be true. Still and all, the house is mine. And the laundry.

Megan and Elizabeth appeared to be using poor Alicia as a Barbie Doll. They'd try out different outfits, from Alicia's small closet and from each of the girls – mix and match – do her hair in various dos, and bring her downstairs for my approval. After three days of this I decided to put a stop to it.

They came down the stairs, dragging Alicia as usual, and presented her. She had on a pair of skintight, ultra-short blue jean cut-offs, over-the-knee socks that were horizontal stripes of magenta, periwinkle, and mauve, Lucite stacked three-inch ho shoes they found in the back of my closet (Halloween costume – don't ask), and a tie-dye scarf they'd tied around her chest making a strapless top with no back and very little front.

'Girls, who gave you permission to go into my closet?'

This left Alicia, as usual, speechless, while Megan and Elizabeth began literally pointing fingers at each other. 'Never mind,' I finally said. 'Take the shoes back upstairs before Alicia falls down, but leave Alicia here, please.'

I smiled at Alicia; she tucked her head down

305

and refused to look at me.

'Mom! It's not Alicia's fault...' Elizabeth started.

'I'm not saying it is. I know, actually, that it's not. I have something else to talk to her about and I would like to do it in peace. So please take the shoes, like I told you, upstairs to my closet then go to whoever's room you were in, and stay there. Alicia will be up in a minute.'

Megan and Elizabeth looked at Alicia's back, then each other. Then me. I smiled. They didn't seem to accept that at face value, but resolutely had Alicia sit down so they could take off her (my) shoes, and then headed upstairs, glancing down at Alicia and me as long as they could without getting their heads stuck between staircase and ceiling. Finally they were gone.

Alicia sat before me with her face made up like a child playing with make-up, which I guess they really were, and in her modified ho outfit (minus the shoes), and looked at her lap.

'Look up, Alicia.' She did, catching my eye, but she couldn't hold it. She looked to the side.

'Are you going to lie to me?' I asked her.

She jerked and looked me in the eye. 'No, ma'am!' she said.

'Then please look at my face. I know it's hard to keep eye contact when you're not used to it, but I hope, between the two of us, we'll get you there.' She nodded her head and looked into her lap. I put a finger out and raised her chin up.

'Oh! Sorry,' she breathed.

'I don't want to make you uncomfortable, Alicia. But you need to try to look people in the face when they talk to you. And,' I said, taking a deep breath, 'you need to stand up for yourself. Do you *like* playing dress-up every day?'

She shrugged. 'Sure,' she said, her chin going down.

'Uh-oh,' I said. 'Your chin went down. Are you telling an untruth?'

She shrugged again, her head down. Finally she lifted her face to mine. 'I'm not crazy about it,' she said.

'Then tell the girls that. You *are not* their new Barbie Doll.'

'Yes, ma'am,' she said, her head going back down.

'OK, that's an untruth. I can tell by your body language,' I told her.

Her head came up. 'You can?' she said, her eyes wide. 'How?'

'Honey, I hate to say it, but you're pretty easy to read. If your head goes down after a straight affirmative or negative statement, then you're probably lying.'

She thought about that for a moment. 'Huh,' she said.

'Which means you're not going to tell the girls you don't want to play dress-up,' I said.

'Ohhhh,' she said, thinking hard about it.

'I love my daughters, Alicia, but they *will* run all over you given half the chance. You need to learn early to stand up for yourself. What would you rather be doing than playing dress up?'

Her answer was quick. 'Going swimming! We only have a few weeks left before school starts and the pool closes.' Her smile was huge. 'I'd never been in a pool before, and I really like it. I think I'd like to learn to swim.'

'OK, next year at the beginning of summer, I'll sign you up for individual lessons. I know one of the teachers and she's really good.'

'Am I too old?' she asked.

'Maybe for the classes – they're all for little kids, but for individual lessons no problem. I saw one of the teachers working with a woman in her eighties last summer. Got her swimming, too.'

'Thank you!' she said and tentatively moved toward me. I reached out and hugged her and she hugged me back.

'You're welcome,' I said, and she ran up the stairs, hopefully to tell off my other two daughters.

That evening Willis drove the girls to a movie and, being Wednesday, Graham went out with Lotta. Having the entire house to ourselves, Willis and I invited Luna over to discuss the stalker.

'I take it you two have discussed this before,' Willis said.

'Ad nauseum,' Luna said.

'Sorry if our near-death experiences bore you,' I said.

Looking at me, Luna said, 'You could make them a little more interesting.'

I flicked her earlobe with my finger and she glared at me. Willis said, 'Girls, please. No touching.'

Getting serious, he said, 'So, who is this guy?'

'Like we know?' I said, glaring at him.

'Yes. We all know. Or someone knows,' he said. 'This is someone we've met. Or someone Elizabeth has met. And how many people out of school has she met that we haven't?'

'It's the whole Aldon thing that makes this so spooky,' I said. 'Where did this guy get that information?'

'It's not a secret,' Luna said. 'There are plenty of people still here in Black Cat that were here when the Lesters were killed.'

'But this guy, this stalker, is fairly young...'

'What about someone who was a teenager back then? One of Monique's friends?' Willis said.

My stomach heaved. I thought I was going to vomit. 'Where are the Rushes?' I asked.

Willis and Luna looked at each other then at me. 'Shit,' they said in unison.

We – Luna, Willis and I – sat in the living room staring at the walls. We were waiting for a phone call Luna had made to be returned. We'd been waiting entirely too long. Instead of the phone ringing, however, the doorbell chimed.

Willis stood up and walked to the door. Luna and I were right behind him. Standing in front of us was a young African-American woman in a cop's uniform, a tidy, short Afro, and an adorable face. Looking behind Willis at Luna, she held up a sheaf of papers and said, 'I got it!'

'Come in,' Luna said. 'You were supposed to call.'

'No way,' the young woman said. 'I want in on this. It's too cool.'

Luna took the papers roughly from her hand and sat down. Turning to us, the young woman said, 'Hi, I'm Bethany Douglass. I'm a computer tech.'

Willis and I introduced ourselves, then Willis said, pointing at the papers Luna was perusing, 'Whatja got?'

We all sat down and Bethany said, 'Bad news on the Rushes. Mrs Rush died of breast cancer in the funny farm about five years after her sentence. Mr Rush was heading up a Right to Life group down in the Valley and got shot by one of his cohorts, and Ruth Rush, their daughter, committed suicide a year ago.'

I grabbed Willis's hand as he sat beside me on the couch. 'What about Eric Rush? Their son?'

Bethany shook her head and started to speak, but Luna interrupted. 'What do you mean here,' she said, pointing at the papers in her hand. 'There's no record on Eric Rush?'

Bethany said, 'The last record we have on him is his school record at Black Cat Ridge High School. There's no record, in Texas anyway, of him going to another school. The sister died in Houston, and he was in her custody when he left here.' Bethany shrugged. 'As far as I can tell, he's off the grid.'

'It's him!' I said, beginning to feel hyperventilation coming on.

'We have no proof of that,' Luna said in her cop voice.

'Oh, come on, Sarge,' Bethany said, then got still when Luna gave her a look.

'You're right, Elena, we have no proof,' Willis

said. 'But you know it's him.'

Luna sighed. 'Of course it's him,' she said.

'Now what?' I asked.

'Where can we get a picture of him?' Luna asked.

'No school records—' Bethany started.

'Can you do age progression?' I asked Bethany as I stood up.

'Of course. My computer can mend your socks and make French toast. What do you have?'

'Just a second,' I said, as I went into my office. I found the right filing cabinet and a folder marked 'church'. In the back I found one of the old church directories, from the time Berry Rush was our minister.

Thumbing through, I found a picture of the three of them, what we thought at the time was the entire family, but no individual picture of Eric. I handed the directory to Bethany. 'That's him between his parents. Can you do something with a picture that small?'

'Is the Pope Catholic?' she said. She headed for the door. 'You got a fax?' she asked over her shoulder.

I grabbed a pen and a slip of paper and wrote the number down and handed it to her as she rushed out.

It was incredible how much the age-progression picture Bethany sent via fax looked like Christine. I made a copy of the fax, drew in some glasses and a long pageboy and, voila, Christine. I didn't think Eric could hide from us again. If he showed his face, we had him.

But that in itself was the problem. He rarely showed his face. Like most stalkers and rapists, he was a coward. He came up from behind. Part of me felt sorry for him, for what his life had been like. Carrying the secret he did for so long at so young an age, telling it to Monique, only to have her and most of her family killed because of it. Losing his mother to an asylum, his father to ideology, and finally his sister, so damaged by her parents, to suicide. He would be about twenty-four now, I thought, too young to have lost so much. But too old to think what he was doing would fix anything. What had life been like for him after Black Cat Ridge? Why had he been off the grid? Why hadn't he gone back to school? I had so many questions only Eric could answer, and I couldn't wait until Luna had him behind bars and would ask those questions for me.

BLACK CAT RIDGE, TEXAS, 1999

The following things happened as a result of that evening's events:

1. Berry Rush was let out of jail and eventually left town – no one knows where.
2. Rosemary Rush was put in the police ward of the hospital because of the concussion she received when I jumped off the roof on to her back. She was later declared unfit to stand trial and was sent to a state asylum.
3. Our house was totaled and we moved in to the Lesters' house, until ours could be rebuilt.

4. Ruth Rush, Rosemary and Berry's oldest child, was let out of the institution where she'd been kept for five years and, now over the age of twenty-one, took custody of her younger brother and moved out of town, no one knows where.
5. The First United Methodist Church of Black Cat Ridge, Texas, had a new minister. He was OK.

We sat in the living room, me reading a book while Willis alternately watched a ball game and used a back scratcher in the tiny space between leg and cast. The kids were playing on the carpet in front of us.

Megan grabbed Bessie and began to tickle her, rolling over on top of her. Bessie began to scream. 'Mommy! Mommy!'

I jumped up and ran to where the girls were. Megan had scooted away from Bessie, staring at her. Graham sat still, his eyes as big as saucers. Willis strained to get up.

Bessie threw her arms around my neck, her eyes squinched shut. 'Mommy, get off, get off!' she cried.

I had a sudden vision. The killers in the hall upstairs. Shots ringing out. Aldon dead. Roy dead. Terry running to Bessie's room. Bessie's not there. She's sleeping with Monique again. Terry runs in there, screaming at her daughters to wake up. The killers come up behind her. They shoot her in the back. Her body falls on the sleeping Bessie. Then they shoot Monique, who stood at her mother's demand, flinging her body against the back wall. And the killers leave.

They don't know about the four-year-old trapped under her mother's dead weight. How long did she lie there? How hard did she have to fight to get out from under Terry? At what point did her mind shut down?

'Mommy! Wake up! Wake up, Mommy!' Bessie screamed.

Holding her tight, I turned to Willis. 'Call Elaine,' I said.

GRAHAM, THE PRESENT

The girls were in the family room watching some chick flick, Dad was in the garage puttering, as Mom called it, and she herself was in her boudoir doing God knows what. I was in the living room with my laptop, checking out what all I was going to do to the Valiant at the J.C. Whitney site. Man, they've got some shit. Then the doorbell rang, and someone banged on the door at the same time. I jumped up to get it before the entire house went ballistic.

Who should be standing there looking like a geek but skater-dude. I thought we'd given him up for Lent.

'What?' I said.

'So she's got a new boyfriend, huh?' skater-dude challenged.

'Who?' I said. Did he know Lotta? What was he talking about?

'Your sister! My Megan! What's she doing, man?' he said, almost in tears. 'I love her!'

'Gimme a break!' I said and tried to slam the door. Unfortunately there was a skateboard blocking it.

'Well, at least I came in the front door, man!' skater-dude said, sniffing like a baby. 'I don't creep around to the back like he's doing.'

I rolled my eyes and started to slam the door again when I got a clue. 'Who?' I asked.

'That guy!' he said, pointing toward the side of the house. 'I've seen him out here like every night! And tonight he goes sneaking around the house and he grabbed the ladder your dad left by the garage—'

I grabbed him by the scruff of the neck. 'Stay here! Don't move! If he comes around front, throw your skateboard at him!'

'Huh?' he said, as I ran back into the house.

I opened the door to the garage. 'Dad,' I whispered, 'he's here! You go to the back door, I'm going out the front and around!'

Dad grabbed my arm. 'No! You stay in the house—'

'Call Luna!' I said, jerking my arm away and heading for the front door.

Skater-dude was still standing there when I burst through. 'You think I can talk to Megan now?' he asked as I flew past.

'Just stay there! Watch out for him!'

'Who?' skater-dude asked.

My last thought as I rounded the corner of the house was: 'Megan can do better than that!'

ELIZABETH, THE PRESENT

I went upstairs to use the bathroom. I don't like to use the half bath downstairs because everybody can hear your business. I flushed and headed into the hall.

That's when he grabbed me. With his hand over my mouth, he whispered in my ear, 'Hush, Bessie. It's me, Aldon. Everything's going to be OK now.'

I stood perfectly still, then nodded my head. Slowly he lessened his grip on my mouth and slowly moved his hand.

I let out the most ear-piercing scream I could muster. And believe me, I could muster a heck of a scream.

Graham came out of my room, somehow, Megan and Alicia came running up the stairs, Megan with a baseball bat and Alicia with one of Mom's decorative rolling pins. Mom and Dad followed behind.

Graham grabbed the stalker around the neck and Megan and Alicia began beating him about the body. It was all Mom and Dad could do to save the guy from being beaten to death by the girls or choked to death by Graham. Personally, I wanted to jump on him and scratch his eyes out, but it looked like we weren't going to be able to do that.

Mrs Luna rushed in the front door, saw the commotion on the top of the stairs and came up, followed by a uniformed police officer. Megan, Alicia and Graham were being held back by my parents, all three breathing hard. 'Aldon' was sitting on the floor, rubbing his neck with one hand while the other arm hung loosely at his side. Something had broken it – either a baseball bat or a rolling pin. Who knew? Who cared?

I got to ask my questions in person, not through Luna. She let me go in first, by myself, to talk to Eric Rush.

'Why?' I said, looking at him, at his bruised neck, his arm in a sling.

He looked at me blankly for a long moment, then said, 'We're the only ones left. We belong together.'

It took me a moment, then I asked, 'You mean the only ones left out of both families? The Lesters and the Rushes?'

He nodded. 'And I owe Monique.' His face crumbled and he began to cry. 'I'll never be able to repay her for what I did! It was all my fault! I need to take care of Bessie. I need to be her big brother because she hasn't got anyone else!'

I touched his hand, as repugnant as it was to me. 'But she does, Eric. She has a big brother, Graham. And two sisters and parents. She has us,' I said.

He ripped his hand from mine and stood up, backing against the wall. 'Liar! Infidels! You aren't her family! I'm the only one who can be her family!' He lunged for me and Luna opened the door.

She had him back in the chair and his one good hand cuffed to the table before he could touch me. I stood up and left the room. I had all the answers I'd ever need.